Tales From The
SPACEPORT BAR

NOW JOIN US FOR

ANOTHER ROUND AT THE SPACEPORT BAR

Other Avon Books Edited by
George H. Scithers & Darrell Schweitzer

TALES FROM THE SPACEPORT BAR

ANOTHER ROUND AT THE SPACEPORT BAR

edited by
George H. Scithers and
Darrell Schweitzer

AVON BOOKS ◆ NEW YORK

ANOTHER ROUND AT THE SPACEPORT BAR is an original publication of Avon Books. This work has never before appeared in book form.
This is a work of fiction. Any similarity to actual persons or events is
purely coincidental.

AVON BOOKS
A division of
The Hearst Corporation
105 Madison Avenue
New York, New York 10016

Copyright © 1989 by George H. Scithers and Darrell Schweitzer
Front cover illustration by Doug Beekman
Published by arrangement with the editors
Library of Congress Catalog Card Number: 88-91353
ISBN: 0-380-75650-1

First Avon Books Printing: April 1989

AVON TRADEMARK REG. U.S. PAT. OFF. AND IN OTHER COUNTRIES, MARCA
REGISTRADA. HECHO EN U.S.A.

Printed in the U.S.A.

K-R 10 9 8 7 6 5 4 3 2 1

ACKNOWLEDGMENTS

"In Vino Veritas?" by W. T. Quick. Copyright © 1988 by W. T. Quick. An original work used with the kind permission of the author.

"The Far King" by Richard Wilson. Copyright © 1978 by Davis Publications, Inc. Reprinted with the kind permission of Richard Wilson, Jr.

"The Altar at Midnight" by C. M. Kornbluth. Copyright © 1952 by Galaxy Publishing Co., Inc. Reprinted with the kind permission of Mary Kornbluth.

"Princess" by Morgan Llywelyn. Copyright © 1988 by Terminus Publications, Inc. Reprinted with the kind permission of the author.

"The Subject Is Closed" by Larry Niven. Copyright © 1977 by Larry Niven. Reprinted with the kind permission of the author.

"The Persecutor's Tale" by John M. Ford. Copyright © 1982 by TSR, Inc. Reprinted with the kind permission of the author.

"Longshot" by Jack C. Haldeman II. Copyright © 1978 by Davis Publications, Inc. Reprinted with the kind permission of the author.

"Finnegan's" by W. T. Quick. Copyright © 1988 by W. T. Quick. An original story used with the kind permission of the author.

"The Oldest Soldier" by Fritz Leiber. Copyright © 1960 by Mercury Press, Inc. Reprinted with the kind permission of the author.

CONTENTS

vii

INTRODUCTION

"In Vino Veritas?"
by W. T. Quick

"Hey, bartender, a scotch and soda over here."

Maybe you've done it like that. Gone into a place where the lights are low and the music good and found an open stool on the far end of a long oak bar. You prop an elbow and raise a finger and, "Hey, bartender . . ."

That's where I come in. I take the bottle of Dewar's in one hand, a soda gun in the other, apply both to a glass full of ice, and make you a card-carrying member of that night's doings down on the corner.

I'm a bartender.

I've built that martini and popped that beer several nights a week for almost twenty years, off and on. I've done it in joints where they check you for .38s and blades at the street, in mom-and-pop places where the granddads who first opened the doors bring the grandkids in for their twenty-first birthday beer, and in crystal palaces that revolve forty stories above the ground while the waitresses trade you an arm for a Ramos Fizz, a leg for Keoke Coffee.

After twenty years of this, I have a few observations. One of them is everybody has a story. The only question is how much Budweiser or Bacardi is needed to bring it out. Did you ever go camping? Remember late at night, around the fire, as the wind died down and the coals began to crackle, somebody would start: "Did I ever tell you about . . . ? Remember when . . . ?"

That's what happens in bars too. Bartenders, contrary to popular opinion, are rarely asked for psychological advice. Good bartenders discover soon enough that the stories are one way, and all that is required is an occasional nod, a steady eye to show that someone, please God *anyone,* is listening.

And people will tell you the damndest things.

They'll also tell the human next to them the same, provided the *vino* glass is half full—or half empty, take your pick. I once refereed a hellacious argument over that question.

Another thing I've noticed is that most of the stories aren't very interesting. There is a drab sameness to the complaints, to the whines, even to the triumphs. "I made it across the Golden Gate Bridge in only twenty minutes" has been fairly popular in my place lately. But the exceptions to this rule can be spectacular, particularly in California. Would you like to know what Liz Taylor's hairdresser really did? Or how the Pacific Stock Exchange almost went under? I know, but I'm not telling. That's part of being a bartender in a real bar, too—knowing when not to tell.

Which brings me to the kind of bars science fiction writers love to immortalize. Oddly enough, many of the characters in these stories *are not drunk*. This is sort of like going to a hospital and finding that none of the patients are sick. Romanticists may believe that bars are witty places, full of slightly tipsy gaiety, but the brute truth is that people go to bars to drink. I deal with an awful lot of alcoholics, and that can be sad at times. But the good stories don't come from the guy who tips a single beer and leaves. They come from the regulars, the long-termers, who start happy hour about three in the afternoon and finish whenever the money in their wallet runs out.

I have a regular who was on late night shot-and-beer terms with presidents, who once knew everybody who was anybody in New York City. He dines out on these stories now, and the chronicle of his fall is numbing. But he remains cheerful and warm, a good compatriot and a compassionate man. He knows a million tales. Not a single one is about aliens. He talks about humans, and sometimes he just tears your heart right out.

Of course all the stories are true, right? Everybody knows that. *In vino veritas*, in wine truth. Well, not quite . . .

The opposite is closer to the mark. The biggest lies come after the sixth hammer, or the seventh. The real whoppers are often told in voices so slurred it's hard to make them out. Any bartender who tries to take stock advice to the bank, even when the advice comes from the local banker, will die a poor man.

Is there any difference between the bars SF writers like to chronicle and the real McCoy? Only that the writer tries to distill an effect, pin down a vision into single, sensible words. Life is messier than that, and bartenders often complain, when *they* get together, about how pointless things seem to be. Bartenders are cynical folk. But where do they go, to relax, to talk, to hoist a few?

Somebody else's bar. Because that's where the action is. The bar—any bar—is where they sell you what you need. Only you know what it is. Only you know what it costs. And only you know whether it's worth it.

Real bars are often boring, very often depressing, and sometimes downright repulsive. Science fiction bars rarely are any of these. But life, like art, rises to the occasion. And when it does, somebody—always—will order another round and start a new story.

There's a black lady who comes in. Her face looks like the primordial map of too many bad roads. She's not from here originally (who is?) and maybe the tangled California years have done it, but she remembers snow. Night after night, pouring down Chardonnay by the endless glass, she builds fantasies of white. For her the flakes are always falling through the trees, in the dark, piling up incredible drifts of sparkling memory. White dreams.

It's lunacy, of course. And at bottom it's absolute, wonderful truth. As are all the lies and terrors and wonders a bartender hears every day.

In the end what they sell in bars, whether of the science fiction or the mundane kind, is dreams. And the occasional nightmare, those tickets on a hell-bound train.

So pull up a stool, prop your elbow and raise a finger. "Hey, bartender . . ."

Here are eighteen of the finest. Have one on me.

THE FAR KING
by Richard Wilson

*Royalty . . . romance . . . extraterrestrial intrigue . . .
in Chicago, of course.*

It was ironic that Ann Bagley got mixed up with a bunch
of extraterrestrials in a nightclub at the top of the Mile-Hi
Building in Chicago. But maybe it was inevitable. She was
the daughter of the minister of a flock in a place like Zion,
Illinois, home of the ecclesiastical fig newton, only it was a
smaller place. I won't name it here, or name him. Ann
Bagley or, as she was later called, NoNo McCanless, is not
her real name.

I'll call him the Rev. Ezekiel Bagley. His sect is one of
many that interpret the Bible literally. But his own interpretation includes the belief that there are alien lands that have
been touched by the hand of God. He used the concept once
in a sermon and it evoked such a response that he kept it in
and soon built his gospel around it. He is pastor of the
Church of the Rediscovered God of Earth and Undiscovered
Lands Beyond, as he renamed it.

His children, three girls, were born in sin, he believed,
because the Book had it so and therefore he was as harsh
with them as he was with his wife and himself. He lived an
austere and humorless life as he strove, with limited wisdom,
to make the world a better place by denouncing its pleasures.
Only in this way, he was convinced, could there be salvation in another world.

He never said in his sermons, or to his family, where that
other and better world might be or how to get to it. He read
books he'd bought secondhand or ordered cheap by mail. He
had shelves of works that mixed fundamentalist dogma with

far-out philosophies that took his fancy or provided a peg for a sermon. He was not above lifting other people's stuff, knowing it would go unrecognized by his congregation of simple folk. Sometimes he preached a weird one:

"Think not that you are the only ones chosen of God. We on Earth are mere dust motes in the sunshine of His far-flung radiance. Many there are on other worlds on whom His mercy shines. These aliens—alien to us, not to Him—may please Him more than we do. In fact I think it likely that we sinful creatures find least favor in His eyes. Do you doubt? Then let me share with you, my fellow sinners, the discovery by a learned man who proved that at least three other planets within our reach have intelligent life. Mathematically one of these could harbor God-fearing creatures with intelligence vastly greater than ours. Is this not, my brethren, a humbling thought?"

And so on. He'd quote from his latest secondhand book and hold it aloft. He'd give his flock glimpses of pertinent passages underlined in red.

"Go and repent, my brethren, and pray forgiveness, and seek salvation through Christ Jesus whom we must recognize as but One of a number of Sons of God doing His work throughout the cosmos."

Her father's sermons had a somber effect on the daughter who was to be NoNo McCanless. Their impact was greater because she'd gone to his study and had read for herself the underlined passages and the paragraphs around them. He hadn't made anything up. It hadn't been revealed to him in a supernatural way. Other people were saying the same things and these things were published in books. She'd always had respect for books.

Maybe this is what planted in her young mind the belief that one day she'd travel to a far world and meet the living Savior. Christ was dead on Earth, or at least gone from it, but maybe on a sister planet His Brother lived and walked among men, unfettered by limitations of space and time. Maybe on that other world He was mortal yet and she'd find Him. And He'd—He'd— It was too fantastic a thought to pursue—who could fathom the mysteries?

She tingled in her teenage way and daydreamed. What would Jesus' Brother's name be? He'd be a Stepbrother, of

course, but His title would also be Christ, which meant
King. Her own father had said it was possible. His books
said so. She might meet Him, one day, if there were a way
to get there. Or He might come here in His magical way,
for surely the Divine Brothers would be in communication
and would visit Each Other. Exalted, she went to bed and
dreamed of her Far King.

I knew her then as a down-the-block neighbor in a village
with no secrets. Her father preached to a small but full house
each Sunday noon. His words thundered out to his little
multitude. I was unwillingly among them, between my
parents, and I knew the effect of the words on them.

I didn't know then where he'd got the words. His daughter
Ann was to show me. At a church supper, urged by her
mother, who knew mine, she asked me to help serve the
apple cobbler. We took ours to a table at the far end of the
basement kitchen. She called me by name. Everybody knew
everybody else in the village but we hadn't formally met.

"I really admire your father," I said. "I used to hate
church before he came." I politely bent the truth.

She ate daintily, half as fast as I. She put down her fork
and chewed and swallowed before she replied. "He has a
lot of books in his study. Would you like to see them?"

I said I would and she took me there. "He reads all the
time," she said. "Mama says 'Come to bed' and he says
'In a minute' and he keeps reading and making notes. Once
I got up in the night because—excuse me—I had a cold and
Mama'd been feeding me juices and I had to go to the
bathroom and he was still up, reading and writing. I asked
him what he was doing and he said 'One day you'll know,
my child.' "

I took a slim green volume from a high shelf. I was
intrigued by its title, *The Far Kingdom.* She said: "I've
looked at that too. It's underlined a lot." We were fourteen
or fifteen then.

I went back often, at his invitation, relayed by her. I
wasn't allowed to borrow the books but I could consult them
there. At first I read out of curiosity but the more I read the
less strange they became. Each was persuasive in its own

way but one often contradicted another. I began to see what Ezekiel Bagley had done. They weren't *his* books—he hadn't written them—yet they were peculiarly his because of the way he'd annotated and crossbred them. He'd made a careful selection of the theories of their authors about extraterrestrial life and God's role in it. He'd built a working synthesis that he preached to his flock. Perhaps it was significant that a boy and a girl should have been caught up in this mass of words.

Once when I was engrossed in the green volume or one like it, Ann, sitting close beside me, read to herself from the Old Testament. I supposed she was going back to the accepted text to seek better evidence for her dream of a Far King. She was reading the Song of Solomon and had come to one of the parts that describe the body of the Shulamite maiden: "Thy two breasts are like two young roes that are twins." She read it aloud to me, then said: "I wonder if mine are. I never thought about it." She unbuttoned her blouse to look for herself. Young girls didn't wear brassieres in those days, at least not in the Bagley family, nor was she wearing a slip.

I must have gasped when she exposed her young breasts and regarded them with new interest. "Do you think mine are like roes?" she asked, moving so I could see better. "Young roes are fawns, you know."

I stared, unable to speak, then turned away.

"No; look and tell me," she said. "Breasts aren't bad or they wouldn't be in the Bible."

I looked again, knowing my face had gone red.

"Well, are they?"

"I don't know," I said finally. "I thought it said, uh, breasts like pomegranates." She shook her head. "But I know where you mean: 'As a piece of pomegranate are thy temples within thy locks.' Solomon also says, 'Thy plants are an orchard of pomegranates' and that must mean another place. I'm only talking about breasts. Do you think mine are like twin roes?"

"How does the Bible mean that?" I asked. "Their shape, or—"

"He also says in Chapter Seven 'thy stature is like to a palm tree, and thy breasts to clusters of grapes.' "

"Your—yours are more like grapes, I guess."

She cupped them one at a time, then with both palms. "I guess so. They're hard and soft both. What do you think?"

It seemed to be an invitation and I reached out a hand. She took it and drew it toward her.

There were footsteps at the end of the hall. Without haste she let go my hand, rebuttoned her blouse and turned the pages from Solomon's Song to Revelation. Her father opened the door and came in. He nodded. "Nothing I like more than to see young people reading Scripture together," he said.

"We wanted to know if another Jesus is mentioned in the Bible," she said, cool as could be.

Her father gave us a little sermon on original sources and the Apocrypha/Lost Books of the Bible but I don't remember much about it. I can't even remember whether I touched her breast or, if I did, whether it was like a cluster of grapes.

We were youth-pure then, still to taste the world. Had I not left the village we might have met often, talked and truly touched and loved, married and raised typical children in a typical small town. But I left and she and I did not meet again until many years later in the 5280 Club in Chicago's Loop.

I'm Jack Norkus and I come into the story here and there, now and then.

I'd spent many years in the Mile-Hi Building, a day visitor among aliens from worlds unknown to our space explorers, when Ann Bagley came in one cold night. I scarcely remembered her as she stood at the door, cold from the wind and wet with snow, seeking shelter denied her by the YW, overbooked that New Year's Eve.

"What made you come here?" I asked.

She was looking around the 5280 Club in amazement, as well she might. It was not yet the dawn of interplanetary, let alone extrasolar, commerce as far as she and most of the other people of Earth knew.

Boots the bartender welcomed her in his transuniversal way and said, "What will be yours?" and I led her to a far booth, away from the stranger residents.

"I knew you'd gone to Chicago and I needed somewhere

to stay," she said. "What is this place, anyway? Some kind of circus—theater?"

I explained that most of them had arrived at one time or another on the Midnight Shipment. They were traders, businesspeople, scholars. For starters, I introduced her to a few of them—they slithered, rolled, oozed, or floated over to the table. She met Mogle, who's a triped; Diskie, who disappears when sideways; JorenzO the Black Magician; and Lopi of All-Planets Films. She was polite to them and they to her; she was taking it well for a person who had expected to spend that night at the YW. She also met Dan and Joe and Keith and Frank, Sam and Moe and Leif and Hank: a handful of Earthlings who, like me, had gained entrée by accident or because the aliens needed them in their commerce and gave them guest privileges.

I don't want to go into a long explanation of how people from a dozen worlds speak the languages of the others. They don't. Some of us can hardly speak our own. If anybody cares, there's an operating manual on the linguapathophone in the message center that's run by Dan McQuarrie, a graduate student in linguistics who commutes from South Bend twice a week. He's a serious young man with a B.Sc. from Glasgow University. If you let him he'll talk you numb about linguapathic telecommunication, for which the Mile-Hi Building is wired in its upper stories. It's a kind of voluntary bugging. Everybody wears a skin-colored plug behind his ear, or whatever he has that gathers sound waves. Not everybody has skin, either, but the device adapts. One of the alien traders—it was Luo of Ulo—had brought its forerunner with him and sold Boots the Chicago concession. It's since been refined; it no longer weighs six pounds. Luo weighs 2,370 pounds, so don't let him step on your foot. Before that, I'm told (I hadn't explored the Mile-Hi Building then, though I lived in its shadow), communication was by sign language or pointie-talkie or other primitive means.

Things are simpler now. For instance, when Eosho wants to trade Daemonian dream capsules for ropes of red licorice, the linguapathophone puts the whole transaction in cross-cultural socioeconomic terms, simultaneously computing the current rate of exchange.

Thus if I buy a rope of Chicago licorice for two cents and

Eosho's dream capsule costs him the equivalent of a nickel, we trade at five of mine for two of his and we are satisfied. I don't know what he gets for red licorice on Daemonia but I bet it's a bundle. I can get up to twenty bucks on the street for one of his dream pills. It beats delivering pizza, which is what I was doing when I discovered that the Mile-Hi Building was not entirely empty above the tenth floor, as most people supposed in those New Depression years.

The Mile-Hi Building rises like a gleaming needle implanted in the lime-rind of earth. It was built by a visionary architect named Fallon and became known as Fallon's Folly when the New Depression hit and the building failed to attract tenants above the tenth floor. The upper stories were closed off to cut maintenance costs and no one knew that aliens had taken over at the mile-high level.

Then, by means of the Midnight Shipment, the top several stories filled with alien beings who used the upper quarters for offices, trade, and recreation. Mayor Daley's successors never knew there were extraterrestrials among them, trading with Earthmen without the sanction of the Chicagoland Industrial Board, trafficking in strange goods without the knowledge of the Chamber of Commerce, helping the economy of Earth and other places without the imprimatur of the Metropolitan Development Council.

In somewhat the same way that the linguapathophone works, the various reconstituted alien atmospheres are blended into a mutually acceptable mixture that, when I first noticed it, was faintly pink and smelled agreeably of Christmas tree tinsel burning on the third rail of a toy electric train track. Now I'm not aware of it anymore.

Somewhere once I'd seen a directory that listed the tenants of the higher stories. I don't remember whether it was in the upper building itself or at the base of that yawning vertical cavern which joins the inhabited areas. The shaft, designed by Fallon to carry a high-speed freight elevator, had been converted by the aliens to house an antigrav platform activated by a bypass button known only to the aliens and those they trusted to use it discreetly. It was the most frightening thing in the world when I first had to use it, delivering pizza from the mundane world below, but now I find it as routine as riding an escalator. Except for JorenzO the Black

Magician and a few others, the aliens don't use it. They make contact with the surface of Earth in other ways.

The directory has since disappeared. As I recall, it looked something like this:

All-Planets Films; Lopi, Producer-Director	528-4
Archives & Library; Skwp, Scribe	528-7
Club; Boots, Manager	528-1
Combined Earth Intelligence	528-19
JorenzO the Black Magician	528-13
Laurel-Eye, Madam	527-2
Midnight Shipment	529
Mogle; Agent	528-6
Society for Prevention of Space Travel	528-18
Zichl, A.; Imported Spirits	527-1

I wasn't sure how factual the board was. Was it significant the Society for Prevention of Space Travel adjoined Combined Earth Intelligence? Were either or both a joke? or a cover for another kind of operation? I'd heard that Diskie was a double agent for Earth and the Extrasolar Consortium, whatever that was.

Anyhow, everybody talks his own particular patois and everybody else understands him. Not always perfectly, of course. Dan McQuarrie goes on about that if you let him; he's full of shoptalk and linguistic anecdotes. Sometimes he gets excited and lapses into gutter Glasgowegian; he was lowly born, like most of us. That's when I tune out his clear speech and listen to him through the bug. Then everything is plain.

So that's why NoNo McCanless, as Ann Bagley came to be known, and the future Far King, when she finally found him, were able to talk each other's language. Literally, that is. As it happened there were basic misunderstandings on each side. Even when we're culturally close, ambiguities befall us. In NoNo's case nobody, least of all NoNo, blamed them on the linguapathophone.

NoNo McCanless had become a regular in the 5280 Club long before the arrival of the Far King, then Leo Reo, heir apparent to the throne of Farland. Probably she's seen as

much of hard times as the rest of us terrestrials since she left
home, as I had earlier, to seek her way in a world beyond
the confines of that narrow village. I could sympathize with
her ambition, which I supposed was to make a good
marriage, not necessarily a romantic one, with a man who'd
provide for her comfortably, with whom she could be
compatible and beget a child or two for immortality's sake.
As I say, I could sympathize with that. But it was hard for
me to accept the way she passed the time among us while
she waited for her prince to come.

Over the years I've seen a few women in the 5280 Club,
all of them Earthwomen except Laurel-Eye, the alien madam
who sometimes relaxed there away from her duties in her
own establishment a floor below. The visitors to the club are
women such as are found in any bar and, because the club
has its own special way of being exclusive, most of them
are normal adventurous women who offer more than their
bodies and brighten our existence with wit and charm and
their special viewpoints on life. That's the kind NoNo
seemed to be. She was lively and had a skill. She worked
in clay, making figurines of the characters who drifted in—
up from the Loop or down from the Midnight Shipment. She
made witty effigies of Diskie and Boots and Mogle and Dan
McQuarrie and me. She always made two and fired them up
and presented one to her subject. A thoughtful thing to do.

But later she grew morose. She spent a lot of time in the
far booth that had become hers and read a lot in books,
sometimes marking the pages as her father had done years
ago.

But sometimes she'd rouse herself into an antic state. Oh,
we all knew NoNo. We knew her somewhat; not well. She
rebuffed familiarities that were more than superficial. She'd
drink your liquor and eat your meals and give you bright,
witty conversation. She'd kiss you if the mood was on her
but it had to be her kind of mood—the hell with yours. She'd
run into you somewhere in Chicagoland and you'd have a
drink and drift over to her place and neck for a while but
in a cool way, interspersed with high-minded conversation.
The next day you'd be practically strangers again.

Sometimes at the club she'd fling herself into our laps, if
we were Earthmen, and we kissed her and hugged her and

laughed and danced energetic dances with her and perspired
a lot. But her kisses were quick, biting, tongue-darting—no
warmth or duration. And nobody, really, sat and talked to
NoNo McCanless. Not meaningfully, intimately. It wasn't
only into human laps that NoNo flung herself when she was
in her hyperactive state and the spirit of seeming abandon
was upon her. It may be that she learned from her father
that all creatures, from whatever world, were God's
creatures. She was as apt to arouse an alien by ruffling its
rufa or tantalizing its tertiary talon as she was to tease a
terrestrial in the way we all knew and, in our frustrated
enjoyment, deplored. (   ) the inscrutable said once out of
his experience with her: "If she biffles my iffle one more
time I'll wurble her what into a permanent plerm." Knowing
the powers of (   ), it was an awesome threat.

I knew how he felt. After one such exhibition when NoNo
seemed to be teasing me more than any other in that mad
group before abandoning us all, in my frustration I visited a
sperm bank on North Clark Street. It was a place where
customers for my Daemonian dream pills sometimes hung
out. None was there this night and I required rent-beer-food
money, so I gave of myself. Some give free at such empor-
iums because the means of extraction is so interesting. I went
only for the money, I told myself.

Later, NoNo was more skilled at sending off males. It was
still important to her to be liked and she was likable up to
a point—a point she defined in her own way.

JorenzO the Black Magician, who reads minds, listened
one night as we discussed NoNo in her absence. "She's a
mystery woman," Dan McQuarrie said. "Why try to explain
her?"

"I can explain her," JorenzO said in his pompous way.
"I have studied her psyche and know why she is as she is.
Will you hear?"

We protested that trespassing on her mind was repugnant
to us, that we really didn't. No, no, we said; then yes, yes.

He began. He told us theatrically, weaving mind images
that made us reluctant but fascinated voyeurs. It was as if
we were portraits on a wall that looked down on all that had
happened to her.

NoNo, then Ann Bagley, had once married. She'd wed a

weak man who'd threatened suicide if she wouldn't have him; it was clear that he intended to go through with the threat. But then, married, there were no children, though both said they wanted them. It was her fault, he claimed; all his ancestors had had children right away, mostly male. Obviously he thought male was better. He taunted her in company, despite tests that had shown them both fertile, telling anyone who'd listen: "I'm all right. If only I had a real woman." Knowing it was no more her fault than his, unable to be with him after that, she left him. But, knowing that she could conceive and wanting not to, except with her chosen man, she fended off all others. Not only did she never let a man get close to being physically amorous, she allowed for fallibility or accident by using every possible precaution as it came along: the pessary, the pill, the coil.

And when the demand came, as it sometimes did when her other creative ways failed her, she'd fling herself among whoever was present and laugh and sing, and twist and shout but not give out, and achieve a kind of release to tide herself over to a new day when she might read a book and mark it, or sculpt a likeness, or write in her notebook. Or sit and wait for her prince.

NoNo came in as JorenzO finished his oral dissection of her. She went to her far booth. JorenzO disappeared in his magickal way. Boots set up a drink for her, on the house. She thanked him and looked around. We raised our glasses to her. Poor NoNo! She was dear to us that night.

NoNo's notebooks were private, she thought. She didn't know about Boots's attenuated pseudolenses which could snake across the room more invisible than spiders' strands to see what she wrote.

She didn't know about the talents of Diskie, a two-dimensional Slivian. Diskie looks like an oversized coin under a foot in diameter. Because he has no third dimension he's weightless and can hover at any level. And because of his lack of substance he can go through things or beings, or stay inside them. When he's not on end he's shimmery, like a silver dollar with a big face on the obverse that changes at his whim from terrestrial to extrasolar. On the reverse of his coinlike body appear and disappear mottos in English, which is the *bêche-de-mer* of the upper reaches of the Mile-Hi Building: Thin is Beautiful, Tomorrow the Whorl, Absorbed by Another, or The Inside Story. Diskie wasn't born or hatched, he said, he was minted; and when he entered NoNo it was in an asexual way. Thus he too was able to help flesh out the story I might have called Inside NoNo McCanless.

Nor was NoNo aware of the extraordinary ability of Skwp the alien scribe to receive, file, and retrieve anything verbal from anywhere.

According to my youth-learned standards none of them should have spied on NoNo and later on her and Leo Reo, nor should they have let me or anyone else see or hear the transcriptions. But because my standards have withered I can summarize a selection from NoNo's supposedly private journal and tell about things that happened later.

Listen to NoNo, writing in the third person and supposedly only to herself:

Nobody knows you when you're old and gray, they say, and she wanted none of that. If an occasional strand of gray marred the glory of one so young she'd pluck it out; if there were many telltale strands she'd dye them and their neighbors. Once she'd let it all go back to natural and had been aghast at what had happened in so short a time. Actually it had been a number of years—five? six?— but she'd stopped counting.

One's youth flits away the timelessness of the early years. For a while it's springtime and summer but all too soon the leaves have turned. The future becomes less vast, less limitless than it was. The years, once ever-extending, become finite and countable. A person wonders for the first time how long she's got. Is there time to do all she wants to do? If there's a chance that there is, hadn't she better get started? Hadn't she better activate the dreams, influence the future, delay the drift? Isn't it time to steer the no-longer-everlasting now toward a foreseeable future?

One thinks about this abstractly at first, then more demandingly as the seasons change—especially if one is no longer a girl but a woman addressed by strangers as "ma'am."

One's dreams of the future, once so pleasant, become

nightmares of anxiety. Once it had been all so possible, so put-offable, because one was so young, so full of promise; but now youth was running out, her promise only a perhaps.

A kind of panic set in for her. All the time in the world had dissolved into a disturbing fear that the once-bright future had shortened, clouded over. This was a sad situation for a woman of fewer than forty years. It resulted in her flinging herself into life as she thought it should be lived. It was a panic reaction that need not have been, if she'd settled for less. But NoNo had vowed to settle for no less than the best. Someday her Prince would come. Of that she was certain. Someday he would ride to her from wherever he'd been to wherever she was. He would be radiant and she would glow and there'd be electricity in the meeting, thunder and lightning, a sound like temple bells, a throbbing in the psyche, and all the other manifestations of a meeting ordained.

It happened almost that way with the arrival of Leo Reo, the future king of Farland.

There were alien snicks and clackings when one of us of Earth talked about the fine figure Leo Reo, the future Far King, cut as he favored the Mile-Hi Building with his presence. The total of this twittering in alien tongues—not that all of them have tongues—was that they knew better. Chances were slight that one from another world could be so like a human being as the visitor was. The impression was that his shape was one he'd assumed for the purpose of his voyage.

There was speculation about that purpose. Not even Skwp, the alien scribe, was yet able to give us hard facts about Farland. It was a place too recently known, to have been programmed into his data bank.

Laurel-Eye contributed to the scuttlebutt. She said she'd heard from a customer that the Farlanders were so new that they were still experimenting eugenically to learn what shape they should be to adapt to their adopted land. Not only was their agriculture in flux, with their farmers seeking the best alien corn, but the species itself awaited improved hybridization. The new planet had been artificially cooled to a habitable state and was facing problems that arose from accelerated evolution. The best breed of cattle and other food animals had not been stabilized; and the people themselves were in a transitory state, still seeking the optimum means of copulation for maximum growth of population. So much for Laurel-Eye's contribution.

Lopi of All-Planets Films claimed Leo Reo was Lopi's own creation. Lopi said he'd been canning a quickie on Quintus V some millennia ago and had hired an itinerant for a supporting role. If that hadn't been Leo Reo, or maybe his great-grandsire, Lopi said, he'd ingest his intaglios. But who can believe a showman?

(   ), our disembodied voice, said he knew a Far King from long ago as a perennial wanderer under an intergalactic curse who leapt from planet to planet as often as was necessary to flee his Nemesis, breaking hearts along the way.
(   ), the inscrutable, who was something of a moralist, said he recalled an incident on Taurus 20 where the being called the farking—the words joined and lowercased—had found A, a trisexualite; and B, an assenting amoralist; and that C had ensued, with long-range effects on the local proprieties.
(   )'s stories tend to get diffuse and I put this in for the record.

Diskie told of a far place in a time past. He had been whirling invisibly sideways, to avoid being obliviated, when a corporeal creature very like Leo materialized and spoke in a prophetic way, causing consternation among the populace. Leo forthwith became a God for Whom to this day Faraway-Long-Agos set out hollow burls of warmed kvish which they ceremonially inhale. Zichl purveys a similar product but most of us prefer Boots's brew.

The universal drink in the 5280 Club is beer, but not the bloating, carbonated product that passes for the working man's beverage on Earth. Boots's beer is an alien elixir, cheap, satisfying, mind sharpening. Boots brews it from an ancient formula, and it's what we need to warm ourselves in the evening of a trying day as we relax and let our minds roam free, comfortably open to pleasing thoughts and to companionship in this haven high above Earth's problems.

Boots has other potions behind his bar and will dispense them on demand; but his beer is the best and far cheaper.

Some say it is less an intoxicant than a tension-easing drug, concocted to keep peace in the club, an antidote to or substitute for hard liquor, pot, and whichever mysticism you found helpful.

Whatever it is, we like it, and like its price.

Mogle was the most skeptical about the royal lineage of Leo Reo, potential Far King. "If he's a prince," Mogle said, "I'm an octopus." But Mogle *is* a sort of octopus.

JorenzO said: "I've seen him before, gallivanting around the safer planets, enjoying the local pleasures. Sure he's a prince—his daddy rules a kingdom the size of Winnetka. Someday, if he lasts, he may be the two-bit king of a minor world."

"You have to admit he cuts a good figure," Boots said. Like all bartenders, he was a diplomat. "Leo lends class to the joint."

"Only because he squinches a lot and leems," said (   ), inscrutably.

"Here he comes," Boots said. "He usually buys for the house. Anybody who objects to that can withdraw." Nobody withdrew and all drank Leo's health in their refilled glasses, myself included.

"A pleasure to see you all in such amity," Leo Reo said, letting his eyes roam to the far booth. NoNo McCanless was absent from it.

Leo Reo's first stop on Earth was the Mile-Hi Building, and he never got beyond it. As a matter of fact, having debarked from the Midnight Shipment, he went no lower than the 528th floor. Of all the aliens who'd traveled to Earth this inhabitant of Farland was the only one with a completely terrestrial look. None of the others could pass for very long. JorenzO the Black Magician did at times but he practiced his deception from a stage and never mingled with the audience.

Each saw Leo Reo as he or she (NoNo) expected to see him. The aliens in the 5280 Club found his nonhuman shape as acceptable as any of their own. They also knew how he appeared to terrestrials and would not consider disclosing his secret.

It was part of the code of the interstellar trader: protect your buddy against the outsider. No matter that we of Earth considered ourselves the insiders; to them the top of the Mile-Hi was no Earthly holding but an alien enclave. So NoNo and I and all others of Earth saw not the reality but what he projected to our minds—a princely being of pleasing Earthly shape. The illusion must have been all the more titillating to them later as they observed certain goings-on between NoNo and Leo Reo in the far booth. The secret of the prince of Farland was safe. Even Boots, NoNo's friend, held his tongue, or whatever he did in his idiom. He might disapprove of the alien's actions but he'd not betray them.

Some have said cynically that if it hadn't been for Leo's royal lineage NoNo wouldn't have given him the time of day, except to sit in his lap and kiss him in her brief and darting way and twist and shout but not give out.

As it happened, he made the first advance. NoNo had come in, looking neither right nor left, and had gone straight to her far booth and read a book with yellow marking pencil in hand. The book was a compendium of the great thoughts of man. She had marked Blaise Pascal's Pensée No. 355:

"Princes and kings sometimes play. They are not always on their thrones. They weary there. Grandeur must be abandoned to be appreciated. Continuity in everything is unpleasant. Cold is agreeable, that we may get warm. . . ."

Leo sent NoNo a drink. She sent back a note: "Join me." He did and I ached to listen. Others eavesdropped and I knew later what was said. I reproduce the essence, skipping the dull parts:

Leo: "We haven't met."

NoNo: "A pity. Rectifiable. NoNo McCanless."

Leo: "Leo Reo. Enchanted."

NoNo: "You don't look enchanted. You look ordinary. *Nice* and ordinary."

Leo: "I'm just a guy. You keep yourself marvelously well. You must be happy."

NoNo: "Happy is relative. Are you?"

Leo: "Mostly. I am a royal relative. There are gaps; surely you know."

NoNo: "I know sadness. I know nothing."

Leo: "A conundrum? What do you read?"

NoNo: "Like Hamlet, words."

Leo: "I know his words. I read thoughts. Shall I read yours?"

NoNo: "If you dare."

Leo: "Your thoughts are chaotic, inchoate. You have the body supreme but ask whether your mind is its equal. You have dreams that reality denies. You know there is more than you have known so far. Am I wrong?"

NoNo: "You are astute. Are you more than clever? Are you the one I've waited for?"

Leo: "I am myself, here, now, and we have met by chance. Often I distrust chance but not tonight. Do I sound like everyone else? It serves me right."

NoNo: "It serves you well. I have waited for years, it seems, filling in the hours, not diluting myself. I read, I learn, but years pass. Once I was seventeen and all that it meant. Now I'm wiser but I deteriorate."

Leo: "You must have been magnificent to have deteriorated to your present perfection."

NoNo: ". . . Shall I sit in your lap?"

Leo: "Do. Hurry."

NoNo: "You advise haste?"

[At this point NoNo McCanless closed her book, drained her drink and moved to his side of the booth. She put a leg across his lap and an arm on his shoulder. Back to the edited transcript:]

Leo: "Cozy. NoNo? You are badly named."

NoNo: "I am mistress of my fate. You smell good, Leo, if that is who you are. You content me."

Leo: "I am myself. You see we have an audience. But if I placed my hand so, who, from afar, would notice?"

NoNo: "None. I notice, though, and I am moved. Are you moved, Leo? Are you the one I've waited for? Are you the king of beasts?"

Leo: "Are you the queen of breasts?"

I tell you, the eavesdroppers could hardly contain themselves. Would NoNo McCanless succumb? Would the heir apparent commit himself to a liaison? Were we watching a game? Who would win? Could there be a winner?

Leo Reo spoke again: "Shall we go?"

A pause by NoNo. Then: "Not to my place, nor to your place here. But to your place in Farland. The way it must be."

A pause by him. An equivocation? He spoke finally: "Are you content to wait?"

Her pause was brief. She spoke eagerly. Too eagerly? "No but yes. Yes."

"Then I'll wait, too. I'll try to send for you. Would you come?"

"Yes. Yes. I'll come."

There was no mistaking their language. His question had been in the conditional. Her answer was in the future positive. If it was a game, he'd won. NoNo could not have known it then.

Skwp the alien scribe—the *w* in his name pronounced *oo* as in *cwm*—looked like a department store mannikin seated behind a desk on rollers. It was hard to say whether the desk was attached to him or whether he was the desk. Whatever the combination, it was functional. There was the oval work surface bounded by printout screens. Built-in data boxes lit when summoned and talked when spoken to. There were transmitters and receivers and filers and retrievers; and Skwp had, or was, all of them. He was a repository of facts. He was strongest on extrasolar statistics but skimpy about Earth. He'd tell you why: Terrestrial data were readily available. If you needed to know who'd won the fifth at Belmont on a certain Saturday, or wanted a list of unsuccessful vice presidential candidates, you could have it at the flick of a switch from Data Central-USA or from Combined Info-UN. Or find it in an almanac. For a Karloff filmography, a Beiderbecke discography, that kind of thing, you wouldn't go to Skwp. But if you were after the day's prices on the wodible market at Blech or the latest scores from the Tertiary Griads in Esteddis, O.D.K., Skwp could supply them at the touch of a mandible. His three mandibles snaked over the top of his desk or wandered around under it. His head was androidal. He had it made for him when he'd been assigned to Earth. His facial expressions were conventionally human, simulating smiles, frowns, thought, and joy, but they were far from convincing.

Skwp—may I call him Scoop from now on?—can I call him he?—was an agreeable fellow but his responses to terrestrial ways were limited. Once I showed him a frame from a film that had been banned in Des Plaines, Illinois, though hardly anybody anywhere was banning anything anymore. Scoop caressed a series of stops that produced a readout that read "Whoo-whoo!" He disappointed me. Of course, he'd ingested the frame into his info banks and that was the important thing for him. I'd have been more pleased if he'd chuckled indulgently and told me about the complicated copulatory activities of the trisexuals of Taurus 20, as ( ) had done.

But I needn't apologize for Scoop's lack of humor. I was grateful for the information he'd gathered, on short notice and despite communication difficulties, on Leo Reo in his own far land and what had made him the way he was. For my benefit Scoop described Leo's background in terrestrial terms, to help me understand an alien ambience that didn't translate well.

When Leo Reo was a younger man he was not the heir to the throne. He had an older brother who was hale and handsome, lean and learned, virile (having already sired sons and daughters) and valiant. Everyone knew the brother would be king one day and Leo's fate as son secundus was to preside over a principality far from the seat of power. So no one paid much attention to him, not even his father and mother. His father the king had him in to hear his lessons or to bestow on him a leftover family honor not worthy of the firstborn. His mother the queen saw him more often. She measured him periodically for height and weight and gave him ancestral trinkets from her side of the family. She told him of ancient glories and kissed him a lot in a dutiful way. They were close for brief lengths of time, but there were weeks when they were apart.

Longing for companionship, Leo found a friend. His father had an adviser on interpersonal relations who was many years younger than the king and not so many years older than Leo. His name was Neel, and Leo came to adore him. He liked the way Neel looked (tall, lean), the way he smelled (spicy, inviting), the way he dressed (flamboyantly, with hidden rustlings), and the way he spoke to the young prince (intimately, excluding all others).

It was inevitable that they should become lovers. Neel's will and Leo's lack of direction made it happen. Even as it happened Leo wondered if it were a princely thing to do. Occasionally, as he pondered the possibility of his elder brother dying, he questioned if it were kingly. Because of the lack of issue from this kind of relationship and because he knew that if he pursued it he might lose the ability, or the will, to know women in a productive way, he was disturbed and confused about his duties to the crown.

But his friend and lover (and adviser to the king) told him it didn't matter: in the rare chance that he survived his brother into majesty they'd work it out. It was the transfer of semen that mattered for progeniture, not the physical or amatory contact with the other sex. Their science had ways to preserve and transfer it, warm and pulsing still, to the wombs of waiting women. A detail.

So Leo's friend persuaded him to fully enjoy their secret life, knowing that, if Leo's brother died, he'd still be capable of siring princes and a potential king.

There was of course more than the physical in their association. There was a meeting of minds the like of which the young prince had never known. It was possible, with Neel, to speak of anything. Sometimes, interlocked in odd ways, they discussed art and poetry, architecture, and music. They sang together or composed verses.

"But you must live in the other world as well," the teacher told his protégé. "You must learn to simulate and dissemble." And so Neel taught him how to be charming to people of all kinds, including those of the other sex. Leo learned to stimulate women mentally and lead them subconsciously to desire him physically.

Such was the teaching that when his brother died in a sporting accident and, after appropriate mourning, he went out into society as the heir apparent, a countess and two princesses fell in love with him purely because of his conversation. He squired them impartially. Such was his success as a dashing and romantic public figure that one day his father summoned him. He congratulated Leo on his popularity but urged him to moderate his activities lest he give the impression that his father the king was ill or impaired.

Leo gladly curtailed his social life, as if in fealty to his father, and again took up his private life with Neel. Neel began to groom him for kingship, amid their pleasures, devising ways to ensure continuity of the throne without the need to take a queen.

Forward in time to the Mile-Hi Building. Inside NoNo McCanless, via Diskie and Scoop:

> I was content today. My friend Leo Reo left a note which said: "I am not far, but am elsewhere than with you, which pains me."
>
> I spent the evening in my booth and worked on two figures. One is of him. One looks like the me as I would want him to see me. I gave them to Boots, who put them on a shelf behind the bar and bought me a drink, two drinks; three drinks. He likes me. Does Leo Reo?
>
> Now that I look again at the figures, the one I made of me looks a little bit pregnant. I didn't consciously make her that way.

Scoop delivered the fateful message.

Leo had been squiring NoNo in his charming way for nearly a week. According to the eavesdroppers, there had been a hottening up of the atmosphere in the far booth of the 5280 Club. He, Leo, was interested in her and she, NoNo, was absorbed in their companionship. They had not gone much beyond conversation but their hands and knees had touched, their minds had met, confidences had been exchanged, and there had been tentative exploration of a number of possibilities.

Again, however, there was ambiguity in the language, despite the efficiency of the linguapathophone. Leo spoke in certain tones which the eavesdropping aliens recognized as laden with reservations, and NoNo spoke in a feminine hyperbole whose nuances men forever misinterpret. It appeared that each had for the other an attraction unmatched

in previous encounters, although the guard of each was up.
To Leo, NoNo seemed to be offering herself as his latest
far-flung conquest, with the aim of making his list and
boasting of it afterwards. The atmosphere was torrid,
electric; the players cool. But I feared that his cool,
compared to hers, was that of an iceberg to an ice cube.

I'm getting to the part where Scoop rolled in on his self-
contained desk and delivered the message. Boots saw him
first. He set up a drink and asked for a preview.

"It requires public dissemination," Scoop said, and
toggled for amplification. The message, as Anglicized,
boomed out of Scoop for all to hear, NoNo included:

"Hear! All concerned, pay heed. Hear! Leo Reo, heir
apparent, my duty commands me say that your honored
father, Potent VII, has chosen sleep as preferable to
continued but impaired existence. The Council of Regents
orders you to most expeditiously return and receive the
scepter of the late king. You will be known, in direct
descent, as Potent VIII. Reply immediately."

Leo Reo, suddenly the Far King, stood to attention. He
replied: "I return at once, on the Midnight Shipment. I,
Potent VIII, the Far King, hear and, for the last time,
obey."

NoNo listened to the Far King's words with quickening
heartbeat. She must have hoped for a mention of herself (a
queen so soon?) but there was none. But surely he had it in
mind and she looked at him with confident eyes when he
turned to her in the booth.

"Goodbye, my dear," he said. "As you heard, I am
commanded to go. Be assured that if ever you reach my land
you will have a most royal welcome."

NoNo chose to read into his words more than was there.
"I hear you, O Prince, O King." I think she had drunk too
much and he resented it on the occasion of his elevation.
She went on: "I hear your call and I shall come, as soon
as I am able. But, Leo, why not now? Surely—"

All of us heard him put her off with explanations of the
solemn ritual and the preordained, inflexible rites. So she
said she understood. She kissed him and let him go to
prepare for his journey. She ordered another drink. She took
out clay and went to work on two new statues. They were

like the ones she'd done before, of him and her, only this time they wore crowns and the female figure was definitely pregnant. She gave them to Boots, who put them behind the bar with the others.

Leo Reo, the potential Far King, had been gone several months by our reckoning. No one could say with certainty whether his time was our time but certainly it passed with excruciating anxiety for NoNo.

Then one night she floated into the 5280 Club waving under our noses, or whatever we had, a validated ticket on the Midnight Shipment. "My king calls and I, his subject and future queen, must obey," she said. "I will send postcards, if postcards there be. You will always be in my thoughts. Now, Boots my friend, farewell drinks for all on me until the loading gong rings."

We drank her health and fortune and pretended to rejoice with her about the arrival of the ticket. The pretense was necessary because Scoop had already told us she'd bought it herself. There'd been no communication of any kind from the Far King.

There was a lot of scurrying around topside when the Midnight Shipment was due. It wasn't every midnight, of course; Earth didn't merit more than one or two transfers a month. Some of us suspected that when Leo Reo, a minor monarch, went to take up his royal duties on Farland no special embarkation had been arranged; more likely Scoop had delayed the fateful message to coincide with a scheduled shipment.

Outsiders were excluded from the sky deck when the Shipment was due. Insider-outsiders like myself were expected to keep out of the way and mind our business. Yet we couldn't help seeing cargo spew out of offices to be levitated to the deck. At the same time extrasolar cargo was offloaded and disappeared into the offices or storage spaces reserved by the resident aliens. Things and people came and went. NoNo went. I'd missed her more before. Neither of us wept.

For a long time there was no communication with Farland. Scoop said that was to be expected from civilizations that had not stabilized themselves. Not to mention communication priorities when a hundred worlds tried to get through simultaneously, convinced that their trivia was as vital as official communiqués.

But eventually there was a bleep—a mere peep—that Scoop fixed on intently because it was addressed to Boots. It was from NoNo. It said, in its entirety: "Bootsie: No one here makes a cocktail the way you do. Keep up the good work and save one for me. NoNo (YesYes)." Boots concocted one on the spot and put it at the back of the freezer, labeled NN/YY.

Scoop sent his circuits searching for another transmission and found this, which is what NoNo McCanless wrote to her former classmates at Carrie Chapman Catt College, for publication in the alumnae magazine, *Sisters Rising:*

"Greetings, sisters, from a far land called Farland. My message: Don't come unless you're officially invited and are well connected. I came insufficiently prepared, having forgotten my Girl Scout training. I was taken in, you might say; I expected more than I got, having assumed a contract. I was misled, having chosen to believe I would be the first among women, which I am not by far. This humbles me, too late for rectification. You can learn from me, though. Heed what I say. . . ."

NoNo's message, which she sent under her real name, Ann Bagley, went on for a thousand words or more. Scoop reported that the editor of *Sisters Rising,* a contemporary in her thirties, found it incomprehensible and spiked it.

From NoNo to All Those at the 5280 Club, delivered by the Midnight Shipment, on the back of a triveofax showing a fuchsia landscape dotted with avocado umbrella trees under a rare triple sunset:

"It's better where you are. At least it's familiar. Who yearns for an alien shore? I, once. No more. Hey, Jack, 'I shall return.' Warm my booth."

Let me, Jack Norkus, say in an aside what my father once told me, back when I first knew NoNo. He said Norkus was a corruption or simplification of the name for a four corners in England where his father and their ancestors had always lived. There were two such intersections in the highland they saw from their village. The nearest was the North Cross. I was reminded of a story about a man called Snooks who'd been jilted by a social-climbing woman who decided she could not live with the name. But then he was accepted by a more imaginative woman who gradually changed Snooks to Senoks and finally to the lordly Sevenoaks. "So," my father told me, "if you ever need it, know that you are not only a Norkus, which has been good enough for many generations, but also a Northcrosse. I hope you won't need it, but you should know it."

I guess he was saying we're as good as they are, whoever they are.

Next from NoNo was a poignant transmission, she not knowing it had been scanned and, in a freak of atmospherics, transmitted from Farland to the cosmos, including the 5280 Club, via Scoop, for our edification, or voyeurism. It was probably lifted from her notebooks after she made the most of the few moments her royal friend gave her for old time's sake. Thus poor NoNo out there with nothing to relate to except him and his indifference, giving her a small part of the time of his day, squeezing her into his schedule out of kindness or guilt. Listen to her, if you can stand it:

We'd sit and talk sometimes, in an Earth-style night-club he'd reconstructed to assuage my homesickness. He'd say "Sit in my lap, you gorgeous sex object" and I'd get all fired up and cuddle close to him, gradually wriggling onto his lap, tousling his hair and seeking subtle erogenous zones like his lower lip, to nibble, or his collar bone, to run my fingers along.

This was exciting to me, with him. I'd done it so often with others, firing them up and then ducking out on them. I guess what it had achieved for me was a kind of orgasmic experience which didn't require going off with one particular man and all the complications and letdowns that would have involved. Forever free, that was me, flitting from one to another, using them for my gratification as long as they interested me, without delivering myself. It was grand while it lasted, though I don't know why they put up with it. It lasted until I met Leo Reo and emigrated at his behest. (Had he really asked me?) I'd come from Earth for him but had he really wanted me? The real me? As it turned out, no. All that mattered to him was the future of his race. I, there unbidden, but one of a number of catalysts that helped create the atmosphere he required before he bedded down.

His other helps, I learned, were exotic perfumes, potions and philtres of an aphrodisiac nature, erotic films, and certain organic foods. He used me and the other catalysts to ensure the success of his repopulation plan. After he'd aroused me he'd say something like "Well, it's time for beddy-by" or "Got to catch up on my beauty sleep" or "Can't keep the programmer waiting." And he'd dismiss me!

My handmaidens would appear as he excused himself to go to his unisexual six-poster, leaving me to get through the night as best I could. Some of my handmaidens had ideas about that, I could tell, from the way they anointed me, singly or in pairs, vigorously, daringly, giving me substitute pleasures for those I'd wanted with him. I never succumbed to their enticements, not so they knew, though I was tempted several times by their expertise and their insinuating ways. What always put me off was their smirking. I wasn't going to wind up as one of them, or give in to their voluptuous invitations. I treated them all as hired masseuses as I masked, while enjoying, the responses their skills evoked.

I'm through with him now, I guess. I have some residual feelings. I much admire the shape of his nostrils and the full curve of his lower lip. I value the conversations we'd had.

I'd like my child, if male, if there could be a child, to resemble him. If I permitted it to happen, knowing I could mold the new male in my way, not his, to Earth ways, not Farland's. . . .

It's up to me, of course. He's supremely indifferent. He's used me, as I've used others, and I don't like it.

But if there were to be a child it would be mine, not his, and maybe it would have the qualities I admire in him and none of his faults. Maybe it would have my good qualities, my talents.

He or she, my son or daughter, the poor bastard, could be the potential president, the someday scientist, the nouveau novelist, the future filmmaker, the artist supreme—or, in my poor deluded father's vision, the future Intergalactic Savior, spreading the gospel according to the Rev. Ezekiel Bagley across the galaxies.

An angry NoNo, at a later time writing in her notebooks about her former adored, the Far King, Potent VIII:

He's about as potent as the bum who sells his dirty blood for a bill at a blood bank on North State Street. Not only didn't he know where anything was, he didn't care. He didn't have to know. It was done for him. Maybe that's the way of royalty—his kind of alien royalty—but it's not what he'd led me to expect.

His idea of a good sexual experience was to lock himself into his royal computing center and get his technicians to program a world-premiere wet dream. Oh, he made a fine kingly ceremony of it but basically it was as romantic as the village idiot wandering around, hand in pocket, pulling his pud.

There he was, my former hero, in his ermine pajamas or the Farland equivalent, supine in his six-poster bed, alone in its sybaritic vastness, with electrodes at temples and gonads, the harness positioned to catch his climactic emission, oblivious to everything but his programmed pleasure.

What a waste of royal beefcake, I thought. But of course nothing was wasted. The technicians, hovering dutifully on the outskirts of his dream, saw to that. His precious seed was saved for sowing far and wide. Instead of having his philoprogenitive fluid wastefully trapped in a solitary female who might or might not conceive, the fellatioid machine ensured that every conceivable iota was preserved, frozen, banked. Later at intervals his input, as I've no doubt they call it in their antiseptic jargon, was thawed and distributed with impartial beneficence to unremarried widows, to unmarriageable maidens, and to wives of impotents. Any leftover stuff, restored to throbbing warmth, was introduced into culture dishes with pulsating, waiting-to-be fertilized eggs taken at their prime from maidens at the height of their nubility.

Nothing was wasted on Farland. Certainly not at the royal level. One component met the other, generation gaps notwithstanding, and lo! in time there was a child, and another and another, ad infinitum. Many turned out well. I've seen hundreds of products of matings past. They're strong, intelligent, handsome, and—it would seem—virile.

I have the making of such a child. It's with me always, chilled inside a capsule in an insulated locket between my warm breasts. Any doctor who has kept up with the abstracts can open the locket and make me the mother of a prince or princess.

One day, maybe. I'm young yet, I tell myself. One day, when I can forget my dreams of royalty and accept reality, I'll have a master carpenter build a six-poster bed and commission technicians to attach me to electrodes. Right now I'd mind terribly. O Leo Reo, what have you become?

But one day, when the pain has dulled, as it must, I'll take out the special tape he sent me with the locket and pretend I'm again with the king of Farland.

I won't have to pretend very hard—if I make up my mind to it and accept the indignity of the programming, it can be very like the real thing. There'll be quasi-connubial bliss with the essence of the Far King in the wedding bed of my design. I'll be the uncrowned queen, along with a thousand or two others whose bastard children are entitled to wear his bar sinister. If I want it. If I succumb.

Would you accept me then, Earthman? Would you have me if I came back riding a half-alien child on my hip? If you would, my friend, I'd no longer need to sit alone in a far booth and brood. Maybe once in a while you'd take me up to watch the Midnight Shipment come in from lands beyond. Maybe then I'd belong somewhere.

This is Jack Norkus again. Or John Northcrosse, whoever the hell I am, speaking to you in Earth tones. Or as Earth-toned as one can speak in the Mile-Hi Building. Was NoNo talking to me, Earthman Jack, in the spied-upon entry in her private journal?

Would I accept her? Would she accept me without first taking to her mock-up six-poster and having her electrodal, computerized coupling with her absent but real enough dream king—and then having her locket opened by a doctor or a competent technician to impregnate her with the real seed of the Far King?

Noble as he is, and impersonal as the method might be, I don't think I'd want to be the stepfather of his farthest-flung child.

They could have managed a better homecoming for her. Maybe it should have been up to me as her friend on Earth but I couldn't get enthusiastic about arranging a celebration for the woman who had jilted me—though she probably never considered that I might have been courting her. Possibly my feelings had never been expressed, had been mostly in my mind.

Anyhow, I regretted that no one had made a special effort to welcome her back. I'd almost forgotten that most of the people at the 5280 Club are aliens and that their ways differ from ours and each other's. To them she was one of hundreds or a thousand transients who make their way among worlds.

So when the Midnight Shipment deposited her and she debarked among the handful of passengers and the multifarious cargo, she was cleared with impersonal inefficiency, just like everyone else. She surrendered her voyage papers, paid the mooring fee, made her mark on the roster, and went to the slide to seek her luggage. She had trouble finding it among the jumble and miasma of other creatures' belongings. She saw me then and gave a wan smile as she gestured helplessly. I went to help her sort through the alien mound and, alas, I believe I said by way of greeting, "How many pieces do you have?"

"Three," she said. "I should have carried them. Hello, Jack. How are you?"

Her words almost tore my heart out but there was little time for talk. She spied a bag and went for it among the jostling nonterrestrial passengers who muttered, "Surbis, surbis," as they made their way in and out of the mass. Something seemed to have her mark on it and, when she nodded, I grabbed it from under what looked like a five-hundred-pound mottled egg about to hatch. She saw the third, finally; and we withdrew to the 5280 Club.

"Shall we sit a moment?" I asked, not knowing her plans; and she nodded. I saw her eyes go to the far booth. It was occupied by a creature of fluid shape that also filled all four seats and the space beneath the table.

"I shouldn't have expected them to save my place," she said. We looked for another.

But then Boots came from behind the bar and, lightly touching her on the shoulder, said to the off-white creature in the booth, "Surbis, sir; reserved," (for our benefit) and chittered away in another tongue until the occupant undulated in a revolting obloid way to a table atop which it repositioned itself, assuming a shape like a giant pulsating haggis with a central sheep's eye that blinked in an offended way. Boots took the creature's drink, bubbling in an oversized egg cup, from the far booth and sat it atop an unoccupied corner of the haggis's table. He suctioned clean the seats and table of the far booth, and ushered us there with professional ceremony.

As we sat opposite each other and thanked him he said, "The usual, I presume, miss?" and gave me a shrug that meant I'd get a beer.

"Beautiful Boots," she said and arranged her bags on the seat beside her. "It's good to be home."

"It's good to see you back," I said automatically. Our conversation died until the drinks came.

Then JorenzO the Black Magician stopped by in his stage regalia and said, "Have I got an act for you!" and proposed a carnival tour to exhibit the only woman of this world who'd been to another. She would lecture on her personal experiences, using holograms which Lopi could supply from his All-Planets library of exotica and erotica, faking NoNo into the picture. She thanked him politely; and he backed away, saying he'd draw up an itinerary, an outline of the act, and a tentative contract.

She and I had little time to talk amid the callers. It was a satisfying welcome after all. Even A. Zichl, the imported spirits person, who'd always been stingy with his expensive trade product, came by. He delighted us with an

OmniOmelet, made of eggs of five planets and seasoning of six others, and a small unlabeled decanter of a mellow brew.

So maybe it was better that each of us welcomed her in his own way and that instead of a big formalized hello there were lots of little ones.

Relaxed and sleepy but with no place to go, she was granted a special dispensation by her alien friends and given one of the club's guest rooms for a couple of nights. I understood from them without being told that I could have shared it or used a connecting one, if that was what she and I wanted. Wordlessly she and I decided otherwise and I went to my place outside. I carried on what trade I could in the streets during the day and visited the club nights.

She was different now, this person who had gone away and returned. She was calm, more thoughtful, and often seemed lost in reverie as she sat once again in her booth. I didn't intrude. She'd look up and nod when I came into the club but didn't invite me to join her. She read, or wrote in a notebook or did her sculpture. Once or twice she shuddered as if in the grip of an unpleasant thought and put up her hand to feel through her blouse as if to be sure the locket was still there. She drank rarely now and in the days that grew into weeks after her return she did not become antic or wild.

She was again a regular in the club but not a mingler.

I learned what she was writing in her journal—a handbook with the title "Alien Sex Customs: A Guide for Earth Women."

She still answered to NoNo or Miss McCanless but she had a new name, according to the byline under the title. The name was Nina Queen.

NoNo and I had said little to each other since her return and I was even less inclined to seek her out after my discovery that she was using, if only privately, the pen name Nina Queen. Probably it was merely merchandising, to help her sell the book. Nevertheless I felt that her royal pseudonym reflected a continuing fantasy, a delusion that she still might one day meet a Far King, of the kind her father had preached so persuasively. I thought: NoNo the Ice

Queen, retreating from human contact within a fortress of frost.

And did she not still wear between her breasts—were they warm now?—that damned locket of his chilled sperm? It had become an unconscious gesture of hers to touch it through her clothing, to caress it lightly, as her eyes looked far beyond any of us.

Damn those breasts and those eyes and that symbol of potential consummation! Damn NoNo and the effect she was having on me still, despite my growing conviction that I should forget her and find someone uncontaminated by aliens, not warped by the preachings of a father obsessed by visions that had come not from his God but from readings in crackpot tracts. I should quit this sick outpost of space and its gallery of sideshow specimens and look for peace beyond the shadow and memories of the Mile-Hi Building. It should be possible to find someone like Kipling's "neater, sweeter maiden in a cleaner, greener land." Somewhere such a maiden must exist for me, if I had the sense to seek her. Somewhere away from the Ice Maiden, the absurdly but aptly named NoNo McCanless, lost and lonely and undoubtedly brave but rapidly becoming a character to be pointed out to tourists.

I went, saying goodbye to no one, but went perhaps not as far as I should have. I found a lake in a neighboring state where I rented a cabin and a rowboat. It was early spring. I bundled up and rowed, watching the season change and the green appear in that clean land.

I went to the village library and looked through books, wondering where in Kipling's poetry I'd read of that sweet maiden. I didn't expect to find her in "Mandalay," in among all the rousing thunder and exotic sounds of the East as voiced by a Tommy shipped home to gritty, drizzly London. Hidden in the next-to-last stanza, embedded like a jewel, it is one of the few lines in the entire poem not distorted by a Cockney accent: "I've a neater, sweeter maiden in a cleaner, greener land!"

I went back to Chicago, to that silver needle stuck in the green rind of an Earth fruit not yet ripe enough to welcome the aliens living among but aloof from them in its mile-high eye.

I went back with nothing resolved, my plans no clearer, not knowing whether I'd speak to NoNo or she to me. It just seemed to me that I was going home to a big city's special neighborhood that had accepted both NoNo and me.

They asked where I'd been, said they'd been looking for me, there was a message from Leo Reo.

"For me? Why me?" As far as I knew, the Far King hadn't communicated with any of us since he left. The message was a Scoop Special, a facsimile of the ornate scroll in which the original must have left the royal palace of Farland. It said:

My dear chap—
First permit me to congratulate you on the happy news. I regret that I will be unable to be present at the nuptials but my fond wishes go to you both. There will be a suitable gift at the proper time for you and your fiancée. I am not writing separately to Ann, for reasons that you and I as men of the world can appreciate. As one of your proverbs has it, "Once smitten, too often bitten."
This then is solely for your eyes . . .

I looked up. Boots, JorenzO, and Scoop were pointedly paying no attention to me. I knew damn well every one of them, and any number of others, knew what Leo had written. They were at the bar, a discreet distance away. NoNo was not in the club.

. . . and I leave it to your excellent judgment how much of it, if any, you will wish to communicate to Ann.
Here is what I must tell you—you may consider it another wedding present or you may curse me:
The locket which Ann Bagley, alias NoNo McCanless, wears between her sweet breasts carries no sperm of mine. It was perhaps cruel to let her think it did and that with it she could conceive, at her pleasure, a royal prince.
If it was cruel of me, it was crueler to let the deception continue. But it was a way of speeding NoNo's departure from Farland—with what she thought to be a token portion of my actual self. I had not summoned her, you must know, and her presence here had begun to cloy.

But you must know that your people and mine are incompatible genetically. The club members must have told you that I am not humanoid but can appear that way if I wish it. Had I appeared in my own shape there could have been no companionship with NoNo, because there are no points of contact. Would she have been smitten if she had seen me the way Skwp once clinically described me, as "a malappendaged monstrosity, often unstable"? No, no.

I give no empty gifts. There is something of value in the capsule NoNo wears but nothing of mine. It is a human seed, Jack. It is yours.

You see, when I was considering a suitable farewell gift to NoNo and decided on the locket, I knew its contents would have to be special and appropriate. Because she and I were incompatible, in more ways than one, I dispatched a trusted emissary to the Northside sperm emporium you are sometimes forced by nature of your business, and by your own nature, to patronize. Your specimen was resold to my trusted messenger and packaged for star travel to Farland.

Was this merely a royal jest? I think not. It was my way of ensuring that NoNo would have a human child if she wanted one in this way, and not a space monster. The decision, with the happy news I've had of your impending marriage, is now yours, my friend.

Whether you value its contents, the locket itself is valuable. Tiffany's would give you a breathtaking estimate. Consider that if you are tempted to destroy it.

I have news of my own. My first true and sanctioned royal son is soon to be born. He will take my former name, Leo, and when he succeeds to the throne he will be Leo IX. Not a jest, but amusing, is it not?

An affectionate farewell from afar.

Potent VIII

Having read the astonishing document I yelled at the group at the bar: "Who the hell said I was going to marry NoNo?" The reply was a combination of alien shrugs.

"Damn it," I said, waving Leo's letter, "what have you been up to?"

"Have a drink on the house," Boots said. "Sit down and talk about it, whatever it is."

"Don't pretend you haven't read every word of it." I accepted the beer. "I want to know what else you've been up to."

"Good news about Leo Reo's boy," JorenzO said. "Kings should have male heirs." He raised a glass. "Here's to everybody's happiness."

"Not a word about any of this to NoNo," I said.

"Words of honor," Boots said. "Whatever she is to know must come from you."

"And what is she to know, you conspirators?"

"What you tell her," he said. "No conspiracy here."

"A pseudolensing eavesdropper, a black magician, a scribe who knows everybody's secrets—and you tell me nothing is going on?"

"It's your move, actually," Boots said.

"What do you mean? Do you see something?"

Diskie appeared out of nowhere. "NoNo is coming," he said. "Oh, hello, Jack. Congratulations."

"Now listen—"

"Inside NoNo McCanless today is tranquility." Diskie spun sideways and disappeared, then came back in sight. "Inside Jack Norkus, on the other hand— You're all riled up, aren't you?"

"Just stay the hell out of me," I yelled. "And out of NoNo too."

"I think he's beginning to move," Boots said.

NoNo came in then. There was a spring in her step and she smiled when she saw us. "Hello, boys. Hello, Jack."

"Hello, N— Hello. I've got to talk to you."

"Call me NoNo. I don't mind. Come to my booth."

"And give these galoots an earful?"

"Oh, that kind of talk. They're going to know anyhow, sooner or later, so it might as well be sooner."

"Know what?" I asked. Was she doing it, too?

"Whatever there is to know. What anybody says anywhere." She was smiling again. She looked good, head high.

"What the hell," I said. "We'll take the booth. Want a drink?"

"A little white wine over ice."

I purposely dropped my voice. "And I'll have another beer."

Boots had them at the table almost before we sat down.

"Surbis?" Boots said. I sensed that under his furry face he was all smiles. "If you want anything else just think—I mean *ring*." He went back to the bar.

"Why so merry, my lady?" I asked.

"Compared to my previous morbid state? The book goes well, for one thing."

"What book?"

"What book? Nina Queen's book. Everybody knows what book. Don't pretend."

"Writing it out of your system?"

"It or him. But it's more than just that. Another him is in it, too."

"Your father."

"Yes, and other hims. I think of you sometimes when I write and you do creep in now and again. Then there's the capital-H Him that father preached about, Christ's extraterrestrial brother."

"You could call it 'The Hymn of Him.' "

She laughed. "That would be better than my working title."

"Is it fiction or nonfiction?"

"A little of both, I suppose."

"May I read it?"

"It's still rough. Could we have another drink?"

Boots was there instantly, serving us. "Actually, it reads very well," he said. "Surbis."

"Damn you, Boots," I said. "Get out of here."

"Thank you, Boots," NoNo said. "But tell Jack I didn't give it to you to read."

Boots nodded and went away.

"He was grinning, wasn't he?" I asked.

She agreed. "Twinkling, I'd say."

"All right. We know there's no privacy. What's this about a wedding? You're aware of the talk?"

"I have been for some days. I think it's rather amusing. And sweet."

"I just heard about it. I've been away, thinking."

"I've thought a lot lately, too."

"That's what we've got to talk about," I said. "Everybody knows what you and I are thinking except you and me. How did you hear about the wedding? Who told you?"

"Nobody told me. It just came into my mind one evening as I sat here and I knew it must have come from one of them. I'd had no thoughts like it before, at least not since we were kids reading Father's books together, and that childish thought was mixed up with others about finding my Prince Charming on Mars or Venus."

"Is it still a childish thought? What was your reaction aside from its being amusing and sweet?"

"That was my reaction to them for putting it in my mind. About such a wedding—I don't reject the idea utterly. On the other hand, I haven't sent announcements to our near and dear."

She was no longer smiling and I realized I had been grilling her about an intimate matter without giving her an indication of my feelings. "Surbis," I said. "I'll admit I've thought about marriage more recently than that time in your father's study. Marrying you. We are talking about you and me, aren't we?"

"Yes. That is the hypothetical subject. Did you think about that before or after I went—chased off after Leo?"

"Before," I said. "Only before, until today."

She put her hand on the table, close to but not touching her glass, and I took it. It was a gentle clasp and we looked at each other without speaking. After a little while we were grinning and broke into laughter.

"You tell me," she said.

"I was thinking that my thoughts were so mixed up that I'd have to ask the eavesdroppers what was really in my mind."

"Me too."

Boots was there again before I said, "I'm starved," and before I realized he hadn't brought another round of drinks but was setting sandwiches before us.

"So that's what you were thinking!" NoNo said, laughing.

"I assure you that was the least of his thoughts, my dear," Boots told her.

As we ate we talked about inconsequential things.
Then I said: "Now we have to talk about the locket."
"I was afraid of that," NoNo said.

After the sweetness of that scene I decline to detail the
agony of our talk about the locket. Boots and his buddies
heard it all, and Scoop can retrieve it for you if your interest
is more scholarly than prurient—or even if it isn't.
I told NoNo I'd had a letter from Leo. That surprised her,
and she asked to see it. I said he had written in confidence
and I would respect that trust. She spoke angrily about trust
for a man who had betrayed her. I said he was not a man.
She said she knew him better than I and that he was a man.
I said she had been deceived, opthalmologically, linguapath-
ophonically and in other ways. I explained. She wept. She
said that if that was so he'd been kind not to let her see him
as he really was. I agreed it was a kind of kindness. I said
it had been gracious of him to tell no one that he had not
sent for her, that she had bought her own ticket to Farland.
More tears.
Because he was not a man, I told her, she could not have
his child. The species were incompatible, I said, ignoring
the other incompatibility of which he'd spoken. All things
were possible, she said. He would not have given her the
locket if— Exobiologists disagreed, I said. I'd plumbed
Scoop to his depths on the subject. Besides—
She blew her nose and wanted to know besides what. I
hesitated, but she seemed to have recovered her composure,
and after a long pause I told her it was not his seed in the
locket. Not his, but— I had to blurt it out: not his but mine.
All the antagonism was wiped from her face as she tried
to understand, to accept. Her voice was dull, her face blank
as she asked how that could be. Ashamed, I told her. Her
face clouded.
It wasn't true, she said at last. Leo had heard the rumors
of a wedding—rumors planted, no doubt, by our well-
meaning but meddling otherworldly friends—and was lying
to be kind. She didn't believe my exobiologists. Whatever
it might cost us, she would have his child.
But I could not let her have that child, knowing it mine,
if she believed it his. Not if we were to marry.

We needn't marry for her to have the child, she pointed out. These weren't the old days.

They were the old days for her father and mother, the grandparents, I pointed out. Had she thought of them?

Often, she said. She thought her father would accept the child, whatever its form, and baptize it in vindication of his belief, and that her mother would go along, as she always had.

But what about me, I asked, hurting. If it turned out, and I believed this, that it was my seed, was I to be denied fatherhood?

She said I'd denied it when I went to that filthy place and sold a piece of myself. Leo had bought and paid for it but that didn't prove it was in the locket.

I said she had sent me there in frustration because of the way she had carried on with me among a dozen males, most of them aliens, during the wildest of her wild ways, in whatever frenzy was upon her then.

She wept again, saying that was long ago and she had hoped we were different now, able to accept the once unacceptable, to be friends and live with the realities of today and of the future.

I was weeping with her and said I'd like us to have a new start. Let's the two of us go off to a cleaner, greener land and sink the locket in the lake I'd found and go on from there together.

With a conventional wedding night and everything, she said. Was that what I wanted?

I said yes it was. Sink the damned locket and go to bed on our honeymoon with nothing between her breasts but her own sweet skin. Without a seed that had been exposed to God knows what influences on two journeys through space.

You're asking for everything or nothing, Jack, aren't you? Take it off, sink it, forget all it may mean and the hell with my feelings.

Yes, I am. For both of us.

No, Jack. There are three of us now. Never, Jack. No. No.

I must have been deranged after that talk with NoNo to seek out JorenzO the Black Magician. But he'd often been kind to us. Furthermore she'd never flung herself into his lap, probably because his awesome dignity would not have permitted it.

"I know you're not a seer," I told JorenzO, "but your other magickal powers might help me."

JorenzO smiled down at me from his seven feet of metal body and costume. He was black as an old kettle except in the stiff steel fiber of his iron-gray hair.

"You are here at the right time. I have just purchased the mechanicals of an act of Spanish seers, a trio accredited by the Futurology Society. For half a century, your time, they were prognosticators without peer. Even you must know of them. They billed themselves as Prog, Nost, and Kate; or, in Hispanic, Prog, Nost, y Kate. I have bought their book for a sum that will permit them to live out their lives in comfort in Barcelona. I had to be generous, for they know how long that will be."

"Fine," I said. "I congratulate you. Can you help me? I have no money."

Always magickal, he was now oracular. Lofty but friendly, he said he would find a solution by probing the future. He was between tours and would do this for me in friendship.

He told me how it would be. I'd be flung into an alternate future, one of several I told him I'd considered. In that future I'd rejected NoNo after she had rejected me and had her child from the locket.

"Expect nightmare," he said. "Expect the unexpected you have asked for. I will show you a future you may not like, though it is there."

I told him I needed to know, however repugnant it might be.

"Then tomorrow night we travel," JorenzO said. "You will see it plain and then must choose whether it is to be or whether there is another way."

Boots took me aside and said, surprising me by his criticism of a fellow alien: "Don't rely too much on JorenzO. It will be chancy, especially to someone like you who can't know the effect it will have on you. Consider that its complexities may have been too much for those of us who have traveled part of that path, then retreated to find a haven

here in a backwater of the cosmos—forgive me, Earthman—
where things are easier and, if there's little excitement,
there's a kind of peace. Talk to NoNo again. Don't fling
yourself so far that you can't get back."

But we had talked, NoNo and I. God how we'd talked.
In the club, downside at her place, my place, at cafeterias
and bars, in parks.

Both of us wanted peace, comfort, ease, and laughter
whether together or apart. We were honest about that. We'd
prefer together, having known each other a long time,
although in scattered segments. Was there another for her or
me? For her, no, unless she still believed in a far prince.
For me, only my neater, sweeter maiden, who might well
be she—not another person but herself returned and different
(why did I think repentant?)—and was I vengeful, demanding
that she renounce her dreams yet again? I may have been;
I too have my wild side. Inside myself (Diskie knows) I've
been as frantic as she; but I stored it up, not giving it out
except those times at the sperm bank when I'd succumbed,
as she never had. Could she be my almost virginal bride?

We came to no conclusion after again exploring the possibilities. One: She could have the child of the locket, hoping
and believing it Leo's. Or she could agree that it was mine
and decline it, preferring the real me, not a surrogate but my
flesh in hers. (Fat chance, from all she'd said.) There was
still unbridgeable distance between us, despite all the
conversation.

We reached the hour JorenzO had set for my journey in
space and time. He must have known there'd be no resolu-
tion and that his experiment would be the alternative.

We were in a small auditorium. Its edges were dark; I
could see no walls. The stage was dim with shapes that had
no meaning. Boots had seated NoNo and me a good distance
apart on a curving riser. He sat between us, next to her.

JorenzO appeared on the stage in a cloud of black smoke.
Diskie entered, glimmering almost subliminally, then winked
out. Scoop came and occupied an aisle, needing no seat, all
attuned, all business.

JorenzO said: "We are assembled to help our friends. Let
the record show this."

Diskie reappeared from inside JorenzO. "The record will

show what it will show. Action now, words later. Like Lopi making a film.''

"First prologue,'' JorenzO said, recapitulating as if for archives. "NoNo has declined to destroy the locket. She is no longer positive it encloses the seed of the Far King but still believes there is a chance to bear a royal child. If she believed the seed to be Jack's, destroying it would be a betrayal of Jack, of whom she is fond. She is also residually fond of the Far King. Both men have been cads, but all men are cads, she reasons. Jack will not have her while she wears the locket. Impasse. Let the drama begin.'' He left the stage to sit near me.

A disembodied voice spoke from among the dim shapes before us: "The time is future, and what you will see is reality. NoNo, estranged from Jack, had the child of the locket. The child was male and human, as she expected it to be, whoever the father. She called him Star Kin. Kin, not quite King. Kin grew and developed normally. NoNo, who thought of herself as Ann Bagley, was happy. She invited Jack to visit, to see the child. He visited once, knew the boy to be his, convinced the child was his, certain of it but unwilling to forget that NoNo had chosen to risk the possibility of it being Leo Reo's. Jack was unwilling to be friends with her. She half hoped there might be a reconciliation but it seemed impossible.'' The voice went on and the shapes began to assume scenes from the narrative:

Jack brooded, refused to visit again.

NoNo left Chicago with Kin and returned to her father's house. She was the prodigal daughter, welcomed, accepted by grandparents proud of their Kin. She was content, a good mother, and read again in her father's books and worked on her own.

Kin continued to grow, but no longer normally. His development accelerated. Eight months after birth he had the body and mind of a boy of six years. Kin's grandparents marveled. A miracle! Kin talked but said little. He read much, mostly in his grandfather's books and in his mother's manuscript.

NoNo marveled at her son. Not a miracle to her, but evidence that Leo had lied, or Jack had lied, and that she had indeed borne the child of a Far King, lord of a realm where time is different.

The minister's village and flock were not yet ready either for a miracle or a star-begotten child; and Kin was kept in the house, as if he were still an infant.

Word of the phenomenal growth reached Jack, who believed neither in a miracle nor that the child was Leo's. He was convinced that Kin was his, born of a seed that had traveled twice across the cosmos, first with Leo's emissary, then back in NoNo's locket, subjected to unknowable extrasolar emissions and influences.

Jack's brooding intensified. He was granted live-in privileges at the 5280 Club and abandoned his business to spend hours poring over theological works Scoop produced from alien archives as well as from his growing terrestrial collection. As a boy in Ezekiel Bagley's study, Jack never thought he'd accept literally any of the clergyman's hand-me-down ideas. Who could have foreseen that the catalyst to his conversion would be the fruit of his own loins, implanted antiseptically in the womb of Ann-Bagley-become-NoNo-McCanless? Anyone who lived among the aliens in the 5280 Club eventually became a little crazy, but Jack took pride in the fact that his research didn't persuade him that he was Jesus Christ. Too many had done that bit. No, sir, he was father to the Jesus of the worlds afar. His son Kin was the Other Christ. Kin, son of God, brother to Jesus, son of God, and immaculately conceived.

Having heard that Kin—one year old in Earth time— looked, acted, and *was* twelve years old, Jack heard another Word and kidnapped his son.

Kin went willingly with his father to the Mile-Hi Building, as if he'd been waiting for his ministry to begin. At the 5280 Club Jack asked JorenzO the Black Magician to seek a place beyond the world that already had a Christ. JorenzO said there'd be no fee; he'd take a profit some way.

JorenzO said: "Board the Midnight Shipment and transfer at The Wait. Ask for Darkohl; everybody will understand. Think Dark Hole. It's a bar not unlike this one. Give Captain Black Otro this card. He'll book you and the boy on the shuttle to Dyson. It's the only way and the only place. Do you know what you're doing? Only you can judge."

Jack said he was sure and took the card. Boots was in the background, saying nothing but seeming to lean toward disapproval.

Kin and Jack reached The Wait and found the shuttle. They were assigned places below and awoke for the glide down to Dyson. Maybe Kin was growing faster now or maybe his sleep below in star time contributed, but when he set foot on the planet he looked a tall, strapping, bearded twenty-one.

It was a good place for them to start, in this craggy desert land whose people could have been their Earth brothers of Biblical times but who had never heard the Word.

For now Kin carried out his first ministry and he and his father (and, presumably, his Father) were content.

But one morning Kin went to his human father and said, "I have had a vision." Jack was pleased until Kin continued. "Mother tried to die because of what we have done."

Jack was troubled. "I am sorry to hear that. But what is done and will be done is the Lord's work."

"I understand but I am saddened. Grandfather found her in time and with God's help she will be restored to health."

"Praise the Lord," Jack said.

"But she is distraught and disturbed. She spends her time sculpting little statues. There are so many that the church is selling them to help its building fund."

"When did it happen, this that you saw in the vision?"

"It seemed that it was a time ago." They spoke no more of it. Later they stood on a mountaintop, leaning on their staffs, content with their work in the valley behind them. Ahead lay another place that needed the Word. And, when they had gone down and enlightened them, there would be other places, other worlds eager to receive them. So spoke Jack to his son, the Son of God, for was it not written that there were many worlds to which God's Majesty reached? That it was not only the bipeds of Earth that He watched over but also the creatures of lands beyond who were as dear to Him, in their various shapes, as were they?

They went down the rocky path and came to a marketplace. A stall displayed figures of bestial shape. Heathen idols, Jack thought, and raised his staff to smash them. But Kin grasped his wrist and bade him look more closely. Could it be a miracle? Was it a sign of the Lord's interstellar omniscience? On that distant planet was evidence that Another had preceded them.

The old woman who tended the stall proffered first one, then another of the clay figures. They were exquisitely made, representing creatures of a dozen worlds whose like he had seen before—Boots and JorenzO and Diskie and Lopi and Mogle and Scoop. Memories of the alien-touched Earth he had renounced! Memories of NoNo—who else could have sculpted them?

But he ignored the old woman's offerings because on a shelf back of her were larger, choicer pieces so true to life that his limbs began to tremble. One was of Leo Reo in a robe that made him look like a Judas. The other was of his son Kin, with a halo over his head. Jack purchased the second, thinking it strange that the halo was attached at the front. When they reached the inn to which they were traveling they saw that the halo had broken off, leaving a scar where it had been fastened to the forehead.

In a dream at the inn that night Jack was troubled by a thought that his son was not his but Adam's and that Kin would slay not his brother, because he had none, but his father.

Had NoNo cursed him across the cosmos? He awoke in sweat, trembling to hear his son suggest that they leave the marked path for a way through the cane fields. He was sore afraid to go but in the end he went, as he knew he must.

Kin's smiling lips and his mother's eyes beckoned him and he followed his son into the barren landscapes where the dead husks rustled in the hot breeze and the alien sun was a blood-red disc behind a haze.

Kin was arrested, charged with and found guilty of patricide, and executed at the scene of the crime as the new crop came up in the cane fields. Method of execution: crucifixion, head down. A multitude of people on the primitive planet watched. Contrary to folk tales, there was no resurrection. Kin's body was taken down and incinerated. His ashes fertilized the field.

The multitudes of the primitive, Earthlike planet vanished as the houselights came on full. "What the hell goes on here?" Lopi yelled. "Who said you could use my set?"

I shuddered and felt nauseated as I was yanked back from the future drama where I'd been both spectator and participant. I blinked in the glare and looked past the audience of aliens to NoNo. She was touching her locket in a questioning way and seemed relieved to see me alive.

"It was a JorenzO production in a good cause," Boots said mildly. "An attempt to solve the problems of two friends."

"When I need a coproducer it won't be JorenzO," Lopi said. "You damn amateurs! Did you damage any of my props?"

"Only a halo on a little statue," NoNo said. "I'll make you another. And we almost lost Jack."

"We did lose him," JorenzO said, giving Lopi a black look. "We saw—lived—the future. It happened in the part of time that is a projection of now. What has happened is past and therefore true."

"It was a projection all right," Lopi stormed. "My stage manager says you ran a tape of my epic in progress, *The Death of God in Dyson*. It should make a mint wherever they eat missionaries." He turned to JorenzO. "And you thought you could pass it off as one of your feats of magick? I should sue you for plagiarism, you fake necromancer."

"It happened," JorenzO said with dignity. "All of us saw. Fortunately the future is reversible."

"Sure," Lopi said. "You rewind the tape."

"Excellently put," Boots said. "Have you considered, Lopi, that All-Planets Films could be liable for invading the privacy of two of our guests?"

Lopi was adaptable. He said: "Okay, I won't show it in the solar area. You drop invasion of privacy, I drop plagiarism. Now will you get the hell out of my screening room and let me work? NoNo, dear, the halo statue; this time make the scar a little more visible, okay? Sorbis, Jack, for killing you off, but it's only a picture, for Christ's sake. Did you like your son?"

"Up to a point," I said, feeling better. "Cane fields aren't my thing."

"I adored him," NoNo said. "I'm going to have him."

Lopi stayed and the rest of us went to the club for restoratives, Boots buying. It was good to be back in the familiar now, the future nightmare dimming as the tape rewound.

NoNo and I sat in her far booth and the others grouped around. There was camaraderie. Accommodation seemed possible. Boots served NoNo a glittering luminescent wine and gave me a beer with bubbles golden and tangy.

There we were, Norkus, Bagley & Co. It sounded like the pair of professional mountebanks we were in JorenzO's purloined scenario, flinging ourselves across the cosmos in an orgy of revenge, blaming our derangement not on our faulty selves but on the Rev. Ezekiel Bagley's charming and terrible interpretation of the Bible. Scoop said the old boy might be right about there being some higher plan in the diversity of worlds but that it probably would take an intercosmic ecumenical congress to work it out.

Having lived vicarious years during the screening—for NoNo and me it was decades—we had come back to ourselves changed. Earlier the different time of Farland had subtly aged NoNo. Now I felt tired to my bones. Had part of myself gone on that future journey? Had it happened? JorenzO said it had, even if reversibly. Everything that could happen on one path or another had happened and it had depleted me.

Now I saw that NoNo had aged once more. It was physical, a bit, in the way she carried herself, the way she spoke. But deeper than that was a new look of maturity and wisdom.

I suppose I was different and wiser too. Thoughts relayed by the aliens flew between us. We had been drifters. We had been barren, not just of children who could be our only immortality, but of purpose. An aimless future lay ahead, unless—

Neither of us wanted to experience another possible future unless it was one we controlled, having just been through a thoroughly nasty one. Theatrical and semifictional as it was, it had been a catharsis.

NoNo and I exchanged glances and little smiles as the alien telepathy worked to catalyze and exchange our thoughts. Of course they'd had it in mind, those clever conspirators, to jolt us in this way or another into reconsidering our once inflexible positions.

Now NoNo and I were touching hands and talking, oblivious to the alien eavesdroppers we knew would always be with us, all friends, all honorary godfathers.

When NoNo voiced the solution, which seemed to have sprung simultaneously from the massed minds of a dozen planets, it received unanimous approval. Boots was particularly happy. He was the last of his kind.

NoNo spoke for all of us:

"My friends, listen. Only recently I still believed, or hoped, that I would be the queen of a far king, if not the Far King I'd known. I was proud and arrogant but I've been humbled by the concern that my friends, old and new, have shown for me. Now I think the coming king is not one I'll marry but one I'll mother. As JorenzO has shown me, he is Kin, but as all of you have assured me, he will live a different life than that of Lopi's scenario.

"And Kin will have a twin, conceived in a private old-fashioned way, but who, with the help of our new-fashioned eugenics, will be a girl. In her lifetime she will have the opportunity to be the queen of a far land, but probably she'll be just as happy to be the consort of a man here on Earth— a prince of a fellow, if not of alien seed.

"Will anyone know which of the twins was star-begotten and which the product of a conventional conception? Possibly you will know but I think it better that you never tell the parents."

It was lump-in-the-throat time as Boots refilled our glasses and we toasted each other.

Then Scoop became animated and produced a scroll from one of the outputs of himself and said: "Hear! A message from the Far King, once Leo Reo, now Potent VIII of Farland, as follows: 'The next Midnight Shipment will bring as my nuptial gift to the happy couple two royal lockets for their twins, should they aspire, in a score of years, to leave Earth in a vicarious way by seeking far mates. For now, give them a fond kiss from their stepfather."

NoNo and I locked eyes and I told Scoop to send Leo a message: "I appreciate the thought but on receipt of the lockets, whatever their intrinsic value or contents, we'll take them to another state and sink them in a lake I know. Sign it John Northcrosse, formerly nobody, now mate-to-be of the former NoNo McCanless, now a new person.''

NoNo, the dear Ann of our youth, said: "Tell Leo I agree absolutely. And tell him to go jump in the lake.''

Dan McQuarrie assured us there was a linguapathic equivalent for the idiom that Leo would understand.

Now, in a special alien suite a mile above Earth with a window overlooking the Midnight Shipment, NoNo and I, content, await the birth of our terrestrial twins.

Richard Wilson was a Futurian, a member of that celebrated group of science-fiction fans who virtually took over the field in the early 1940s and are the subject of Damon Knight's memoir, The Futurians. *Wilson went on to become an editor for various news services and later the Director of the Syracuse University News Bureau. Since he was a part-time writer, his output in science fiction was not large, but it was extremely distinguished, including the Nebula Award–winning novelette "Mother to the World" and such satirical novels as* Those Idiots from Earth *and* The Girls from Planet Five.

He died in 1988.

THE ALTAR AT MIDNIGHT
by C. M. Kornbluth

For any technological advance, for the opening of any new frontier, there is always a human price to be paid.

He had quite a rum-blossom on him for a kid, I thought at first. But when he moved closer to the light by the cash register to ask the bartender for a match or something, I saw it wasn't that. Not just the nose. Broken veins on his cheeks, too, and the funny eyes. He must have seen me look, because he slid back from the light.

The bartender shook my bottle of ale in front of me like a Swiss bell-ringer so it foamed inside the green glass.

"You ready for another, sir?" he asked.

I shook my head. Down the bar, he tried it on the kid— he was drinking Scotch and water or something like that— and found out he could push him around. He sold him three Scotch and waters in ten minutes.

When he tried for number four, the kid had his courage up and said, "I'll tell *you* when I'm ready for another, Jack." But there wasn't any trouble.

It was almost nine and the place began to fill up. The manager, a real hood type, stationed himself by the door to screen out the high-school kids and give the big hello to conventioneers. The girls came hurrying in too, with their little makeup cases and their fancy hair piled up and their frozen faces with the perfect mouths drawn on them. One of them stopped to say something to the manager, some excuse about something, and he said: "That's aw ri'; getcha assina dressing room."

A three-piece band behind the drapes at the back of the stage began to make warm-up noises and there were two

53

bartenders keeping busy. Mostly it was beer—a midweek crowd. I finished my ale and had to wait a couple of minutes before I could get another bottle. The bar filled up from the end near the stage because all the customers wanted a good, close look at the strippers for their fifty-cent bottles of beer. But I noticed that nobody sat down next to the kid, or, if anybody did, he didn't stay long—you go out for some fun and the bartender pushes you around and nobody wants to sit next to you. I picked up my bottle and glass and went down on the stool to his left.

He turned to me right away and said: "What kind of a place is this, anyway?" The broken veins were all over his face, little ones, but so many, so close, that they made his face look something like marbled rubber. The funny look in his eyes was it—the trick contact lenses. But I tried not to stare and not to look away.

"It's okay," I said. "It's a good show if you don't mind a lot of noise from—"

He stuck a cigarette into his mouth and poked the pack at me. "I'm a spacer," he said, interrupting.

I took one of his cigarettes and said: "Oh."

He snapped a lighter for the cigarettes and said: "Venus."

I was noticing that his pack of cigarettes on the bar had some kind of yellow sticker instead of the blue tax stamp.

"Ain't that a crock?" he asked. "You can't smoke and they give you lighters for a souvenir. But it's a good lighter. On Mars last week, they gave us all some cheap pen-and-pencil sets."

"You get something every trip, hah?" I took a good, long drink of ale and he finished his Scotch and water.

"Shoot. You call a trip a 'shoot.' "

One of the girls was working her way down the bar. She was going to slide onto the empty stool at his right and give him the business, but she looked at him first and decided not to. She curled around me and asked if I'd buy her a li'l ole drink. I said no and she moved on to the next. I could kind of feel the young fellow quivering. When I looked at him, he stood up. I followed him out of the dump. The manager grinned without thinking and said, "G'night, boys," to us.

The kid stopped in the street and said to me: "You don't

have to follow me around, Pappy.'' He sounded like one wrong word and I would get socked in the teeth.

''Take it easy. I know a place where they won't spit in your eye.''

He pulled himself together and made a joke of it. ''This I have to see,'' he said. ''Near here?''

''A few blocks.''

We started walking. It was a nice night.

''I don't know this city at all,'' he said. ''I'm from Covington, Kentucky. You do your drinking at home there. We don't have places like this.'' He meant the whole Skid Row area.

''It's not so bad,'' I said. ''I spend a lot of time here.''

''Is that a fact? I mean, down home a man your age would likely have a wife and children.''

''I do. The hell with them.''

He laughed like a real youngster and I figured he couldn't even be twenty-five. He didn't have any trouble with the broken curbstones in spite of his Scotch and waters. I asked him about it.

''Sense of balance,'' he said. ''You have to be tops for balance to be a spacer—you spend so much time outside in a suit. People don't know how much. Punctures. And you aren't worth a damn if you lose your point.''

''What's that mean?''

''Oh. Well, it's hard to describe. When you're outside and you lose your point, it means you're all mixed up, you don't know which way the can—that's the ship—which way the can is. It's having all that room around you. But if you have a good balance, you feel a little tugging to the ship, or maybe you just *know* which way the ship is without feeling it. Then you have your point and you can get the work done.''

''There must be a lot that's hard to describe.''

He thought that might be a crack and he clammed up on me.

''You call this Gandytown,'' I said after a while. ''It's where the stove-up old railroad men hang out. This is the place.''

It was the second week of the month, before everybody's pension check was all gone. Oswiak's was jumping. The

Grandsons of the Pioneers were on the juke singing the *Man from Mars Yodel* and old Paddy Shea was jigging in the middle of the floor. He had a full seidel of beer in his right hand and his empty left sleeve was flapping.

The kid balked at the screen door. "Too damn bright," he said.

I shrugged and went on in and he followed. We sat down at a table. At Oswiak's you can drink at the bar if you want to, but none of the regulars do.

Paddy jigged over and said: "Welcome home, Doc." He's a Liverpool Irishman; they talk like Scots, some say, but they sound like Brooklyn to me.

"Hello, Paddy. I brought somebody uglier than you. Now what do you say?"

Paddy jigged around the kid in a half-circle with his sleeve flapping and then flopped into a chair when the record stopped. He took a big drink from the seidel and said: "Can he do this?" Paddy stretched his face into an awful grin that showed his teeth. He has three of them. The kid laughed and asked me: "What the hell did you drag me into here for?"

"Paddy says he'll buy drinks for the house the day anybody uglier than he is comes in."

Oswiak's wife waddled over for the order and the kid asked us what we'd have. I figured I could start drinking, so it was three double Scotches.

After the second round, Paddy started blowing about how they took his arm off without any anesthetics except a bottle of gin because the red-ball freight he was tangled up in couldn't wait.

That brought some of the other old gimps over to the table with their stories.

Blackie Bauer had been sitting in a boxcar with his legs sticking through the door when the train started with a jerk. Wham, the door closed. Everybody laughed at Blackie for being that dumb in the first place, and he got mad.

Sam Fireman has palsy. This week he was claiming he used to be a watchmaker before he began to shake. The week before, he'd said he was a brain surgeon. A woman I didn't know, a real old Boxcar Bertha, dragged herself over and began some kind of story about how her sister married a Greek, but she passed out before we found out what happened.

Somebody wanted to know what was wrong with the kid's face—Bauer, I think it was, after he came back to the table.

"Compression and decompression," the kid said. "You're all the time climbing into your suit and out of your suit. Inboard air's thin to start with. You get a few redlines—that's these ruptured blood vessels—and you say the hell with the money; all you'll make is just one more trip. But, God, it's a lot of money for anybody my age! You keep saying that until you can't be anything but a spacer. The eyes are hard-radiation scars."

"You like dot all ofer?" asked Oswiak's wife politely.

"All over, ma'am," the kid told her in a miserable voice. "But I'm going to quit before I get a Bowman Head."

I took a savage gulp at the raw Scotch.

"I don't care," said Maggie Rorty. "I think he's cute."

"Compared with—" Paddy began, but I kicked him under the table.

We sang for a while, and then we told gags and recited limericks for a while, and I noticed that the kid and Maggie had wandered into the back room— the one with the latch on the door.

Oswiak's wife asked me, very puzzled: "Doc, w'y dey do dot flyink by planyets?"

"It's the damn govermint," Sam Fireman said.

"Why not?" I said. "They got the Bowman Drive, why the hell shouldn't they use it? Serves 'em right." I had a double Scotch and added: "Twenty years of it and they found out a few things they didn't know. Redlines are only one of them. Twenty years more, maybe they'll find out a few more things they didn't know. Maybe by the time there's a bathtub in every American home and an alcoholism clinic in every American town, they'll find out a whole *lot* of things they didn't know. And every American boy will be a pop-eyed, blood-raddled wreck, like our friend here, from riding the Bowman Drive."

"It's the damn govermint," Sam Fireman repeated.

"And what the hell did you mean by that remark about alcoholism?" Paddy said, real sore. "Personally, I can take it or leave it alone."

So we got to talking about that and everybody there turned out to be people who could take it or leave it alone.

It was maybe midnight when the kid showed at the table again, looking kind of dazed. I was drunker than I ought to be by midnight, so I said I was going for a walk. He tagged along and we wound up on a bench at Screwball Square. The soap-boxers were still going strong. As I said, it was a nice night. After a while, a potbellied old auntie who didn't give a damn about the face sat down and tried to talk the kid into going to see some etchings. The kid didn't get it and I led him over to hear the soap-boxers before there was trouble.

One of the orators was a mush-mouthed evangelist. "And oh, my friends," he said, "when I looked through the porthole of the spaceship and beheld the wonder of the Firmament—"

"You're a stinkin' Yankee liar!" the kid yelled at him. "You say one damn more word about can-shootin' and I'll ram your spaceship down your lyin' throat! Wheah's your redlines if you're such a hot spacer?"

The crowd didn't know what he was talking about, but "wheah's your redlines" sounded good to them, so they heckled mushmouth off his box with it.

I got the kid to a bench. The liquor was working in him all of a sudden. He simmered down after a while and asked: "Doc, should I've given Miz Rorty some money? I asked her afterward and she said she'd admire to have something to remember me by, so I gave her my lighter. She seem' to be real pleased with it. But I was wondering if maybe I embarrassed her by asking her right out. Like I tol' you, back in Covington, Kentucky, we don't have places like that. Or maybe we did and I just didn't know about them. But what do you think I should've done about Miz Rorty?"

"Just what you did," I told him. "If they want money, they ask you for it first. Where you staying?"

"Y.M.C.A.," he said, almost asleep. "Back in Covington, Kentucky, I was a member of the Y and I kept up my membership. They have to let me in because I'm a member. Spacers have all kinds of trouble, Doc. Woman trouble. Hotel trouble. Fam'ly trouble. Religious trouble. I was raised a Southern Baptist, but wheah's Heaven, anyway? I ask' Doctor Chitwood las' time home before the redlines got so thick—Doc, you aren't a minister of the Gospel, are you? I hope I di'n' say anything to offend you."

"No offense, son," I said. "No offense."

I walked him to the avenue and waited for a fleet cab. It was almost five minutes. The independent cabs roll drunks and dent the fenders of fleet cabs if they show up in Skid Row and then the fleet drivers have to make reports on their own time to the company. It keeps them away. But I got one and dumped the kid in.

"The Y Hotel," I told the driver. "Here's five. Help him in when you get there."

When I walked through Screwball Square again, some college kids were yelling "wheah's your redlines" at old Charlie, the last of the Wobblies.

Old Charlie kept roaring: "The hell with your breadlines! I'm talking about atomic bombs. *Right—up—there!*" And he pointed at the Moon.

It was a nice night, but the liquor was dying in me.

There was a joint around the corner, so I went in and had a drink to carry me to the club; I had a bottle there. I got into the first cab that came.

"Athletic Club," I said.

"Inna dawghouse, harh?" the driver said, and he gave me a big personality smile.

I didn't say anything and he started the car.

He was right, of course. I was in everybody's doghouse. Someday I'd scare hell out of Tom and Lise by going home and showing them what their daddy looked like.

Down at the Institute, I was in the doghouse.

"Oh, dear," everybody at the Institute said to everybody, "I'm sure I don't know what ails the man. A lovely wife and two lovely grown children and she had to tell him 'either you go or I go.' And *drinking!* And this is rather subtle, but it's a well-known fact that neurotics seek out low company to compensate for their guilt feelings. The *places* he frequents. Dr. Francis Bowman, the man who made space flight a reality. The man who put the Bomb Base on the Moon! Really, I'm sure I don't know what ails him."

The hell with them all.

Cyril M. Kornbluth (1923–58) was a prodigy, a regular contributor to the pulp magazines while still in his teens. He went on to produce many of the most distinguished short stories of the '50s, including "The Little Black Bag," "The Marching Morons," and "Shark Ship." In collaboration with Frederik Pohl, he wrote one of the great classics of science fiction, The Space Merchants, *in addition to* Gladiator-at-Law, Search the Sky, *and* Wolfbane. *His solo novels,* The Syndic, Takeoff, *and* Not This August *are also superior work.*

Unlike some authors of SF·bar stories, Kornbluth actually did his research on location. He had a wide variety of drinking companions from all walks of life; and, like a true writer, he listened to what they said.

PRINCESS
by Morgan Llywelyn

They all loved her, even the smallest among them.

One of them heard someone call her "princess" and after that they all called her "Princess," thinking it was her name. They did not understand the sarcasm implied in princess or honey or baby, applied to a tired woman in middle years with an aching back and work-reddened hands.

They would come trooping in close to closing time, chattering among themselves, and crowd close to the bar, demanding drinks. "Orange bitters, Princess," or "Whiskey, plenty of whiskey. In a big glass, Princess." The tops of their heads hardly reached the level of the bar, and when she brought the drinks they would jump up, their wrinkled gray faces and bald skulls flashing into her vision as they caught glimpses of the glasses. Then a scaly hand would come over the lip of the bar and seize the drink. Out of sight there were gurglings and the smacking of lips, then the hand deposited the empty glass back on the polished wood.

Feet pattered toward the door. "Good night, Princess!" one of them always remembered to call.

A pile of coins glittered in payment for the drinks.

She neither laughed at them nor shrank away from them as the other townspeople did. Who was she to laugh at anyone? Homely old maid eking out a thin living in a run-down bar on the wrong side of a dying town. Her looks had always been a magnet for caustic comments, so she could feel a certain empathy with the ones who came in just before closing time, because the bar was emptiest then.

Every night she polished the glasses on her apron and rearranged the bottles and jugs behind the bar, glancing through the smeared window from time to time as if she were waiting for someone special. But there was no someone special, never had been.

She polished and waited as the smoke got thicker and thicker in the room, then what patrons she had began to straggle out, back to shabby houses and depressing flats not very different from her own. Gray lives.

At last the door swung inward instead of out and she felt the cold air blow in with them. If there were any people left in the bar, they always left then. No one seemed to want to stay.

People whispered that they had a mine of some sort up in the hills. Whatever it was, they made enough to pay for their drinks, though they never left any extra for a tip. But in time she noticed that the windows of the bar sparkled in the morning when she came down from her seedy apartment on the floor above, and the step in front was swept clean. Sometimes a jug of wild flowers waited for her just outside the door. One night it rained and she had forgotten to bring in the laundry, her threadbare clothes and stained towels. In the morning she found them neatly folded and stacked under the overhang of the eaves, safe and dry.

One night one of the few regulars had too much to drink and said ugly things to her. He wasn't a mean man, but his tongue was rough. She would have cried if her tears had not all dried up long ago. Then the door swung inward; from behind the bar she could not see who entered, but the townman did. He started to get up and then his face changed color and he sat down again, hard, on the barstool. She could hear the broken vinyl creak on the seat cushion. A thin thread of saliva dropped onto the man's chest from his parted lips. He drained his glass quickly and staggered out.

No one said ugly things to her after that.

Sometimes, lying on her narrow bed above the bar, she dreamed of a handsome man coming for her, driving up in front one day with a screech of tires. He would carry her away in a big car that smelled new inside, and she would never look back.

She knew it was a dream. But she still glanced out the window, sometimes. The few cars she saw were battered and dusty, like everything else in the town.

Still, she felt strangely content. Not happy, because she had never been happy and could not have identified the feeling if it crept up on her. But her life began to seem full and she had companionship of a sort.

"Princess," one of them would say out of her sight, over the edge of the bar, "you look nice tonight." They could not possibly see her, and she did not try to lean across and look down at them; it was better if you didn't look at them. But she would smile to herself and give her thinning hair a pat.

"Make me something hot to drink," the voice would say. "The night is cold; it's frozen the flanges of my nose."

Small titters from his companions. Not laughter; they did not laugh like people. They laughed as squirrels might, fast and shrill.

When they were in the bar no new customers entered. What business there was fell off. In time it was safe for them to come in the afternoon; there was no one in the room anyway to stare at them. The business, always shaky, should have failed completely. But it didn't. There always seemed to be just as much money in the register at the end of the day as there had been when townspeople came. And she liked it better, not having to put up with the problems townsfolk brought.

She was standing on the other side of the bar one day, down at the end with her back toward the door, trying to repair the broken vinyl on the barstool with a piece of tape. She was holding her lower lip between her teeth and a wisp of hair kept falling down in her eyes. She was so preoccupied she didn't hear them come in. She thought she was alone until she felt the touch.

It was as light as cobweb, trailing up her leg. Under her skirt. Not attacking, not even invading. Just . . . exploring, with a gentle and innocent curiosity, like that of a blind person touching the face of a stranger.

She froze.

No one had ever touched her there before.

But an unaccustomed feeling of warmth permeated the core of her being, a feeling with a color—rose-gold—and a fragrance, the scent of honeysuckle blooming. She closed her eyes and stood immobile.

At last the touch ceased. The colors faded, the fragrance too. When she opened her eyes the bar was empty. But she knew something wonderful had come to her.

The next time the liquor wholesaler called on her she bought better brands of whiskey and some imported beers. She had never ordered good stuff before. The townspeople only drank the cheapest and wouldn't have known the difference. But the first time she poured the good liquor the stack of coins left on the counter afterwards was higher.

In fact, there seemed to be more money altogether, though she couldn't have explained how. When she added up her receipts, she found she could afford to replace the seats on the barstools—not that anyone used them anymore. The only customers she had now were too short to climb up on them. She thought of ordering shorter barstools, then decided that would be vaguely ridiculous. No one was complaining.

Instead she went to the town's only emporium, which featured dead flies lying feet-up in the windows, and bought herself a new blouse. Soft, pretty, a sort of rosy-gold color. She got a little bottle of perfume too. One that smelled like honeysuckle to her.

When she asked the salesgirl for face cream she was rewarded with a strange look, but the other women didn't dare say anything. No one made any smart cracks about her anymore.

She rubbed the cream into her skin every night, in the flat above the bar. When she peered into the mirror she couldn't see that it made any difference, but her skin felt better. The wind off the desert had dried it out; now it was soft to the touch. She ran her fingertips across her cheek wonderingly.

The next night one of them put coins into the old jukebox in the corner that had been dead for fifteen years. It came to life with a shudder and a screech, and a baritone voice began celebrating "The Way You Look Tonight."

The seasons passed; the town finished dying. There were no battered cars left to park on the streets, which were abandoned to blowing dust and an occasional tumbleweed, rolling along like a spidery bouquet. She didn't go out for food. There was always something in the pantry when she went to look for it. And when she emptied a bottle for her customers she began finding a full one behind it on the mirrored shelves back of the bar. Everything she needed was already there.

On the lazy afternoons and in the long, blue evenings there were only eight of them in the bar, the seven little creatures and the hunchbacked albino woman. But it was enough.

Morgan Llywellyn writes both fantasy and historical fiction, including Red Branch, The Horse Goddess, *and* The Lion of Ireland. *(For the latter she received an unusual honor, a fan phone call from a president of the United States.) She lives in Ireland.*

THE SUBJECT IS CLOSED
by Larry Niven

Perhaps there are a few topics that are out of bounds even in that most celebrated of interstellar watering holes, Draco's Tavern.

We get astronauts in the Draco Tavern. We get workers from Mount Forel Spaceport, and some administrators, and some newsmen. We get chirpsithtra; I keep sparkers to get them drunk and chairs to fit their tall, spindly frames. Once in a while, we get other aliens.

But we don't get many priests.

So I noticed him when he came in. He was young and round and harmless-looking. His expression was a model of its kind: open, willing to be friendly, not nervous, but very alert. He stared a bit at two bulbous aliens in space suits who had come in with a chirpsithtra guide.

I watched him invite himself to join a trio of chirpsithtra. They seemed willing to have him. They like human company. He even had the foresight to snag one of the high chairs I spread around, high enough to bring a human face to chirpsithtra level.

Someone must have briefed him, I decided. He'd know better than to do anything gauche. So I forgot him for a while.

An hour later he was at the bar, alone. He ordered a beer and waited until I'd brought it. He said, "You're Rick Schumann, aren't you? The owner?"

"That's right. And you?"

"Father David Hopkins." He hesitated, then blurted, "Do you trust the chirpsithtra?" He had trouble with the word.

I said, "Depends on what you mean. They don't steal the

66

salt shakers. And they've got half a dozen reasons for not wanting to conquer the Earth.''

He waved that aside. Larger things occupied his mind. "Do you believe the stories they tell? That they rule the galaxy? That they're aeons old?''

"I've never decided. At least they tell entertaining stories. At most . . . You didn't call a chirpsithtra a liar, did you?''

"No, of course not.'' He drank deeply of his beer. I was turning away when he said, "They said they know all about life after death.''

"Ye Gods. I've been talking to chirpsithtra for twenty years, but that's a new one. Who raised the subject?''

"Oh, one of them asked me about the, uh, uniform. It just came up naturally.'' When I didn't say anything, he added, "Most religious elders seem to be just ignoring the chirpsithtra. And the other intelligent beings too. I want to *know*. Do they have souls?''

"Do they?''

"He didn't say.''

"She,'' I told him. "All chirpsithtra are female.''

He nodded, not as if he cared much. "I started to tell her about my order. But when I started talking about Jesus, and about salvation, she told me rather firmly that the chirpsithtra know all they want to know on the subject of life after death.''

"So then you asked—''

"No, sir, I did not. I came over here to decide whether I'm afraid to ask.''

I gave him points for that. "And are you?'' When he didn't answer I said, "It's like this. I can stop her at any time you like. I know how to apologize gracefully.''

Only one of the three spoke English, though the others listened as if they understood it.

"I don't know,'' she said.

That was clearly the answer Hopkins wanted. "I must have misunderstood,'' he said, and he started to slip down from his high chair.

"I told you that we know as much as we want to know on the subject,'' said the alien. "Once there were those who knew more. They tried to teach us. Now we try to discourage religious experiments.''

Hopkins slid back into his chair. "What were they? Chirpsithtra saints?"

"No. The Sheegupt were carbon-water-oxygen life, like you and me, but they developed around the hot F-type suns in the galactic core. When our own empire had expanded near enough to the core, they came to us as missionaries. We rejected their pantheistic religion. They went away angry. It was some thousands of years before we met again.

"By then our settled regions were in contact, and had even interpenetrated to some extent. Why not? We could not use the same planets. We learned that their erstwhile religion had broken into variant sects and was now stagnant, giving way to what you would call agnosticism. I believe the implication is that the agnostic does not know the nature of God, and does not believe you do either?"

I looked at Hopkins, who said, "Close enough."

"We established a trade in knowledge and in other things. Their skill at educational toys exceeded ours. Some of our foods were dietetic to them; they had taste but could not be metabolized. We mixed well. If my tale seems sketchy or superficial, it is because I never learned it in great detail. Some details were deliberately lost.

"Over a thousand years of contact, the Sheegupt took the next step beyond agnosticism. They experimented. Some of their research was no different from your own psychological research, though of course they reached different conclusions. Some involved advanced philosophies: attempts to extrapolate God from Her artwork, so to speak. There were attempts to extrapolate other universes from altered laws of physics, and to contact the extrapolated universes. There were attempts to contact the dead. The Sheegupt kept us informed of the progress of their work. They were born missionaries, even when their religion was temporarily in abeyance."

Hopkins was fascinated. He would hardly be shocked at attempts to investigate God. After all, it's an old game.

"We heard, from the Sheegupt outpost worlds, that the scientifically advanced worlds in the galactic core had made some kind of breakthrough. Then we started losing contact with the Sheegupt," said the chirpsithtra.

"Trade ships found no shuttles to meet them. We sent

investigating teams. They found Sheegupt worlds entirely
depopulated. The inhabitants had made machinery for the
purpose of suicide, generally a combination of electrocution
terminals and conveyor belts. Some Sheegupt had used
knives on themselves, or walked off buildings, but most had
queued up at the suicide machines, as if in no particular
hurry."

I said, "Sounds like they learned something, all right. But
what?"

"Their latest approach, according to our records, was to
extrapolate rational models of a life after death, then attempt
contact. But they may have gone on to something else. We
do not know."

Hopkins shook his head. "They could have found out
there wasn't a life after death. No, they couldn't, could they?
If they didn't find anything, it might be they were only using
the wrong model."

I said, "Try it the other way around. There is a Heaven,
and it's wonderful, and everyone goes there. Or there is a
Hell, and it gets more unpleasant the older you are when you
die."

"Be cautious in your guesses. You may find the right
answer," said the chirpsithtra. "The Sheegupt made no
attempt to hide their secret. It must have been an easy
answer, capable of reaching even simple minds, and capable
of proof. We know this because many of our investigating
teams sought death in groups. Even millennia later, there
was suicide among those who probed through old records,
expecting no more than a fascinating puzzle in ancient
history. The records were finally destroyed."

After I closed up for the night, I found Hopkins waiting
for me outside.

"I've decided you were right," he said earnestly. "They
must have found out there's a Heaven and it's easy to get
in. That's the only thing that could make that many people
want to be dead. Isn't it?"

But I saw that he was wringing his hands without knowing
it. He wasn't sure. He wasn't sure of anything.

I told him, "I think you tried to preach at the chirpsithtra.
I don't doubt you were polite about it, but that's what I think
happened. And they closed the subject on you."

He thought it over, then nodded jerkily. "I guess they made their point. What would I know about chirpsithtra souls?"

"Yeah. But they spin a good yarn, don't they?"

Larry Niven continues to be one of the leading writers of science fiction. Some recent Niven titles include The Legacy of Heorot *(with Jerry Pournelle and Steven Barnes)*, The Integral Trees, *and* The Smoke Ring. *The Draco Tavern series has always been something · of a departure for him, since his longer work had tended toward the epic and galaxy-spanning, whereas the doings at Draco always have an intimate feel to them, for all they too deal with BIG ideas.*

THE PERSECUTOR'S TALE
by John M. Ford

Of deeds done in darkness, and things thrown into deep water . . .

We were the usual sort of travelers on the Empire's high roads: unspeaking people bound on unguessable business, united only by a direction of motion. If not for the interruption of our journey, I do not think we would have noticed one another at all. I except myself, of course; but my observations are not detected by their subjects. They would be valueless otherwise.

We stopped at a small inn, with just enough rooms for our party; there were no other guests, and the innkeeper freely admitted that guests were rare. This had nothing to do with the quality of the house, which was excellent; but the city of our destination was only two hours farther by the high road, and the cars did not normally even stop.

Tonight, though, Midwinter's Eve, wet snow clogged the tracks, and ice coated the catenary, threatening to bring the wire down. It would be much better that we pause short of our goal than possibly be trapped all night in a powerless car.

There were protests, as is customary when an Imperial service performs less than flawlessly, but they quieted when the motorman assured us that our stay would be paid for by the Ministry of Transport; and they ceased when we saw the inn.

It was of the same stone as the mountains around it, with embrasures and round mock-towers at the corners; it sprawled in a manner that suggested intrigues of design but never vulgar randomness. From its leaded prism windows lights shone soft and amber and warm—from our car, in the storm, to call the effect seductive is no exaggeration.

The innkeeper met us at the car, sweeping snow from the platform, and led us inside; as he did so, a young man hitched a pair of mules to the rings on the car's front end. He gave the whip to the motorman, who cracked it once smartly, and the beasts pulled the car around a tightly curved side track—"spur," the word is—toward a small shed at the inn's rear.

The interior was as well appointed as the exterior had been. There were tapestries and paintings on the walls, intricate parquet floors with carpets in the complex southern style, simply styled furniture scarred with long use. Nothing was remotely modern, and wear showed on every surface, yet the effect was not one of disrepair but of the comfortable patina of age.

A member of our company, a centurion just returned from the Empire's northern frontier, looked in some awe at the massive ceiling beams, and commented that only far beyond his posting could trees of such girth still be found. Another traveler, an electrical engineer, pointed out the paths for wires to the iron candelabra, holes drilled with hand augers long after the beams were raised.

Our host affirmed this, showing us how the candle-holders had been altered for wire and glasslamps. We were impressed (as the innkeeper expected), and not merely with the age of the structure. The times before electricity seem to us, centuries later, as alien, feral, dark in more senses than one.

The only staff at this time of year were the innkeeper's family. His son, who had hitched the mules to the car, now ported our bags, refusing more than modest tips, though there was of course no electric lift. His daughter bustled from room to room, making down beds and checking plumbing for proper function. And his wife was preparing dinner, hot potato-and-mushroom soup followed by a cold collation of sliced beef and mutton. The bread was fresh, from refrigerated dough. Sparkling water came from a spring somewhere on the inn grounds, and the wines were more than good enough. It was said by several of us that the Empress's own chefs could have done no better on such short notice and without their army of potboys and scullery maids, and I believe that to be true. The family were solid, sturdy people, of the sort once called "the hearthbrick of the Empire."

After dinner our party, and our host, sat in the great hall before the main fire, with mugs of hot buttered ale. Snow piled against the windows, and occasionally a gust of wind made whispers and creaks and sucked sparks up the chimney, but it was not hard to forget that there was a storm outside, that we all were kept from appointments in a city leagues away. The glasslamps in the hall were dimmed and tapers lit, both in token of tomorrow's solstice and to conserve generator fuel, and the glimpse recalled of featherbeds upstairs seemed something from a dream.

The innkeeper appeared to notice that our thoughts were straying, and as he refilled our mugs he spoke of this being the longest of all nights, before the shortest of days (touching on the legends of that day), and encouraged us to use up some of the long dark hours in pleasant conversation. Thus it was revealed, gradually, who we were.

I have mentioned the frontier soldier, and the engineer, who was an instructor at a cantonment University. There was another centurion, of the famous 29th Guards, in his violet undress uniform; a young chymist, partner in a firm and of obvious prosperity; a traveling justice, robed in white, with her two clerks in black and gold. I introduced myself as a journalist, which no longer draws the disapproval it did when I was young and beardless, and tonight seemed even to impress my companions.

The last of us to speak was a spare man, gaunt in fact, in a well-cut suit of red and black chequy, the sort that had been most fashionable in Inner Courts some years ago. His watch-chain was of heavy silver links, his cravat of white silk. In a voice that was quiet but by no means soft, he introduced himself as a persecutor for the state.

There was a pause in sound and action, and then all present—save the innkeeper—did those small, half conscious actions that outrun thought. The Guardsman reached toward his weapon baldric (which was empty, of course). The frontier soldier muttered something, apparently a complex oath to some minor god. The justice turned slowly to face the persecutor, stroking her back blindfold at the left temple, while a clerk whispered into her right ear. I stroked one finger minutely against another.

The first of us to speak was the engineer; he seemed very thoughtful, though I was not certain what he was thinking of. "That could be a dangerous admission, in a company of strangers," he said, and we waited in the pause, but he said no more.

The chymist, heedless, did. "Surely you're retired, lord sir. No active persecutor would admit the fact, knowing that one of those present—" and then he seemed to hear the ice cracking under him, and was silent.

For a long moment wind whistled, fire crackled on without us; then the innkeeper rang his ladle on the kettle of ale. He said, "Please, enough silence. It's a pleasure for me that you're my guests; I'll not have you sleeping here displeased. My lord persecutor."

"Yes?" said the gaunt man, his eyes level and his body calm.

"You've dampened all our spirits with your revelations. Do you not consider that . . . unjust?"

I spoke of thin ice; here was a man who danced on warm water. I watched the justice; her tongue moistened her lips. I observed the two soldiers; their poses told me that they were still armed.

The persecutor said "You, sir, asked me to speak."

The innkeeper did not flinch. "To make conversation, not stop it. I ask you . . . is it just?"

"No," said the gaunt man, quite clearly. "It is not just. You have a forfeit in mind, I think?"

"I do, lord sir. Surely you have traveled widely, surely seen things we have not. Would you tell us a tale?"

"About—"

"About what you like." Our host faced me and said "Of course, sir author, you know the legend of tales told on this night."

I nodded, though I knew none such. And I caught the innkeeper's look, and I scanned the hearthside circle.

One might have supposed to find us all preparing to make excuses and retire upstairs, to the safe isolation of stone walls and thick down comforters. Not at all. There was an expectance that whispered like the storm-wind in the flue, drawing up sparks.

Our host dipped more ale, stirred up the fire, and I understood; we would hear a ghost story, told as such stories should be in a circle of warmth, and we would sleep well. I wondered what stories the innkeeper's children had heard, growing up in a lonely inn.

The persecutor looked long at me, as if waiting for some professional cue as to the proper forms; but we all know that tales begin at the beginning.

"There was a young person, of influence and prosperity and a devious intelligence," he said, with gathering tempo. "I'll call him a 'he,' for language's sake; but you'll understand that he could have been, might have been, a she . . .

"He came to decide that, in just one case, for just one act, he was above the law."

Yes. This was just the place to begin.

". . . but the crime, while horrid, was beyond the reach of ordinary law."

"Murder?" said the chymist, leaning forward in his chair.

"Not murder," said the frontier centurion. "For murder there's hanging, or the reaching blades."

"Or electrocution," said the electrical engineer.

"Horrid," said the persecutor, "but secret, for the young man and his lover conspired, and deeds were done in darkness, and things were thrown into deep water. With her he pursued a course of silence. It was mutual blackmail, of course."

I had seen the two legal clerks touch, earlier; now they touched again.

"And then one night he reached out for her, and touched skin, but not her skin; he felt the dead skin of serpents. He opened his eyes, and dead bare bones looked back. And he knew that the persecutor had come for him, and worse, he knew by whom he was betrayed."

The clerks drew apart. The justice moved her head from side to side, as if waiting for a whispered word from one of them.

"The young man screamed."

Wind cried.

"And when he was done screaming, however long it was, he opened his eyes again . . . and he was alone in the room."

The soldier from the frontier said, "And so he fled?"

"No. At the time, he knew better. As I say, he was very intelligent. He sought . . . redemption—"

"Good," said the engineer.

"—but he sought it as an armor of virtue, a sword of righteousness . . . a medal of good conduct."

The Guardsman swirled the butter in his ale, and adjusted his baldric and beribboned jacket.

"And he found the things he sought . . . but none of them was the thing he wanted. He had opportunities to become a dead hero, but he was not ready for that.

"And sometimes, on his cot, in the deepest night, snakeskin would brush his cheek, and the persecutor's bone mask would hover above him. And so he marched to the leaden drum."

Several did not comprehend; the Guardsman explained the phrase to mean the abandonment of a sound military career. In his voice there was something like relief.

A faint, rapid rustling came from somewhere overhead. The persecutor drank some ale and said, "Having found the honor of symbol inadequate, the young man decided to forget honor. He submerged himself in physical things—and I do not mean the fleshly lusts; sex was far too spiritual for him. I mean artifice, technology. Glass and wood and steel, the mechanical mysteries—"

"There is an owl in the rafters," the young chymist said, pointing into the dimness above. We all looked up. The owl is the bird of knowledge, legend says. And of judgment. But that is only legend. What can owls know of the sins of men?

"Indeed there is an owl," said the innkeeper impatiently. "And there is a cat. They share the mice. He's a good owl, my owl; you needn't cover your ale. Please, lord sir, continue."

"I second that," said the electrical engineer. "Could mechanical illumination dispel your young man's darkness?"

"Strange that you should say that," said the persecutor, "for he fancied once to trap the persecutor with carbon arcs and charged wires, and smokes and noise produced by chymistry. And one night his traps all erupted, and he hurried downstairs. He stood at the door to the snare room, hearing the whine and explosion, staring in at the smoke glowing blue-white . . . but he could not go in. He could not bear the thought. So, in his nightclothes, he turned and went out the door.

"There, under the moonless sky, robed all in black with gloves of snakeskin, stood a figure who looked back at him with an eyeless face.

"Then at last he fled, naked."

"It is not justice," said the centurion from the northern marches, "to drive a man mad." The soldier's voice was not heated; it was quite as cold as the northern wind. "It is not justice, whatever law may say; it is—"

"Persecution," said the gaunt man. "And that is what it is called."

The innkeeper's wife appeared, carrying a tray of light sugared pastries, which were more than welcome.

The persecutor ate his sweetcake without haste, then cleaned his fingers elaborately on a linen napkin. He began again: "The man fled more than a locale. He fled himself. He changed his name each time it was asked, wore clothes twice and burned them, became a thousand travellers on a thousand roads."

"What," I said, "did he give as his trade, and how did he earn his way?"

The persecutor looked at me sharply; but he had examined us all as he spoke. "He had studied many things, and desperation hones cleverness. He was always one who could be here come morning and gone come night."

I nodded. So did the circuit justice.

The engineer said, "Were his trades all honest ones?"

"No. And he admitted this, in those western regions where it is admired. I think you are wondering how this could be, with persecution on him; you misunderstand. The law forbids us to intervene, or even to inform an ordinary constable. If he had been caught, I should have visited him in prison." The persecutor plucked at his clothing, removing invisible crumbs from the red and black squares. "Many persons under persecution choose to multiply their identities; very often it is the last phase of events. For when night after night the persecutor continues to appear, the subject knows, first, that he cannot escape the state; second, that whatever he may call himself, he is the same thing within . . . the evil knows its territory.

"There is a third thing he comes to know . . . that a person without an identity is dead. We all need some 'I,' even a collective 'I' such as a flag or a uniform."

The Guardsman said, "I'm proud of my uniform. And the discipline of . . ." he stopped, looked around, then was silent, embarrassed but not without dignity.

The persecutor did not respond. He said, "In time, as happens, he came to see black cloaks by daylight, though of course only his mind put persecutors inside them. He began to wonder, obsessively, which of the people he saw in the day put on robes by night to haunt him."

"And he attacked one?" the chymist said. "You drove him to further crimes?"

"No. That has never happened."

"I wonder why," said the chymist, with what was doubtless meant to be a deep, wise irony but sounded only as petulance.

There was a pause, until the wind and the whisper of falling snow had erased the echo of the chymist's outburst. The persecutor said, "There is no question that we drive our victims. That is the whole object. Some are driven to extraordinary measures, and this young person was one such. In the persecutor's presence, under a half moon, he—"

"Was redeemed?" I could not tell who had spoken.

"—maimed himself, in a bloody and dreadful manner that I shall not describe."

"This has been known to happen," said the justice, in a high, clear voice. Her face was tilted down, and she stroked her blindfold with the fingers of both hands. Her clerks drew back from her.

The centurion from the frontier said "And was blood enough?" His right hand gripped his left wrist. I have heard that northern men keep a small, thin knife hidden there. "Was it enough? Finish the tale."

"The tale is finished," the persecutor said softly. "It has no proper end. No, Centurion, blood is not enough. Blood is nothing, flesh is nothing. Flesh and blood are wracked with iron, in the halls of physical justice. But iron cannot touch the spirit that sets itself above justice. Thus, I."

The Guardsman said, "Spirit," not loudly, and as if he had never heard the word.

"Suppose," said the gaunt man, his face flickering in flamelight, "that a god appeared on earth, and said 'I offer you absolution. It is a gift; there is no obligation. I forgive you, it is done.'

"A strange idea, I agree. But supposing there were such a god, what would we people do? Take the offer, no doubt. And then return to the pleasures of evil . . . and take it again. Steal, be absolved. Kill, be absolved. We all know the value of things that cost nothing—and if gods did make the world they must know it too.

"So a price would have to be established. A transcendent price, that one would have to try and pay . . . and which one could afford to pay only once in one's life."

The engineer spoke. "And in the absence of a god . . . when is the price paid?"

The persecutor stood up. His movements were stiff, as with cold, though it was pleasantly warm in the hall. Perhaps he had been still for too long. He went to the fire and gazed into it. "In the absence of a god, there can be no absolute. I know . . . when I see, and hear.

"And that . . . is the end . . . of my story."

The frontier soldier stood then. "Please pardon my rudeness, but I have been accustomed to a different sunset. I shall be retiring now."

"No rudeness in it," said the innkeeper. "If you rise before I, do come down to the kitchen for early tea."

The centurion bowed slightly and went up the stairs.

"I too am tired," the justice said, and rose on her clerks like crutches. "Good night to you all."

And then the rest of us followed, one by one: "Good night . . . my friends." "Good night and untroubled dreams." "Good night."

As I went upstairs, I heard the innkeeper say, "Do retire, sir, before you fall asleep; a bed will favor your back much more than that chair." And then he walked out of the hall, leaving the Guards centurion sitting straight and alone, looking at nothing.

Overhead, feathers rustled. "Who?" said the owl. "Who?"

I turned at the landing and closed the door of my room behind me.

The room was small, but very neat. A small lamp was lit on the nightstand; a bit of beef and cheese and a covered cup of warm tea were there as well. The crisp bedclothes were turned back, and looked inviting. But.

I opened the inner lining of my kit bag, and took out what was hidden there; put on the shapeless cloak, the skullbone mask, the long gloves of black snakeskin, and the heavy silver ring with its swirling fire opal. A tiny silver pipe went into my throat.

My step has always been light, and our innkeeper kept his doors oiled and true. I opened the one I sought without a sound.

The only light in the gaunt man's room came from the bedlamp. He was reading in bed; the book slipped from his fingers, slipped down the sheets to the floor as he pulled the blankets up. He reminded me of a picture in a book I had read as a child: a drawing in red and black of a little old woman who has heard a noise in the night. It is odd that I still remember it so clearly.

"I heard your tale," I said, the pipe in my throat buzzing and trilling.

He stared at me, as he had looked at all of us in the hall, wondering now the other side of the question; but the mask hid my face, the cloak my body, the throat-pipe my voice. And his eyes were drawn irresistibly to the opal, which blazed in the dim electric light. Perhaps, he would be thinking, I had been none of the guests; a window-peeper in the snow. Or the innkeeper, or the owl in the rafters, or a spirit in the fire. The persecuted think amazing things.

He nodded a little, but did not speak; and I said, "You seem to have learned many things, in your travels."

He found his voice; it was firm, more to his surprise than mine. "It was said that I was intelligent."

"You have recognized who pursues you."

Another nod. "Yes . . . I showed that tonight, didn't I. You're . . . myself. I—I'm sorry if what I did tonight was . . . wrong, or offended—"

I waved my unringed hand. "This has been known to happen," I said, and saw him start, and recalled that the justice had spoken those words. Well. It would not matter. "And do you then know what it is that I am looking for?"

He still clutched the sheets, and stared at his knuckles and wrists like a schoolboy looking for notes cribbed there. Then he looked up at my ring, and then at my black pit eyes.

He said, "No, I do not know." A pause. A breath. Faintly I heard his heart. "But I am willing to take whatever you have for me."

I smiled, though of course there was no outward sign. I extended my ringed hand.

He could not take his eyes from the flickering stone. He bent his head and kissed it lightly.

I brushed the ring against his bare throat, touched a trigger. The fang moved softer than a whisper. His grip on the bedclothes relaxed, and he toppled with a sigh and a rustle of linen.

His face, half-hidden, smiled childishly.

I returned to my room, disrobed, coughed up the silver pipe, and packed the things away. I wrapped myself in a velvet bedrobe and sat by the window to sip the tea and watch for dawn. On such nights I need no sleep.

The morning was bright and crystal clear; and as we all sat at an enormous breakfast the motorman appeared, with the news that the high road was cleared all the way to the city.

I cannot say our pleasure was undiluted; we could think of few finer places to be snowbound. But there were reminders of this business and that, and soon bags were brought down, and goodbyes said to the innkeeper and his family (and more tips paid), and we were all standing on the trolley platform.

The gaunt man stood somewhat apart, looking down the tracks with mingled puzzlement and eagerness, talking with the trolley motorman. "Yes, sir, your ticket is valid to the city," the motorman said patiently. "Yes, these are all the bags you arrived with . . . No, sir, the service doesn't mark coach tickets with the passenger's name . . ."

The electrical engineer listened to this as he finished a

sweetcake. He licked jam from his fingers and brushed crumbs from his nose, and whistled without a tune.

"I think he's a bit mad," said the chymist. "Tries his best to ruin our evening, and this morning acts as if he barely remembers. What he did, or us, or his own—"

"He told a scary story, and it scared you," said the frontier soldier pleasantly. "Who knows what he really is?"

"Maybe even a persecutor," the Guardsman added. "Anyway, you ought to spend a night awake in the dark once in a while. Good for the spirit." The two centurions resumed a spirited discussion of favorite weapons.

One of the legal clerks sat on a large bag; the other stood behind her, his hands on her shoulders. They were not looking at one another . . . but perhaps after long service to a justice one's own eyes become less essential.

I felt a hand brush mine, with a surprisingly intimate touch, and I turned to face the justice. She carried a silver stick, and wore a white silk blindfold. "My best to you," she said, in a voice only I could hear. Perhaps it was only her custom before traveling. Surely so, for she spoke also to the gaunt man, who kissed her hand, and then touched his lips to her bandaged eyes. I noticed the white cravat was missing from his throat.

The motorman rang the bell, and the party filed aboard. I was last, and before I stepped into the car I signaled to the driver; he nodded and closed the door, and the car pulled away without me, its spidery pantograph singing a long fading note on the pristine air.

The innkeeper came out to sweep the platform. Without surprise—I wonder what could surprise him—he said, "You'll be staying a little longer, sir?"

"Yes," I said. "My appointments are postponed a little while. I shall travel on later."

"Pleased to have you, sir." He paused in his sweeping. "Did the thin gentleman board all right?"

"Yes, he did."

"He was all questions when he woke this morning, as well as waking late."

"You seem to have answered them well."

He began to speak, I believe to say an automatic "Thank you, sir," but after a moment he said instead, "My good wife and I have raised two children from birth. The questions were not wholly strange."

He leaned upon his broom, and looked with me toward the now-distant trolleycar. "It's Midwinter's morning, sir. This is the day, they say, that journeys end."

I moved a finger slightly, stroking it across another. The gesture would mean nothing to anyone not a persecutor. Only those who wear the opal ring know that it has two triggers, two fangs, two venoms.

The other brings death by convulsion, often breaking bones.

We call it Remembrance.

I have used both, according to need.

I said, "That is the legend . . . and also the day when lost things are found again."

We went inside, where the fire was warm, the beds were inviting, and the owl slept.

John M. Ford won the World Fantasy Award for The Dragon Waiting. *His other books include several science fiction novels (*The Princes of the Air, *etc.), and Star Trek novels (most recently,* How Much for Just the Planet?). *His short fiction has appeared in virtually all the genre magazines, and he is coauthor (with George Scithers and Darrell Schweitzer) of* On Writing Science Fiction: The Editors Strike Back.

LONGSHOT
by Jack C. Haldeman II

". . . another burned-out spacer with a tale to tell."

"Hot tip? Humph! A sure thing? I don't want to hear about it." The spacer slammed his drink on the bar and looked the robot bartender right in the electronic eye. "I've been from one side of this universe to the other and if I haven't learned anything else, I've learned that there's no such thing as a sure thing."

The bartender whirred and polished another glass.

"Sure I've played the ponies. I've been around. Nags on Old Earth, Bat Flies on Medi IV, Fuzzies on Niven—I've played them all, money on the nose. Was a time you couldn't keep me away from the tracks. Not anymore. I learned my lesson, but good. How 'bout another? A double."

The robot swallowed the empty glass, produced a full one. He sighed deep in his gearworks, afraid that this was going to be another burned-out spacer with a tale to tell.

It was.

The spacer's name was Terry Freeland, although everybody called him Crash, and his story was bound to be a tale of woe. Judging from the stubble on his face and the condition of his clothes, he hadn't lifted ship in a long time. Besides, if he had any money he wouldn't be drinking in a dump like this.

Except for a run of bad luck, thought the robot, *I wouldn't be pulling beers in a place like this, either.* Still, it beat pumping gas.

"It was on Dimian. You know Dimian? Out in the Rigel sector?" asked Crash, sipping his drink.

The robot nodded. He knew Dimian. A real backwater planet.

"Well, I was landing at the spaceport at Chingo. They got a lot of nerve calling it a spaceport, buncha gravel out in the middle of nowhere. Only two bars in the whole of Chingo, and it's the biggest town on Dimian. Some spaceport. Anyway, I was hauling a load of Venusian lettuce mold hoping to swing a big deal for some dutrinium. Wheeling and dealing, that's my game. Those sentients on Dimian really get off on lettuce mold. So I was coming in for a landing, you know, and . . . hey, I don't know what you've heard about me, but it ain't true I make a habit of bustin' up ships. Just had a few hard landings and a little bad luck, that's all. Like that time. They said I was drunk, but I say their null-field wasn't working right. Sure I'd had a shot or two while I was hanging in orbit, but that don't mean nothing. Do it all the time. Came down a little hard, that's all. Bent a stabilizer. Crunched a couple of scouts, but they were parked where they shouldn't 'a been. Anyway . . ."

It was looking to be a near total loss. They were overstocked on lettuce mold and Crash's profits didn't amount to much more than it took to fix the stabilizer and the two scouts. He hadn't been able to carry insurance since that time on Waycross, so everything was out-of-pocket. Still, he'd managed to pick up a load of dutrinium dirt cheap and if they'd ever finish fixing the stabilizer, maybe he'd be able to unload it on some other planet for big bucks.

He was always looking for big bucks. That's why he went to the track. That's why he listened to Whisky John. It was a mistake. Nobody listened to Whisky John. Nobody with any sense, that is.

Whisky John was born bad news.

"I tell you, it can't miss," said Whisky John. "These yoyos don't know the first thing about handicapping."

"You mean they actually race these monsters?"

"Sure. That's the whole idea. Those Dimians don't know nothing. They work 'em in the field till they get too old to cut the mustard, then they turn 'em loose on the track. These Dimians are crazy wild about betting. Most only thing to do around here."

"So where's the edge?" asked Crash.

"What you do is find one that's been out in the field a long time but hasn't done much work. He may be old, but he'll probably have a few kilometers left in him. I got it straight from B'rrax, a stableboy who sweeps out the stalls, that the sleeper of the year is going to be Heller."

"Heller?"

"That's the one. Eighty-five years old and getting pretty long in the tooth. But he was owned by National and they don't do much dredging, so he's had an easy life. He's the longshot. Two hundred to one. *Two hundred to one!*"

Crash cast a doubtful eye over the field. Monsters they were, too. The natives called them something unpronounceable that was roughly translated as "behemoths." It was an understatement. They looked like three elephants piled one on top of another. Had about as many legs, too. Thirty meters high and Lord knows what they weighed. Crash figured they could dredge pretty good, but he had a hard time imagining them racing around a track.

"Two hundred to one, you say? Eighty-five years old?"

"A sure thing. You can't lose."

"If you're so smart, how come you ain't rich?" asked Crash.

"Bad luck and hard times," said Whisky John wistfully. "I've had more than my share of both. Believe me, if I had any cash I'd put it right on the beast's, er, nose. Had to let you in on this. Figure I owe you one from that time on Farbly." He winked and Crash blushed. It had been close on Farbly, that's for sure. They'd been lucky to get out at all.

"I don't know," said Crash.

"How much you got? Cash."

"Free and clear? Let me see, after the stabilizer, uh . . . about 500 creds."

"Think about it. One hundred thousand creds! Free and clear. No taxes on Dimian. You could get a bigger cruiser, anything. Think about it."

Crash thought about it and the more he thought about it the better it seemed. It was all the cash he had and if he lost it he'd have to eat peanut butter crackers till he dumped the dutrinium. But still—*One Hundred Thousand Creds!*

He placed the bet.

Together they climbed into the stands; tall, rickety old wooden bleachers a good half klick from the track. There were a few offworlders scattered through the crowd, even a couple more humans, but mostly it was wall-to-wall Dimians. Whisky John was right about one thing—Dimians were sure crazy wild about behemoth racing.

Crash didn't know much about the Dimians, except that he thought they were weird. They probably thought Crash was weird, too. They looked like crickets, were about a meter tall, and talked in a high, squeaking rasp that Crash couldn't understand. Whisky John could speak it a little on account of his being marooned on Dimian for a good many years waiting for his ship to come in. Every time he got a few creds ahead, he'd blow it away with some crazy scheme. Whisky John was a mite irresponsible.

Down on the track, several Dimians were herding the behemoths toward the starting line. Crash noted with pleasure that Heller was still listed on the tote board at 200-1.

The Dimians moved the beasts along with huge prods, never getting closer to one than necessary. Crash didn't blame them, they were dwarfed by the massive animals. Looked like mountains being led around by small bugs. Hairy mountains.

"Where are the jockeys?" asked Crash.

"What jockeys? You couldn't pay a Dimian enough to climb on top of one of those monsters," replied Whisky John.

"How do they get around the track?"

"Sometimes they don't. When that starting gun goes off they go where they damn well please. Mostly they head around the track, though, since that's the way they're pointing at the beginning. They ain't too smart."

"Which one's Heller? I can't make out the numbers."

"It's easy to tell. He's the one on the left."

"No!"

"Yes."

If behemoths were mountains, Heller was a mountain with rickets. Most of his hair had fallen out. He was a mountain with a bad case of the mange. Half his legs didn't look like they worked right. Where the others had gleaming tusks, Heller had rotten stumps. Where the others had blazing eyes, Heller had sad, dull orbs. He had loser written all over him.

"You mean my money's on *that?*"

"Smart money, too. You can't tell a book by its cover, I always say. He can still hit the fast ball, probably tear the track apart." Whisky John was an incurable optimist, especially with other people's money.

"He's blind as a bat. He can't walk. He looks like he's a hundred years old."

"Eighty-five," corrected Whisky John.

"If he's eighty-five, how old are the others?"

"Average out about thirty, I reckon. That's good for an old behemoth. But remember he's two hundred to one. He's had an easy life."

"Easy life? He looks like a hundred miles of bad road." Crash was trying to figure out if he had time to strangle Whisky John and still run down to get his money back before the race started.

He was too late. The race started.

Crash could tell the race started because the Dimians in the crowd went wild, screaming and jumping up and down. It was harder to tell by looking at the behemoths, though, because they just seemed to be wandering aimlessly around, bumping into each other.

"This is a race?"

"Exciting, isn't it?" said Whisky John.

Three of the behemoths started lurching more or less down the track and the spectators went wild. Some of the others followed the leaders, including, to Crash's surprise, Heller. He wasn't last, either. Not if you counted the two behemoths that had fallen down and the one that was going the wrong way. Crash felt a faint hope rising.

"Come on, Heller," he shouted in desperation, pounding Whisky John on the shoulder.

It soon became apparent why the stands were so far from the track. Once the behemoths started, they went any old which way and didn't stop for anything. Unless, of course, they fell down. They were very good at falling down. They were better at falling down than running. Each time one toppled over, the ground shook. One had crashed through the fence around the track and was wandering out into the desert. Heller was in fourth place and losing ground rapidly.

He had to win or it was peanut butter crackers for Crash. Lots of peanut butter crackers.

The track was a jumble of lurching, tottering behemoths. Half of them had fallen down. The falling down part was easy, but the getting up was hard. Some of them just fell asleep after they flopped, only to be woken up by another one stumbling into them. They were the clumsiest animals Crash had ever seen. The lead behemoth got his legs all tangled up and went down in a heap. The second-place one tripped over him. Suddenly everything had changed. Heller was in second place, straining for the lead.

"Atta boy," shouted Crash, pounding Whisky John's arm some more. "You can do it."

They were lumbering down the home stretch now, neck and, er, neck, their bodies swaying with each ponderous step.

"Don't fall down, Heller. Don't fall down!" Crash's heart was pounding furiously. So was his hand and Whisky John's arm was getting mighty sore.

As they approached the checkered flag, Heller was a tusk behind and giving it all he had. Just before the finish line, however, a gleam came into those eyes that had been dull so many years. Something stirred deep in the beast's massive chest. *Pride! Glory!* He straightened his bent back. He rose up on his crippled legs. He gave a mighty leap forward. *Victory!*

Crash about died.

Two hundred to one. He was already spending his money. Whisky John's arm felt like a chinaberry tree hosting a woodpecker convention.

They went to collect the money. Whisky John did the talking. They handed him a large paper bag full of cred slips and a huge coil of rope. Whisky John looked pale.

"I swear, Crash, I didn't know." He had sick written all over his face.

"Know what? That's the money, right?"

"Right. One hundred thousand creds. It's all here. But I swear I didn't know, honest."

"We got the money, so what's to worry about? Let's go."

"It's not that easy, Crash."

"What do you mean? We just walk out and it's party time."

"See this rope, Crash?"

"Yeah. Nice rope. Let's go."

"This rope is for your behemoth."

"My what?"

"Your behemoth. Heller. He's yours. It was a claims race—I swear I didn't know—you just won the money *and* the behemoth, every metric ton of him."

"I won't do it. I'll leave him. Let's go." Crash was having none of this. He wanted to start spending his money.

"You can't just abandon him, Crash. He belongs to you now, at least as far as the Dimians see it. They won't stand for it. Behemoth racing is part of their religion and they take it seriously. If you dump Heller they'll kill you."

"Kill me?"

"Tear you limb from limb."

Gulp. Crash could see this was a serious matter. They walked over to the paddock area where several Dimians were washing down the behemoths with large hoses.

"I guess I could race him some more," said Crash doubtfully. "He probably has a few laps left in him. Maybe even make some money out of it."

"That's it, Crash. Hey, I'll be running along."

"You stay right here."

They looked up at Heller. He was panting at a ferocious rate. He looked terrible close up.

"What does he eat?"

"Volmer sprouts. Only the tender ones. About 10 kilos a day."

"Expensive?"

Whisky John nodded.

"Maybe I can sell him."

"That's it. Sell him. Good idea. I guess I'll be—"

Crash froze him with a stare.

"He doesn't look all that bad," lied Crash, trying to make the best out of a rotten situation. He walked towards the towering beast. "Probably lots of people out there would want a winner like him." He stood directly under Heller, looked up at his chin.

"Don't touch him!" cried Whisky John.

Crash patted Heller's massive toe, looked back over his shoulder. "What?" he asked.

Too late.

Heller rolled his eyes and swished his tail. He moaned with the sound of a thousand breaking hearts.

"Oh Lord," said Whisky John. "Now you've done it. A Love Bond."

"A what?" Heller leaned down and licked Crash on the side of the head. It sent him reeling.

"If you touch a behemoth they fall in love with you. Instantly and forever. It's called a Love Bond and there's no getting out of it. It's the peak of the Dimian's religious experience. If you tried to sell him now . . ."

"I know, they'd kill me."

"Limb from limb," added Whisky John with a serious shake of his head. "You are stuck for life."

Crash could see that Heller loved him. Love just oozed from every pore on the poor animal's massive body. He rolled his eyes with love. He waved his trunk with love. He made soul-wrenching groans of love. It was a pitiful sight. Crash felt sorry for the beast.

"He is kinda cute, at that," said Crash. "A fella could get to like him."

They tied the rope around Heller's neck and led him away. The rope was unnecessary; he followed Crash like a giant puppy dog.

Unfortunately, he made a very clumsy puppy dog. He stepped on a grocery wagon, squashed it flat. Crash dug a handful of creds out of the paper bag. He sideswiped an aircar. Crash dug into the bag. He wiped out ten light poles and three traffic lights. Crash dug into his bag and led him out of town.

On the edge of the desert, out of harm's way, Crash sat on a rock and surveyed the problem. He still had a lot of money. Money could simplify any situation. He was beginning to like Heller.

"You know," he said to the behemoth, "you and I could go places together. Do things."

He sat on the rock and talked to Heller for hours, making plans for the future, spinning dream castles that involved lots of Volmer sprouts and won races. Whisky John counted the money out into little piles on the sand. Heller stood and wheezed a lot. The sun fell low on the horizon.

So total was Heller's love for Crash that it must have been contagious. Or maybe it was the wine Crash was drinking. Anyway, the spacer was so overcome by emotion that he climbed a tree and gave Heller a kiss on the nose.

It was too much for poor old Heller. His heart couldn't stand so much happiness. He smiled a huge lovesick grin, moaned, and fell over dead.

The ground shook. Crash was heartbroken. He had come to love Heller nearly as much as Heller had loved him.

"What am I going to do?" cried Crash.

"Bury him."

"How am I going to go on without him?" wailed Crash.

"You got to bury him," said Whisky John, taking a slosh of the wine bottle. "All very clear."

"What's very clear?" asked Crash, casting a suspicious eye toward the other man.

"It's all Love Bond ritual. Has to be done a certain way. You dig the hole—nobody can help you, got to do it yourself—right where he died. Then you got to get their magical men to come and do their stuff. Then you got to put up a monument, has to be a big one, too. No skimping."

"Sounds expensive."

"A Love Bond is no simple thing."

"How much?"

"See that pile of money there?" He pointed to the rest of the winnings and Crash nodded. "Kiss it goodbye."

"No way out?"

"They'd—"

"I know. Limb from limb. Hole alone'll take me a week to dig."

It took two.

Crash lifted off from Dimian broke as a clam. He ate peanut butter crackers for a long, long time.

"That's how it went," said Crash, setting his empty glass in front of the robot bartender. It was his tenth empty glass. "Learned my lesson." He shook a bent smoke from the crushed pack in his pocket.

The bartender whirred sympathetically. This was one hard-luck spacer. He wiped the counter with the bar rag. Crash got shakily to his feet, headed for the exit.

He paused at the door, turned toward the bartender. "That was the fifth race, you said, wasn't it?"

The robot nodded. Good odds, too.

Jack C. Haldeman II (Jay to his friends) is the author of one solo novel, Vector Analysis, *one collaborative novel,* There Is No Darkness *(with his brother Joe), along with numerous shorter works, including a notably looney series of science-fictional sports stories published in* Isaac Asimov's Science Fiction Magazine *and later* Amazing *during the Scithers editorships of those magazines. Haldeman has been, as he has reported, variously a research biologist, printer's devil, medical technologist in a trauma unit, gardener, beach bum, photographer, statistician, file clerk, pharmacist's assistant, bartender (aha!), mechanic, and chairman of the 32nd World Science Fiction Convention (Discon II in Washington, D.C., 1974).*

He is now, much more sensibly, a full-time writer.

FINNEGAN'S
by W. T. Quick

There are some things technology just can't replace.

I think I missed the bottles the most. After all, I'd made a living almost forty years with those bottles. Black Jack, Dewar's, Johnny Walker, Boodles—I knew them by their shape, their feel. I could tend bar in the dark if I had to. Now the bottles were gone, disappeared into the bowels of something called a Mixtronic.

Finnegan's would never be the same. Probably, neither would I.

Not that I'd never changed. I had. And watched the hairline recede, the gut begin to grow, the wrinkles appear at the corners of my eyes, watched it all in the great cut-glass mirror behind Finnegan's solid oak bar. But it was comfortable change, slow and easy, not like the Mixtronic. They installed it one day and took away the bottles and everything was different.

It worked like this. Come in and sit down. Take out your creditab and slip it into the slot in front of you. Decide what you're drinking and punch the number of the drink on the keyboard. Listen to the soft whir and—*chickachung!*—out pops a perfect drink, measured to the milliliter. In a guaranteed hygienic plastic cup. A *plastic* cup, for chrissakes!

No mess, no fuss, no waste. And no use for a slightly overaged bartender, it seemed.

Thursday night. Usually a slow one—several of the veterans' clubs ran gladiator bingo on Thursday, and my customers like their gambling. I felt at loose ends. Nobody was in the bar. Usually I would have spent the time polishing glasses and wiping down bottles. However, no glasses, no bottles. Outside, the streetlamp glowed dimly through the dusty front window. I noticed the bar odors— stale smoke, old beer, dried sweat. When a bartender is busy, all he notices are customers. I can pick a mumbled drink order out of a conversation at twenty yards, and never hear the conversation.

The quiet was beginning to get to me when the front door creaked open. A stranger came in, a tall, balding man with a thin face, glasses, the look of an accountant. I moved behind the bar and nodded, feeling foolish. I couldn't offer to make him a drink. He had to do that himself.

"Mr. Guardino?" he said, seating himself.

Nobody had called me that in twenty years. I'm Harry, to one and all.

"Yeah, that's me. What can I do you for?"

He reached into a pocket of his suit and took out a long envelope. "I'm sorry to be the one . . ." He let his voice trail off and I knew. After all these years, it had to end sometime.

There was something about the owner's gratitude, and changing times, and there was a check for three months' salary. I took the check and signed the form and thanked the man and waited for him to leave. Then I walked around the bar and sat on one of the stools. It felt strange. I don't think I'd sat at my own bar even once in all those forty years. Bartenders just don't do it. The good ones don't. I didn't.

"Well," I said into the silence. "Let's see how it works."

I took out my smart plastic and fed it into the slot. I heard a faint whirring as the card disappeared. A tiny light glowed at the head of the keyboard. I pressed a button next to the light and a small screen lit up and displayed the names of drinks, one after another. If he desired, a customer could simply punch in the number of his preferred potation, but I chose to let the menu run.

What a litany! Whiskey sour. Sloe gin fizz. Margarita. Martini. Piña colada. Manhattan.

Each name had once meant something, maybe everything,

to some poor frazzled drinker. I waited until my own particular poison, Dewar's scotch and water, came drifting up. Number 347. I punched the number. After a time the dispenser hiccoughed and disgorged a plastic cup filled with ice and light amber liquid. I tasted. Dewars, all right, but the plastic seemed to change the taste a bit. I sipped, crunched ice, and thought.

The man had explained it all. The Mixtronic people would come by, open and close the bar each day. They would keep the machine cleaned, stocked, and operating. Their janitorial service would do the same for the rest of the bar. Their television monitors would keep an eye on the place, alert the police in case of trouble. Hidden loudspeakers would let the monitors talk to the customers, if necessary.

Very neat, it seemed. And no need for the bartender, of course.

I had about twelve or fifteen more and woke up the next day with a screaming hangover, probably the first in fifteen years. There are drunk bartenders and old bartenders, but not very many drunk old bartenders. The stuff cuts the life expectancy a lot of ways, and it's too easy for us to get hold of.

I tried all the usual remedies, none of which helped much, and tottered out to make some phone calls. By the time I had finished it was about five o'clock and I was feeling much improved. A bit of corned beef and cabbage over at the Shanty helped even more, so by the time I walked into Finnegan's I was feeling pretty chipper.

Irish Red was staring into the mirror and saw me come in.

"Hey, Harry," he hollered, turning. "What a rotten thing."

I nodded. "Red," I replied. "You know. Nothing stays the same."

"That's for sure," he agreed. "A drink?"

"Why not?"

"Now if I can just get this damn thing to—" He played with the buttons for a while. A plastic cup finally appeared and he handed it to me with a flourish. "It sure feels funny, me getting a drink for *you*."

I tasted, grimaced.

He looked worried. "What's the matter, ain't it okay?"

"It's close enough, Red. Thanks. Don't worry about it."

Red is an interesting character. He isn't Irish much, just likes to think he is. He drinks Jameson's on the rocks, and I never serve him more than five. I have my reasons and Red respects them. But what the hell, it wasn't my problem anymore.

"How many's that, Red?"

His long, toothy face turned apprehensive for a moment, but then he remembered I wasn't the bartender any longer.

"Three, maybe four, Harry. Why?" He grinned suddenly.

"No reason. Thanks again for the drink, Red." I tipped my drink to him and retired to a back table where I could watch the action.

There were a couple of guys sitting next to Red. One I knew, a meek little man who came in maybe twice a year. The other one I didn't know, but I recognized the type. A skinny dude with frantic eyes and a quick way with a beer. He was really pounding them down.

The door slammed and the Sky Pilot waddled in. He had to waddle—he went at least three hundred pounds and wasn't much over five eight. He threw his beefy arms wide and began to sing "Mother Machree." Jesus. That meant he was on his second quart of bourbon and it wasn't hardly evening yet. His voice was okay, though.

Another drink came my way, courtesy of the Pilot. I sipped slowly. Sobriety seemed like a good idea.

Two hours later the joint was, as they say, jumping.

Fast Freddie was trying to pick up a girl he didn't know. Her boyfriend, whose neck was purest crimson, looked displeased. It made his tattoos quiver.

The Sky Pilot and Lawyer Tom were trying to harmonize, but they kept forgetting the words. Irish Red was well into his ninth or tenth drink; he turned a reddened eye on the frantic beer drinker, who began to eye him back.

Tin Lizzie lost her wig and began to scream at the Mixtronic. "I said a *double*, dammit!"

Overhead the telecams swung back and forth uneasily.

The Schoolmarm was trying to convince Jack the Cap that

yes, Poland had once had an empire, which The Cap fiercely denied.

It wouldn't take much more, I figured. And it didn't. The front door opened and in came Stan the Man, lumbering and myopic, peering dimly through the smoke. His eyes lighted on the Sky Pilot and a slow smile spread across his wide, flat face.

It had been twenty years since I'd allowed the two of them in the bar at the same time. The last time they'd ended up fighting a duel with rusty sabers at three in the morning in somebody's backyard.

Stan tippy-toed over to the Pilot who, warned by an arcane sensibility, turned and swung. The sudden sucker punch was the Pilot's specialty, particularly after two quarts of hooch. His big fist caught Stan square on the money, knocking him into the table where the Redneck was glaring at Fast Freddie. Freddie used to be a Marine, but that didn't help much when the Redneck picked up the table and heaved.

The frantic beer drinker grinned evilly and took a swing at Irish Red, who ducked and swung back.

A whooping siren, like a car alarm, began to screech from the speakers, but nobody paid any attention. Tin Lizzie found her wig and began pummeling the Sky Pilot with it, as he tried to disentangle himself from Stan the Man.

A chair crashed into the big mirror behind the bar. Tin Lizzie, bawling hugely, began to pound on one of the drink dispensers. "A double!" she ranted. Sparks rose from other dispensers, and smoke billowed from somewhere behind the bar.

The speakers kept on squawking, but now you could barely hear them over the increasing tumult.

I waited until I heard louder sirens shrieking up outside. Then I got up, took a leather sap from my hip pocket, and popped the frantic beer drinker behind his left ear. As I'd suspected, he'd been carrying a blade. Irish Red, despite some of his disgusting proclivities, didn't deserve to get his throat cut.

It took about three minutes, I reflected, as I melted out the back door.

What the hell? I hadn't had that much to drink, but I still had a mild hangover. Something was ringing. My doorbell.

I let the tall, thin, balding accountant type into the apartment. His eyes darted behind his glasses.

"What happened?" he asked.

"What do you mean?"

"I reviewed the tapes. I saw you sitting at that table all night. If I hadn't seen with my own eyes, I would have bet you caused it all somehow. For revenge, maybe. But you didn't *do* anything . . ." He sounded puzzled.

"Oh. You mean the bar last night."

"Uh huh. The bar last night. Twenty grand in damages. Three injured. The Mixtronic destroyed. A shambles."

"It looked that way," I agreed.

He shook his head. "Look, Guardino—"

"Mr. Guardino," I said mildly.

He paused. "Oh. Right—Mr. Guardino. Listen, the Mixtronic thing is pretty new. We've tested it, sure, but Finnegan's was one of the first real commercial installations. I've got to know. I mean—if *you* know, that is. What *happened?*" His voice rose slightly.

I let him hang a bit. No use making it sound easy. Come to think of it, maybe it wasn't. How to explain that making drinks is only 10 percent of a good bartender's job? Anybody, even a machine, can make drinks. But tend bar? The rest of it, that is?

I shook my head. "Well, as near as I can figure it, Irish Red had ten Jameson's on the rocks."

He stared at me.

"Yeah. And that damned Mixtronic was serving Tin Lizzie doubles every time she ordered them. Not to mention serving the Sky Pilot at all."

"Does this mean something?"

"Only if you know about Fast Freddie's married life. And Stan the Man's duel. And that the Schoolmarm isn't really a teacher. Unless she's deep into scotch, that is. Also, it helps to be able to read eyes."

"Eyes?"

"Yeah. That's why I sapped that guy. You saw?"

He nodded. "I saw. The cops said he was wanted for attempted murder."

I looked at my hand. "No surprise," I said.

The accountant took a deep breath. "I think I begin to see what you're driving at. And it happened so fast. One minute nice and calm, the next a disaster."

"I've seen it start to blow quicker, but I've always stopped it in time."

He shook his head. "Can I ask you how? How you stop it?"

I shrugged. "I just do. I'm a bartender. That's what I'm paid for."

He sighed. "So you're saying the Mixtronic can't do the job?"

I know people. And I know when to back off. "Listen, buddy, can somebody operate the Mixtronic off a central keyboard? Serious drinkers have a lot of trouble with the little keypads, anyway."

He thought for a second. "Sure. Easy."

"Okay, then. Consider. I know you save a good chunk of money with the liquor measurement. And there's no possibility of theft. How much do you save with no cameras, no monitors, no people running around opening and closing bars?"

He took off his glasses. Something began to shine in his eyes.

Mixtronic attendant doesn't have quite the ring of bartender, but it'll do. At least I know when to make singles and when to make doubles for Tin Lizzie. And Irish Red only gets five. And the Sky Pilot none when he's singing. And I remind Fast Freddie about his wife every once in a while, and I don't serve people with funny eyes.

Pretty much the same. In fact, right now there's only two things bugging me: I wonder if anybody will find out about all the invitations I phoned out for my farewell party that night.

And, dammit, I *still* miss the bottles.

William T. Quick is the author of Dreams of Flesh & Sand; *its two sequels,* Dreams of Gods & Men *and* Dreams of Life & Death; *and* Yesterday's Pawn. *His short fiction has appeared in numerous magazines in the field, most notably* Analog.

THE OLDEST SOLDIER
by Fritz Leiber

A skirmish in a never-ending war.

The one we called the Leutnant took a long swallow of his dark Loewensbrau. He'd just been describing a battle of infantry rockets on the Eastern Front, the German and Russian positions erupting bundles of flame.

Max swished his paler beer in its green bottle and his eyes got a faraway look and he said, "When the rockets killed their thousands in Copenhagen, they laced the sky with fire and lit up the steeples in the city and the masts and bare spars of the British ships like a field of crosses."

"I didn't know there were any landings in Denmark," someone remarked with an expectant casualness.

"This was in the Napoleonic wars," Max explained. "The British bombarded the city and captured the Danish fleet. Back in 1807."

"Vas you dere, Maxie?" Woody asked, and the gang around the counter chuckled and beamed. Drinking at a liquor store is a pretty dull occupation and one is grateful for small vaudeville acts.

"Why bare spars?" someone asked.

"So there'd be less chance of the rockets setting the launching ships afire," Max came back at him. "Sails burn fast and wooden ships are tinder anyway—that's why ships firing red-hot shot never worked out. Rockets and bare spars were bad enough. Yes, and it was Congreve rockets made the 'red glare' at Fort McHenry," he continued unruffled, "while the 'bombs bursting in air' were about the earliest precision artillery shells, fired from mortars on bomb-ketches. There's a condensed history of arms in the

American anthem." He looked around smiling. "Yes, I was there, Woody—just as I was with the South Martians when they stormed Copernicus in the Second Colonial War. And just as I'll be in a foxhole outside Copeybawa a billion years from now while the blast waves from the battling Venusian spaceships shake the soil and roil the mud and give me some more digging to do."

This time the gang really snorted its happy laughter and Woody was slowly shaking his head and repeating, "Copenhagen and Copernicus and—what was the third? Oh, what a mind he's got," and the Leutnant was saying, "Yah, you vas there—in books," and I was thinking, *Thank God for all screwballs, especially the brave ones who never flinch, who never lose their tempers or drop the act, so that you never do quite find out whether it's just a gag or their solemnest belief. There's only one person here takes Max even one percent seriously, but they all love him because he won't ever drop his guard . . .*

"The only point I was trying to make," Max continued when he could easily make himself heard, "was the way styles in weapons keep moving in cycles."

"Did the Romans use rockets?" asked the same light voice as had remarked about the landings in Denmark and the bare spars. I saw now it was Sol from behind the counter.

Max shook his head. "Not so you'd notice. Catapults were their specialty." He squinted his eyes. "Though now you mention it, I recall a dogfoot telling me Archimedes faked up some rockets powered with Greek fire to touch off the sails of the Roman ships at Syracuse—and none of this romance about a giant burning glass."

"You mean," said Woody, "that there are other gazebos besides yourself in this fighting-all-over-the-universe-and-to-the-end-of-time racket?" His deep whiskey voice was at its solemnest and most wondering.

"Naturally," Max told him earnestly. "How else do you suppose wars ever get really fought and refought?"

"Why should wars ever be refought?" Sol asked lightly. "Once ought to be enough."

"Do you suppose anybody could time-travel and keep his hands off wars?" Max countered.

I put in my two cents' worth. "Then that would make Archimedes' rockets the earliest liquid-fuel rockets by a long shot."

Max looked straight at me, a special quirk in his smile. "Yes, I guess so," he said after a couple of seconds. "On this planet, that is."

The laughter had been falling off, but that brought it back and while Woody was saying loudly to himself, "I like that refighting part—that's what we're all so good at," the Leutnant asked Max with only a moderate accent that fit North Chicago, "And zo you aggshually have fought on Mars?"

"Yes, I have," Max agreed after a bit. "Though that ruckus I mentioned happened on our moon—expeditionary forces from the Red Planet."

"Ach, yes. And now let me ask you something—"

I really mean that about screwballs, you know. I don't care whether they're saucer addicts or extrasensory perception bugs or religious or musical maniacs or crackpot philosophers or psychologists or merely guys with a strange dream or gag like Max—for my money they are the ones who are keeping individuality alive in this age of conformity. They are the ones who are resisting the encroachments of the mass media and motivation research and the mass man. The only really bad thing about crackpottery and screwballistics (as with dope and prostitution) is the cold-blooded people who prey on it for money. So I say to all screwballs: Go it on your own. Don't take any wooden nickels or give out any silver dimes. Be wise and brave—like Max.

He and the Leutnant were working up a discussion of the problems of artillery in airless space and low gravity that was a little too technical to keep the laughter alive. So Woody up and remarked, "Say, Maximilian, if you got to be in all these wars all over hell and gone, you must have a pretty tight schedule. How come you got time to be drinking with us bums?"

"I often ask myself that," Max cracked back at him. "Fact is, I'm on a sort of unscheduled furlough, result of a transportation slipup. I'm due to be picked up and returned to my outfit any day now—that is, if the enemy underground doesn't get to me first."

It was just then, as Max said that bit about enemy underground, and as the laughter came, a little diminished, and as Woody was chortling "Enemy underground now. How do you like that?" and as I was thinking how much Max had given me in these couple of weeks—a guy with an almost poetic flare for vivid historical reconstruction, but with more than that . . . it was just then that I saw the two red eyes low down in the dusty plate-glass window looking in from the dark street.

Everything in modern America has to have a big plate-glass display window, everything from suburban mansions, general managers' offices and skyscraper apartments to barbershops and beauty parlors and ginmills—there are even gymnasium swimming pools with plate-glass windows twenty feet high opening on busy boulevards—and Sol's dingy liquor store was no exception; in fact, I believe there's a law that it's got to be that way. But I was the only one of the gang who happened to be looking out of this particular window at the moment. It was a dark windy night outside and it's a dark and untidy street at best and across from Sol's are more plate glass windows that sometimes give off very odd reflections, so when I got a glimpse of this black formless head with the two eyes like red coals peering in past the brown pyramid of empty whiskey bottles, I don't suppose it was a half second before I realized it must be something like a couple of cigarette butts kept alive by the wind, or more likely a freak reflection of taillights from some car turning a corner down the street, and in another half second it was gone, the car having finished turning the corner or the wind blowing the cigarette butts away altogether. Still, for a moment it gave me a very goosey feeling, coming right on top of that remark about an enemy underground.

And I must have shown my reaction in some way, for Woody, who is very observant, called out, "Hey, Fred, has that soda pop you drink started to rot your nerves—or are even Max's friends getting sick at the outrageous lies he's been telling us?"

Max looked at me sharply and perhaps he saw something, too. At any rate he finished his beer and said, "I guess I'll be taking off." He didn't say it to me particularly, but he kept looking at me. I nodded and put down on the counter

my small green bottle, still one-third full of the lemon pop
I find overly sweet, though it was the sourest Sol stocked.
Max and I zipped up our windbreakers. He opened the door
and a little of the wind came in and troubled the tanbark
around the sill. The Leutnant said to Max, "Tomorrow night
we design a better space gun"; Sol routinely advised the two
of us, "Keep your noses clean"; and Woody called, "So
long space soldiers." (And I could imagine him saying as
the door closed, "That Max is nuttier than a fruitcake and
Freddy isn't much better. Drinking soda pop—ugh!'')

And then Max and I were outside leaning into the wind,
our eyes slitted against the blown dust, for the three-block
trudge to Max's pad—a name his tiny apartment merits
without any attempt to force the language.

There weren't any large black shaggy dogs with red eyes
slinking about and I hadn't quite expected there would be.

Why Max and his soldier-of-history gag and our outwardly
small comradeship meant so much to me is something that
goes way back into my childhood. I was a lonely timid
child, with no brothers and sisters to spar around with in
preparation for the battles of life, and I never went through
the usual stages of boyhood gangs either. In line with those
things I grew up into a very devout liberal and "hated war"
with a mystical fervor during the intermission between 1918
and 1939—so much so that I made a point of avoiding
military services in the second conflict, though merely by
working in the nearest war plant, not by the arduously heroic
route of out-and-out pacifism.

But then the inevitable reaction set in, sparked by the
liberal curse of being able, however belatedly, to see both
sides of any question. I began to be curious about and
cautiously admiring of soldiering and soldiers. Unwillingly
at first, I came to see the necessity and romance of the
spearmen—those guardians, often lonely as myself, of the
perilous camps of civilization and brotherhood in a black
hostile universe . . . necessary guardians, for all the truth in
the indictments that war caters to irrationality and sadism and
serves the munition makers and reactionaries.

I commenced to see my own hatred of war as in part only
a mask for cowardice, and I started to look for some way

to do honor in my life to the other half of the truth. Though it's anything but easy to give yourself a feeling of being brave just because you suddenly want that feeling. Obvious opportunities to be obviously brave come very seldom in our largely civilized culture; in fact, they're clean contrary to safety drives and so-called normal adjustment and good peacetime citizenship and all the rest, and they come mostly in the earliest part of a man's life. So that for the person who belatedly wants to be brave it's generally a matter of waiting for an opportunity for six months and then getting a tiny one and muffing it in six seconds.

But however uncomfortable it was, I had this reaction to my devout early pacifism, as I say. At first I took it out only in reading. I devoured war books, current and historical, fact and fiction. I tried to soak up the military aspects and jargon of all ages, the organization and weapons, the strategy and tactics. Characters like Tros of Samothrace and Horatio Hornblower became my new secret heroes, along with Heinlein's space cadets and Bullard and other brave rangers of the spaceways.

But after a while reading wasn't enough. I had to have some real soldiers and I finally found them in the little gang that gathered nightly at Sol's liquor store. It's funny, but liquor stores that serve drinks have a clientele with more character and comradeship than the clienteles of most bars— perhaps it is the absence of jukeboxes, chromium plate, bowling machines, trouble-hunting, drink-cadging women, and—along with those—men in search of fights and forget- fulness. At any rate, it was at Sol's liquor store that I found Woody and the Leutnant and Bert and Mike and Pierre and Sol himself. The casual customer would hardly have guessed that they were anything but quiet souses, certainly not soldiers, but I got a clue or two and I started to hang around, making myself inconspicuous and drinking my rather symbolic soda pop, and pretty soon they started to open up and yarn about North Africa and Stalingrad and Anzio and Korea and such, and I was pretty happy in a partial sort of way.

And then about a month ago Max had turned up and he was the man I'd really been looking for. A genuine soldier with my historical slant on things—only he knew a lot more than I did, I was a rank amateur by comparison—and he had this crazy appealing gag too, and besides that he actually cottoned to me and invited me on to his place a few times, so that with him I was more than a tavern hanger-on. Max was good for me, though I still hadn't the faintest idea of who he really was or what he did.

Naturally Max hadn't opened up the first couple of nights with the gang, he'd just bought his beer and kept quiet and felt his way much as I had. Yet he looked and felt so much the soldier that I think the gang was inclined to accept him from the start—a quick stocky man with big hands and a leathery face and smiling tired eyes that seemed to have seen everything at one time or another. And then on the third or fourth night Bert told something about the Battle of the Bulge and Max chimed in with some things he'd seen there, and I could tell from the looks Bert and the Leutnant exchanged that Max had "passed"—he was now the accepted seventh member of the gang, with me still as the tolerated clerical-type hanger-on, for I'd never made any secret of my complete lack of military experience.

Not long afterwards—it couldn't have been more than one or two nights—Woody told some tall tales and Max started matching him and that was the beginning of the time-and-space-soldier gag. It was funny about the gag. I suppose we just should have assumed that Max was a history nut and liked to parade his bookish hobby in a picturesque way—and maybe some of the gang did assume just that—but he was so vivid yet so casual in his descriptions of other times and places that you felt there had to be something more and sometimes he'd get such a lost, nostalgic look on his face talking of things fifty million miles or five hundred years away that Woody would almost die laughing, which was really the sincerest sort of tribute to Max's convincingness.

Max even kept up the gag when he and I were alone together, walking or at his place—he'd never come to mine—though he kept it up in a minor-key sort of way, so that it sometimes seemed that what he was trying to get across was not that he was the Soldier of a Power that was fighting across all of time to change history, but simply that we men were creatures with imaginations and it was our highest duty to try to feel what it was really like to live in other times and places and bodies. Once he said to me, "The growth of consciousness is everything, Fred—the seed of awareness sending its roots across space and time. But it can grow in so many ways, spinning its webs from mind to mind like the spider or burrowing into the unconscious darkness like the snake. The biggest wars are the wars of thought."

But whatever he was trying to get across, I went along with his gag—which seems to me the proper way to behave with any other man, screwball or not, so long as you can do it without violating your own personality. Another man brings a little life and excitement into the world, why try to kill it? It is simply a matter of politeness and style.

I'd come to think a lot about style since knowing Max. It doesn't matter so much what you do in life, he once said to me—soldiering or clerking, preaching or picking pockets—so long as you do it with style. Better fail in a grand style than succeed in a mean one—you won't enjoy the successes you get the second way.

Max seemed to understand my own special problems without my having to confess them. He pointed out to me that the soldier is trained for bravery. The whole object of military discipline is to make sure that when the six seconds of testing come every six months or so, you do the brave thing without thinking, by drilled second nature. It's not a matter of of the soldier having some special virtue or virility the civilian lacks. And then about fear. All men are afraid, Max said, except a few psychopathic or suicidal types and they merely haven't fear at the conscious level. But the better you know yourself and the men around you and the situation you're up against (though you can never know all of the last and sometimes you have only a glimmering), then the better you are prepared to prevent fear from mastering you. Generally speaking, if you prepare yourself by the daily self-discipline of looking squarely at life, if you imagine realistically the troubles and opportunities that may come, then the chances are you won't fail in the testing. Well, of course I'd heard and read all those things before, but coming from Max they seemed to mean a lot more to me. As I say, Max was good for me.

So on this night when Max had talked about Copenhagen and Copernicus and Copeybawa and I'd imagined I'd seen a big black dog with red eyes and we were walking the lonely streets hunched in our jackets and I was listening to the big clock over at the University tolling eleven . . . well, on this night I wasn't thinking anything special except that I was with my screwball buddy and pretty soon we'd be at his place and having a nightcap. I'd make mine coffee.

I certainly wasn't expecting anything.

Until, at the windy corner just before his place, Max suddenly stopped.

Max's junky front room-and-a-half was in a smoky brick building two flights up over some run-down stores. There is a rust-flaked fire escape on the front of it, running past the old-fashioned jutting bay windows, its lowest flight a counterbalanced one that only swings down when somebody walks out onto it—that is, if a person ever had occasion to.

When Max stopped suddenly, I stopped too, of course. He was looking up at his window. His window was dark and I couldn't see anything in particular, except that he or somebody else had apparently left a big black bundle of something out on the fire escape and—and it wouldn't be the first time I'd seen that space used for storage and drying wash and what not, against all fire regulations, I'm sure.

But Max stayed stopped and kept on looking.

"Say, Fred," he said softly then, "how about going over to your place for a change? Is the standing invitation still out?"

"Sure, Max, why not," I replied instantly, matching my voice to his. "I've been asking you all along."

My place was just two blocks away. We'd only have to turn the corner we were standing on and we'd be headed straight for it.

"Okay then," Max said. "Let's get going." There was a touch of sharp impatience in his voice that I'd never heard there before. He suddenly seemed very eager that we should get around that corner. He took hold of my arm.

He was no longer looking up at the fire escape, but I was. The wind had abruptly died and it was very still. As we went around the corner—to be exact as Max pulled me around it— the big bundle of something lifted up and looked down at me with eyes like two red coals.

I didn't let out a gasp or say anything. I don't think Max realized then that I'd seen anything, but I was shaken. This time I couldn't lay it to cigarette butts or reflected taillights, they were too difficult to place on a third-story fire escape. This time my mind would have to rationalize a lot more inventively to find an explanation, and until it did I would have to believe that something . . . well, alien . . . was at large in this part of Chicago.

Big cities have their natural menaces—holdup artists, hopped-up kids, sick-headed sadists, that sort of thing—and you're more or less prepared for them. You're not prepared for something . . . alien. If you hear a scuttling in the basement you assume it's rats and although you know rats can be dangerous you're not particularly frightened and you may even go down to investigate. You don't expect to find bird-catching Amazonian spiders.

The wind hadn't resumed yet. We'd gone about a third of the way down the first block when I heard behind us, faintly but distinctly, a rusty creaking ending in a metallic jar that didn't fit anything but the first flight of the fire escape swinging down to the sidewalk.

I just kept walking then, but my mind split in two—half of it listening and straining back over my shoulder, the other half darting off to investigate the weirdest notions, such as that Max was a refugee from some unimaginable concentration camp on the other side of the stars. If there were such concentration camps, I told myself in my cold hysteria, run by some sort of supernatural SS men, they'd have dogs just like the one I'd thought I'd seen . . . and, to be honest, thought I'd *see* padding along if I looked over my shoulder now.

It was hard to hang on and just walk, not run, with this insanity or whatever it was hovering over my mind, and the fact that Max didn't say a word didn't help either.

Finally, as we were starting the second block, I got hold of myself and I quietly reported to Max exactly what I thought I'd seen. His response surprised me.

"What's the layout of your apartment, Fred? Third floor, isn't it?

"Yes. Well . . ."

"Begin at the door we'll be going in," he directed me.

"That's the living room, then there's a tiny short open hall, then the kitchen. It's like an hourglass, with the living room and kitchen the ends, and the hall the wasp waist. Two doors open from the hall: the one to your right (figuring from the living room) opens into the bathroom; the one to your left, into a small bedroom."

"Windows?"

"Two in the living room, side by side," I told him. "None in the bathroom. One in the bedroom, onto an air shaft. Two in the kitchen, apart."

"Back door in the kitchen?" he asked.

"Yes. To the back porch. Has glass in the top half of it. I hadn't thought about that. That makes three windows in the kitchen."

"Are the shades in the windows pulled down now?"

"No."

Questions and answers had been rapid-fire, without time for me to think, done while we walked a quarter of a block. Now after the briefest pause Max said, "Look, Fred, I'm not asking you or anyone to believe in all the things I've been telling as if for kicks at Sol's—that's too much for all of a sudden—but you do believe in that black dog, don't you?" He touched my arm warningly. "No, don't look behind you!"

I swallowed. "I believe in him right now," I said.

"Okay. Keep on walking. I'm sorry I got you into this, Fred, but now I've got to try to get both of us out. *Your* best chance is to disregard the thing, pretend you're not aware of anything strange happening—then the beast won't know whether I've told you anything, it'll be hesitant to disturb you, it'll try to get at me without troubling you, and it'll even hold off a while if it thinks it will get me that way. But it won't hold off forever—it's only imperfectly disciplined. *My* best chance is to get in touch with headquarters—something I've been putting off—and have them pull me out. I should be able to do it in an hour, maybe less. You can give me that time, Fred."

"How?" I asked him. I was mounting the steps to the vestibule. I thought I could hear, very faintly, a light pad-padding behind us. I didn't look back.

Max stepped through the door I held open and we started up the stairs.

"As soon as we get in your apartment," he said, "you turn on all the lights in the living room and kitchen. Leave the shades up. Then start doing whatever you might be doing if you were staying up at this time of night. Reading or typing, say. Or having a bite of food, if you can manage it. Play it as naturally as you can. If you hear things, if you feel things, try to take no notice. Above all, don't open the windows or doors, or look out of them to see anything, or go to them if you can help it—you'll probably feel drawn to do just that. Just play it naturally. If you can hold them . . . it . . . off that way for half an hour or so—until midnight, say—if you can give me that much time, I should be able to handle my end of it. And remember, it's the best chance for you as well as for me. Once I'm out of here, you're safe."

"But you—" I said, digging for my key, "—what will you—?"

"As soon as we get inside," Max said, "I'll duck in your bedroom and shut the door. Pay no attention. Don't come after me, whatever you hear. Is there a plug-in in your bedroom? I'll need juice."

"Yes," I told him, turning the key. "But the lights have been going off a lot lately. Someone has been blowing the fuses."

"That's great," he growled, following me inside.

I turned on the lights and went in the kitchen, did the same there and came back. Max was still in the living room, bent over the table beside my typewriter. He had a sheet of light-green paper. He must have brought it with him. He was scrawling something at the top and bottom of it. He straightened up and gave it to me.

"Fold it up and put it in your pocket and keep it on you the next few days," he said.

It was just a blank sheet of cracklingly thin light-green paper with "Dear Fred" scribbled at the top and "Your friend, Max Bournemann" at the bottom and nothing in between.

"But what—?" I began, looking up at him.

"Do as I say!" he snapped at me. Then, as I almost

flinched away from him, he grinned—a great big comradely grin.

"Okay, let's get working," he said, and he went into the bedroom and shut the door behind him.

I folded the sheet of paper three times and unzipped my windbreaker and tucked it inside the breast pocket. Then I went to the bookcase and pulled at random a volume out of the top shelf—my psychology shelf, I remembered the next moment—and sat down and opened the book and looked at a page without seeing the print.

And now there was time for me to think. Since I'd spoken of the red eyes to Max there had been no time for anything but to listen and to remember and to act. Now there was time for me to think.

My first thoughts were: *This is ridiculous! I saw something strange and frightening, sure, but it was in the dark, I couldn't see anything clearly, there must be some simple natural explanation for whatever it was on the fire escape. I saw something strange and Max sensed I was frightened and when I told him about it he decided to play a practical joke on me in line with that eternal gag he lives by. I'll bet right now he's lying on my bed and chuckling, wondering how long it'll be before I—*

The window beside me rattled as if the wind had suddenly risen again. The rattling grew more violent—and then it abruptly stopped without dying away, stopped with a feeling of tension, as if the wind or something more material were still pressing against the pane.

And I did not turn my head to look at it, although (or perhaps because) I knew there was no fire escape or other support outside. I simply endured that sense of a presence at my elbow and stared unseeingly at the book in my hands, while my heart pounded and my skin froze and flushed.

I realized fully then that my first skeptical thoughts had been the sheerest automatic escapism and that, just as I'd told Max, I believed with my whole mind in the black dog. I believed in the whole business insofar as I could imagine it. I believed that there are undreamed of powers warring in this universe. I believed that Max was a stranded time-traveller and that in my bedroom he was now frantically operating some unearthly device to signal for help from some unknown headquarters. I believed that the impossible and the deadly were loose in Chicago.

But my thoughts couldn't carry further than that. They kept repeating themselves, faster and faster. My mind felt like an engine that is shaking itself to pieces. And the impulse to turn my head and look out the window came to me and grew.

I forced myself to focus on the middle of the page where I had the book open and start reading.

Jung's archetypes transgress the barriers of time and space. More than that: they are capable of breaking the shackles of the laws of causality. They are endowed with frankly mystical "prospective" faculties. The soul itself, according to Jung, is the reaction of the personality to the unconscious and includes in every person both male and female elements, the animus and anima, as well as the persona or the person's reaction to the outside world . . .

I think I read that last sentence a dozen times, swiftly at first, then word by word, until it was a meaningless jumble and I could no longer force my gaze across it.

The glass in the window beside me creaked.

I laid down the book and stood up, eyes front, and went into the kitchen and grabbed a handful of crackers and opened the refrigerator.

The rattling that muted itself in hungry pressure followed. I heard it first in one kitchen window, then the other, then in the glass in the top of the door. I didn't look.

I went back in the living room, hesitated a moment beside my typewriter, which had a blank sheet of yellow paper in it, then sat down again in the armchair beside the window, putting the crackers and the half carton of milk on the little table beside me. I picked up the book I'd tried to read and put it on my knees.

The rattling returned with me at once and peremptorily, as if something were growing impatient.

I couldn't focus on the print anymore. I picked up a cracker and put it down. I touched the cold milk carton and my throat constricted and I drew my fingers away.

I looked at my typewriter and then I thought of the blank sheet of *green* paper and the explanation for Max's strange act suddenly seemed clear to me. Whatever happened to him tonight, he wanted me to be able to type a message over his signature that would exonerate me. A suicide note, say. Whatever happened to him . . .

The window beside me shook violently, as if at a terrific gust.

I occurred to me that while I must not look out of the window as if expecting to see something (that would be the sort of giveaway against which Max warned me) I could safely let my gaze slide across it—say, if I turned to look at the clock behind me. Only, I told myself, I mustn't pause or react if I saw anything.

I nerved myself. After all, I told myself, there was the blessed possibility that I would see nothing outside the taut pane but darkness.

I turned my head to look at the clock.

I saw *it* twice, going and coming back, and although my gaze did not pause or falter, my blood and my thoughts started to pound as if my heart and mind would burst.

It was about two feet outside the window—a face or mask or muzzle of a more gleaming black than the darkness around it. The face was at the same time the face of a hound, a panther, a giant bat, and a man—in between those four. A pitiless, hopeless man-animal face alive with knowledge but dead with a monstrous melancholy and a monstrous malice. There was the sheen of needlelike white teeth against black lips or dewlaps. There was the dull pulsing glow of eyes like red coals.

My gaze didn't pause or falter or go back—yes—and my heart and mind didn't burst, but I stood up then and stepped jerkily to the typewriter and sat down at it and started to pound the keys. After a while my gaze stopped blurring and I started to see what I was typing. The first thing I'd typed was:

the quick red fox jumped over the crazy black dog . . .

I kept on typing. It was better than reading. Typing I was doing something, I could discharge. I typed a flood of fragments: "Now is the time for all good men—," the first words of the Declaration of Independence and the Constitution, the Winston Commercial, six lines of Hamlet's "To be or not to be" without punctuation, Newton's Third Law of Motion, "Mary had a big black—"

In the middle of it all the face of the electric clock that I'd looked at sprang into my mind. My mental image of it had been blanked out until then. The hands were at quarter to twelve.

Whipping in a fresh yellow sheet, I typed the first stanza of Poe's "Raven," the Oath of Allegiance to the American Flag, the lost-ghost lines from Thomas Wolfe, the Creed and the Lord's Prayer, "Beauty is truth; truth, blackness—"

The rattling made a swift circuit of the windows—though I heard nothing from the bedroom, nothing at all—and finally the rattling settled on the kitchen door. There was a creaking of wood and metal under pressure.

I thought: *You are standing guard. You are standing guard for yourself and for Max.* And then the second thought came: *If you open the door, if you welcome it in, if you open the kitchen door and then the bedroom door, it will spare you, it will not hurt you.*

Over and over again I fought down that second thought and the urge that went with it. It didn't seem to be coming from my mind, but from the outside. I typed Ford, Buick, the names of all the automobiles I could remember, Overland, Moon, I typed all the four-letter words, I typed the alphabet, lower case and capitals, I typed the numerals and punctuation marks, I typed the keys of the keyboard in order from left to right, top to bottom, then in from each side alternately. I filled the last yellow sheet I was on and it fell out and I kept pounding mechanically, making shiny black marks on the dull black platen.

But then the urge became something I could not resist. I stood up and in the sudden silence I walked through the hall to the back door, looking down at the floor and resisting, dragging each step as much as I could.

My hands touched the knob and the long-handled key in the lock. My body pressed the door, which seemed to surge against me, so that I felt it was only my counterpressure that kept it from bursting open in a shower of splintered glass and wood.

Far off, as if it were something happening in another universe, I heard the University clock tolling: One . . . two . . .

And then, because I could resist no longer, I turned the key and the knob.

The lights all went out.

In the darkness the door pushed open against me and something came in past me like a gust of cold black wind with streaks of heat in it.

I heard the bedroom door swing open.

The clock completed its strokes. Eleven . . . twelve . . .

And then . . .

Nothing . . . nothing at all. All pressures lifted from me. I was aware only of being alone, utterly alone. I knew it, deep down.

After some . . . minutes, I think, I shut and locked the door and I went over and opened a drawer and rummaged out a candle, lit it, and went through the apartment and into the bedroom.

Max wasn't there. I'd known he wouldn't be. I didn't know how badly I'd failed him. I lay down on the bed and after a while I began to sob and, after another while, I slept.

Next day I told the janitor about the lights. He gave me a funny look.

"I know," he said. "I just put in a new fuse this morning. I never saw one blown like that before. The window in the fuse was gone and there was a metal sprayed all over the inside of the box."

That afternoon I got Max's message. I'd gone for a walk in the park and was sitting on a bench beside the lagoon, watching the water ripple in the breeze when I felt something burning against my chest. For a moment I thought I'd dropped my cigarette butt inside my windbreaker. I reached in and touched something hot in my pocket and jerked it out. It was the sheet of green paper Max had given me. Tiny threads of smoke were rising from it.

I flipped it open and read, in a scrawl that smoked and grew blacker instant by instant:

Thought you'd like to know I got through okay. Just in time. I'm back with my outfit. It's not too bad. Thanks for the rearguard action.

The handwriting (thoughtwriting?) of the blackening scrawl was identical with the salutation above and the signature below.

And then the sheet burst into flame. I flipped it away from me. Two boys launching a model sailboat looked at me strangely. I looked at the paper flaming, blackening, whitening, disintegrating . . .

I know enough chemistry to know that paper smeared with wet white phosphorus will burst into flame when it dries completely. And I know there are kinds of invisible writing that are brought out by heat. There are those general sorts of possibility. Chemical writing.

And then there's thoughtwriting, which is nothing but a word I've coined. Writing from a distance.—a literal telegram.

And there may be a combination of the two—chemical writing activated by thought from a distance . . . from a great distance.

I don't know. I simply don't know. When I remember that last night with Max, there are parts of it I doubt. But there's one part I never doubt.

When the gang asks me, "Where's Max?" I just shrug.

But when they get to talking about withdrawals they've covered; rearguard actions they've been in, I remember mine. I've never told them about it, but I never doubt that it took place.

Fritz Leiber is one of the greatest living masters of fantasy. His credits include the Fafhrd and Grey Mouser series, and such classic novels as Conjure Wife, The Big Time, The Wanderer, *and* Our Lady of Darkness. *He has won virtually every award the field has to offer: the Hugo, Nebula, and World Fantasy Award (for individual stories and a special award for Lifetime Achievement). He is nearing his fifth decade as a professional writer, and is currently at work on a new Grey Mouser novel.*

"The Oldest Soldier" is the first of Leiber's "Change War" series, sharing the same background as The Big Time.

THE ULTIMATE CRIME
by Isaac Asimov

Sometimes you can learn the most astonishing things over good food and drink. . . . The solution to a problem which puzzled the greatest deductive mind of an Age, for instance.

"The Baker Street Irregulars," said Roger Halsted, "is an organization of Sherlock Holmes enthusiasts. If you don't know that, you don't know anything."

He grinned over his drink at Thomas Trumbull with an air of the only kind of superiority there is—insufferable.

The level of conversation during the cocktail hour that preceded the monthly Black Widowers' banquet had remained at the level of a civilized murmur, but Trumbull, scowling, raised his voice at this point and restored matters to the more usual unseemliness that characterized such occasions.

He said, "When I was an adolescent I read Sherlock Holmes stories with a certain primitive enjoyment, but I'm not an adolescent anymore. The same, I perceive, cannot be said for everyone."

Emmanuel Rubin, staring owlishly through his thick glasses, shook his head. "There's no adolescence to it, Tom. The Sherlock Holmes stories marked the occasion on which the mystery story came to be recognized as a major branch of literature. It took what had until then been something that *had* been confined to adolescents and their dime novels and made of it adult entertainment."

Geoffrey Avalon, looking down austerely from his seventy-four inches to Rubin's sixty-four, said, "Actually, Sir Arthur Conan Doyle was not, in my opinion, an exceedingly good mystery writer. Agatha Christie is far better."

121

"That's a matter of opinion," said Rubin, who, as a mystery writer himself, was far less opinionated and didactic in that one field than in all the other myriad branches of human endeavor in which he considered himself an authority. "Christie had the advantage of reading Doyle and learning from him. Don't forget, too, that Christie's early works were pretty awful. Then, too"—he was warming up now—"Agatha Christie never got over her conservative, xenophobic prejudices. Her Americans are ridiculous. They were all named Hiram and all spoke a variety of English unknown to mankind. She was openly anti-Semitic and through the mouths of her characters unceasingly cast her doubts on anyone who was foreign."

Halsted said, "Yet her detective was a Belgian."

"Don't get me wrong," said Rubin. "I love Hercule Poirot. I think he's worth a dozen Sherlock Holmeses. I'm just pointing out that we can pick flaws in anyone. In fact, all the English mystery writers of the twenties and thirties were conservatives and upper-class oriented. You can tell from the type of puzzles they presented—baronets stabbed in the libraries of their manor houses—landed estates—independent wealth. Even the detectives were often gentlemen—Peter Wimsey, Roderick Alleyn, Albert Campion—"

"In that case," said Marion Gonzalo, who had just arrived and had been listening from the stairs, "the mystery story has developed in the direction of democracy. Now we deal with ordinary cops, and drunken private eyes and pimps and floozies and all the other leading lights of modern society." He helped himself to a drink and said, "Thanks, Henry. How did they get started on this?"

Henry said, "Sherlock Holmes was mentioned, sir."

"In connection with you, Henry?" Gonzalo looked pleased.

"No, sir. In connection with the Baker Street Irregulars."

Gonzalo looked blank. "What are—"

Halsted said, "Let me introduce you to my guest of the evening, Mario. He'll tell you. Ronald Mason, Mario Gonzalo. Ronald's a member of BSI, and so am I, for that matter. Go ahead, Ron, tell him about it."

Ronald Mason was a fat man, distinctly fat, with a glistening bald head and a bushy black mustache. He said,

"The Baker Street Irregulars is a group of Sherlock Holmes enthusiasts. They meet once a year in January, on a Friday near the great man's birthday, and through the rest of the year engage in other Sherlockian activities."

"Like what?"

"Well, they—"

Henry announced dinner, and Mason hesitated. "Is there some special seat I'm supposed to take?"

"No, no," said Gonzalo. "Sit next to me and we can talk."

"Fine." Mason's broad face split in a wide smile. "That's exactly what I'm here for. Rog Halsted said that you guys would come up with something for me."

"In connection with what?"

"Sherlockian activities." Mason tore a roll in two and buttered it with strenuous strokes of his knife. "You see, the thing is that Conan Doyle wrote numerous Sherlock Holmes stories as quickly as he could because he hated them—"

"He did? In that case, why "

"Why did he write them? Money, that's why. From the very first story, 'A Study in Scarlet,' the world caught on fire with Sherlock Holmes. He became a world-renowned figure and there is no telling how many people the world over thought he really lived. Innumerable letters were addressed to him at his address in 221B Baker Street, and thousands came to him with problems to be solved.

"Conan Doyle was surprised, as no doubt anyone would be under the circumstances. He wrote additional stories and the prices they commanded rose steadily. He was not pleased. He fancied himself as a writer of great historical romances and to have himself become world-famous as a mystery writer was displeasing—particularly when the fictional detective was far the more famous of the two. After six years of it he wrote 'The Final Problem,' in which he deliberately killed Holmes. There was a world outcry at this and after several more years Doyle was forced to reason out a method for resuscitating the detective, and then went on writing further stories.

"Aside from the value of the sales as mysteries, and from the fascinating character of Sherlock Holmes himself, the stories are a diversified picture of Great Britain in the late

Victorian era. To immerse oneself in the sacred writings is to live in a world where it is always 1895.''

Gonzalo said, ''And what's a Sherlockian activity?''

''Oh well. I told you that Doyle didn't particularly like writing about Holmes. When he did write the various stories, he wrote them quickly and he troubled himself very little about mutual consistency. There are many odd points, therefore, unknotted threads, small holes, and so on, and the game is never to admit that anything is just a mistake or error. In fact, to a true Sherlockian, Doyle scarcely exists—it was Dr. John H. Watson who wrote the stories.''

James Drake, who had been quietly listening from the other side of Mason, said, ''I know what you mean. I once met a Holmes fan—he may even have been a Baker Street Irregular—who told me he was working on a paper that would prove that both Sherlock Holmes and Dr. Watson were fervent Catholics and I said, 'Well, wasn't Doyle himself a Catholic?' which he was, of course. My friend turned a very cold eye on me and said, 'What has *that* to do with it?' ''

''Exactly,'' said Mason, ''exactly. The most highly regarded of all Sherlockian activities is to prove your point by quotations from the stories and by careful reasoning. People have written articles, for instance, that are supposed to prove that Watson was a woman, or that Sherlock Holmes had an affair with his landlady. Or else they try to work out details concerning Holmes's early life, or exactly where Watson received his war wound, and so on.

''Ideally, every member of the Baker Street Irregulars should write a Sherlockian article as a condition of membership, but that's clung to in only a slipshod fashion. I haven't written such an article yet, though I'd like to.'' Mason looked a bit wistful. ''I can't really consider myself a true Irregular till I do.''

Trumbull leaned over from across the table. He said, ''I've been trying to catch what you've been saying over Rubin's monologue here. You mentioned 221B Baker Street.''

''Yes,'' said Mason, ''that's where Holmes lived.''

''And is that why the club is the Baker Street Irregulars?''

Mason said, ''That was the name Holmes gave to a group

of street urchins who acted as spies and sources of information. They were his irregular troops as distinguished from the police.''

"Oh well,'' said Trumbull, ''I suppose it's all harmless.''

"And it gives us great pleasure,'' said Mason seriously. "Except that right now it's inflicting agony on me.''

It was at this point, shortly after Henry had brought in the veal cordon bleu, that Rubin's voice rose a notch. "Of course,'' he said, ''there's no way of denying that Sherlock Holmes was derivative. The whole Holmesian technique of detection was invented by Edgar Allan Poe; and his detective, Auguste Dupin, is the original Sherlock. However, Poe only wrote three stories about Dupin and it was Holmes who really caught the imagination of the world.

"In fact, my own feeling is that Sherlock Holmes performed the remarkable feat of being the first human being, either real or fictional, ever to become a world idol entirely because of his character as a reasoning being. It was not his military victories, his political charisma, his spiritual leadership—but simply his cold brain power. There was nothing mystical about Holmes. He gathered facts and deduced from them. His deductions weren't always fair; Doyle consistently stacked the deck in his favor, but every mystery writer does that. I do it myself.''

Trumbull said, "What you do proves nothing.''

Rubin was not to be distracted. "He was also the first believable super-hero in modern literature. He was always described as thin and aesthetic, but the fact that he achieved his triumphs through the use of brain power mustn't mask the fact that he is also described as being of virtually superhuman strength. When a visitor, in an implicit threat to Holmes, bends a poker to demonstrate his strength, Holmes casually straightens it again—the more difficult task. Then, too—''

Mason nodded his head in Rubin's direction and said to Gonzalo, "Mr. Rubin sounds like a Baker Street Irregular himself—''

Gonzalo said, "I don't think so. He just knows everything—but don't tell him I said so.''

"Maybe he can give me some Sherlockian pointers, then.''

"Maybe, but if you're in trouble, the real person to help you is Henry."

"Henry?" Mason's eye wandered around the table as though trying to recall first names.

"Our waiter," said Gonzalo. "He's *our* Sherlock Holmes."

"I don't think—" began Mason doubtfully.

"Wait till dinner is over. You'll see."

Halsted tapped his water glass and said, "Gentlemen, we're going to try something different this evening. Mr. Mason has a problem that involves the preparation of a Sherlockian article, and that means he would like to present us with a purely literary puzzle, one that has no connection with real life at all.—Ron, explain."

Mason scooped up some of the melted ice cream in his dessert plate with his teaspoon, put it in his mouth as though in a final farewell to the dinner, then said, "I've got to prepare this paper because it's a matter of self-respect. I love being a Baker Street Irregular, but it's difficult to hold my head up when every person there knows more about the canon than I do and when thirteen-year-old boys write papers that meet with applause for their ingenuity.

"The trouble is that I don't have much in the way of imagination, or the kind of whimsy needed for the task. But I know what I want to do. I want to do a paper on Dr. Moriarty."

"Ah, yes," said Avalon. "The villain in the case."

Mason nodded. "He doesn't appear in many of the tales, but he is the counterpart of Holmes. He is the Napoleon of crime, the intellectual rival of Holmes and the great detective's most dangerous antagonist. Just as Holmes is the popular prototype of the fictional detective, so is Moriarty the popular prototype of the master villain. In fact, it was Moriarty who killed Holmes, and was killed himself, in the final struggle in 'The Final Problem.' Moriarty was not brought back to life."

Avalon said, "And on what aspect of Moriarty did you wish to do a paper?" He sipped thoughtfully at his brandy.

Mason waited for Henry to refill his cup and said, "Well, it's his role as a mathematician that intrigues me. You see, it is only Moriarty's diseased moral sense that makes him a master criminal. He delights in manipulating human lives and in serving as the agent for destruction. If he wished to bend his great talent to legitimate issues, however, he could be world famous—indeed, he *was* world famous, in the Sherlockian world—as a mathematician.

"Only two of his mathematical feats are specifically mentioned in the canon. He was the author of an extension of the binomial theorem, for one thing. Then, in the novel *The Valley of Fear,* Holmes mentions that Moriarty had written a thesis entitled *The Dynamics of an Asteroid,* which was filled with mathematics so rarefied that there wasn't a scientist in Europe capable of debating the matter."

"As it happened," said Rubin, "one of the greatest mathematicians alive at the time was an American, Josiah Willard Gibbs, who—"

"That doesn't matter," said Mason hastily. "In the Sherlockian world only Europe counts when it comes to matters of science. The point is this, nothing is said about the contents of *The Dynamics of an Asteroid;* nothing at all; and no Sherlockian has ever written an article taking up the matter. I've checked into it and I know that."

Drake said, "And *you* want to do such an article?"

"I want to very much," said Mason, "but I'm not up to it. I have a layman's knowledge of astronomy. I know what an asteroid is. It's one of the small bodies that circles the Sun between the orbits of Mars and Jupiter. I know what dynamics is; it's the study of the motion of a body and of the changes in its motion when forces are applied. But that doesn't get me anywhere. What is *The Dynamics of an Asteroid* about?"

Drake said thoughtfully, "Is that all you have to go by, Mason? Just the title? Isn't there any passing reference to anything that is in the paper itself?"

"Not one reference anywhere. There's just the title, plus the indication that it is a matter of a highly advanced mathematics."

Gonzalo put his sketch of a jolly, smiling Mason—with the face drawn as a geometrically perfect circle—on the wall next to the others and said, "If you're going to write about how planets move, you need a lot of fancy math, I should think."

"No, you don't," said Drake abruptly. "Let me handle this, Mario. I may be only a lowly organic chemist, but I know something about astronomy too. The fact of the matter is that all the mathematics needed to handle the dynamics of the asteroids was worked out in the 1680s by Isaac Newton.

"An asteroid's motion depends entirely upon the gravitational influences to which it is subjected and Newton's equation makes it possible to calculate the strength of that influence between any two bodies if the mass of each body is known and if the distance between them is also known. Of course, when many bodies are involved and when the distances among them are constantly changing, then the mathematics gets tedious—not difficult, just tedious.

"The chief gravitational influence on any asteroid is that originating in the Sun, of course. Each asteroid moves around the Sun in an elliptical orbit, and if the Sun and asteroid were all that existed, the orbit could be calculated, exactly, by Newton's equation. Since other bodies also exist, their gravitational influences, much smaller than that of the Sun, must be taken into account as producing much smaller effects. In general, we get very close to the truth if we just consider the Sun."

Avalon said, "I think you're oversimplifying, Jim. To duplicate your humility, I may be only a lowly patent lawyer, and I won't pretend to know any astronomy at all, but haven't I heard that there's no way of solving the gravitational equation for more than two bodies?"

"That's right," said Drake, "if you mean by that, a general solution for all cases involving more than two bodies. There just isn't one. Newton worked out the general solution for the two-body problem but no one, to this day, has succeeded in working out one for the three-body problem, let alone for more bodies than that. The point is, though, that only theoreticians are interested in the three-body problem. Astronomers work out the motion of a body by first calculating the dominant gravitational influence, then correcting it one step at a time with the introduction of other lesser gravitational influences. It works well enough." He sat back and looked smug.

Gonzalo said, "Well, if only theoreticians are interested in the three-body problem and if Moriarty was a high-powered mathematician, then that must be just what the treatise is about."

Drake lit a new cigarette and paused to cough over it. Then he said, "It could have been the love life of giraffes, if you like, but we've got to go by the title. If Moriarty had solved the three-body problem, he would have called the treatise something like, *An Analysis of the Three-Body Problem*, or *The Generalization of the Law of Universal Gravitation*. He would *not* have called it *The Dynamics of an Asteroid*."

Halsted said, "What about the planetary effects? I've heard something about that. Aren't there gaps in space where there aren't any asteroids?"

"Oh, sure," said Drake. "We can find the dates in the Columbia Encyclopedia, if Henry will bring it over."

"Never mind," said Halsted. "You just tell us what you know about it and we can check the dates later, if we have to."

Drake said, "Let's see now." He was visibly enjoying his domination of the proceedings. His insignificant gray mustache twitched and his eyes, nested in finely wrinkled skin, seemed to sparkle.

He said, "There was an American astronomer named Kirkwood and I think Daniel was his first name. Sometime around the middle 1800s he pointed out that the asteroids' orbits seemed to cluster in groups. There were a couple of dozen known by then, all between the orbits of Mars and Jupiter, but they weren't spread out evenly, as Kirkwood pointed out. He showed there were gaps in which no asteroids circled.

"By 1866 or thereabouts—I'm pretty sure it was 1866—he worked out the reason. Any asteroid that would have had its orbit in those gaps would have circled the Sun in a period equal to a simple fraction of that of Jupiter."

"If there's no asteroid there," said Gonzalo, "how can you tell how long it would take it to go around the Sun?"

"Actually, it's very simple. Kepler worked that out in 1619 and it's called Kepler's Third Law. May I continue?"

"That's just syllables," said Gonzalo. "What's Kepler's Third Law?"

But Avalon said, "Let's take Jim's word for it, Mario. I can't quote it either, but I'm sure astronomers have it down cold. Go ahead, Jim."

Drake said, "An asteroid in a gap might have an orbital period of six years or four years, let us say, where Jupiter has a period of twelve years. That means an asteroid, every two or three revolutions, passes Jupiter under the same relative conditions of position. Jupiter's pull is in some particular direction each time, always the same, either forward or backward, and the effect mounts up.

"If the pull is backward, the asteroidal motion is gradually slowed so that the asteroid drops in closer toward the Sun and moves out of the gap. If the pull is forward, the asteroidal motion is quickened and the asteroid swings away from the Sun, again moving out of the gap. Either way nothing stays in the gaps, which are now called 'Kirkwood gaps.' You get the same effect in Saturn's rings. There are gaps there too."

Trumbull said, "You say Kirkwood did this in 1866?"

"Yes."

"And when did Moriarty write his thesis, supposedly?"

Mason interposed. "About 1875, if we work out the internal consistency of the Sherlockian canon."

Trumbull said, "Maybe Doyle was inspired by the news of the Kirkwood gaps, and thought of the title because of it. In which case, we can imagine Moriarty playing the role of Kirkwood and you can write an article on the Moriarty gaps."

Mason said uneasily, "Would that be enough? How important was Kirkwood's work? How difficult?"

Drake shugged. "It was a respectable contribution, but it was just an application of Newtonian physics. Good second-class work; not first class."

Mason shook his head. "For Moriarty, it would have to be first class."

"Wait, wait!" Rubin's sparse beard quivered with growing excitement. "Maybe Moriarty got away from Newton altogether. Maybe he got onto Einstein. Einstein revised the theory of gravity."

"He extended it," said Drake, "in the General Theory of Relativity in 1916."

"Right. Forty years after Moriarty's paper. That's got to be it. Suppose Moriarty had anticipated Einstein—"

Drake said, "In 1875? That would be before the Michelson-Morley experiment. I don't think it could have been done."

"Sure it could," said Rubin, "if Moriarty were bright enough—and he was."

Mason said, "Oh yes. In the Sherlockian universe, Professor Moriarty was brilliant enough for anything. Sure he would anticipate Einstein. The only thing is that, if he had done so, would he not have changed scientific history all around?"

"Not if the paper were suppressed," said Rubin, almost chattering with excitement. "It all fits in. The paper was suppressed and the great advance was lost till Einstein rediscovered it."

"What makes you say the paper was suppressed?" demanded Gonzalo.

"It doesn't exist, does it?" said Rubin. "If we go along with the Baker Street Irregular view of the universe, then Professor Moriarty *did* exist and the treatise *was* written, and it *did* anticipate General Relativity. Yet we can't find it anywhere in the scientific literature and there is no sign of the relativistic view penetrating scientific thought prior to Einstein's time. The only explanation is that the treatise was suppressed because of Moriarty's evil character."

Drake snickered. "There'd be a lot of scientific papers suppressed if evil character were cause enough. But your suggestion is out anyway, Manny. The treatise couldn't possibly involve General Relativity; not with that title."

"Why not?" demanded Rubin.

"Because revising the gravitational calculations in order to take relativity into account wouldn't do much as far as asteroidal dynamics are concerned," said Drake. "In fact, there was only one item known to astronomers in 1875 that could be considered, in any way, a gravitational puzzle."

"Uh-oh," said Rubin, "I'm beginning to see your point."

"Well, I don't," said Avalon. "Keep on going, Jim. What was the puzzle?"

Drake said, "It involved the planet Mercury, which revolves about the Sun in a pretty lopsided orbit. At one point in its orbit it is at its closest to the Sun (closer than any other planet, of course, since it is nearer to the Sun in general than the others are) and that point is the 'perihelion'. Each time Mercury completes a revolution about the Sun, that perihelion has shifted very slightly forward.

"The reason for the shift is to be found in the small gravitational effects, or perturbations, of the other planets on Mercury. But after all the known gravitational effects are taken into account, the perihelion shift isn't completely explained. This was discovered in 1843. There is a very tiny residual shift forward that can't be explained by gravitational theory. It isn't much—only about forty-three seconds of arc per century, which means the perihelion would move an unexplained distance equal to the diameter of the full Moon in about forty-two hundred years, or make a complete circle of the sky"—he did some mental calculations—"in about three million years.

"It's not much of a motion, but it was enough to threaten Newton's theory. Some astronomers felt that there must be an unknown planet on the other side of Mercury, very close to the Sun. Its pull was not taken into account, since it was unknown, but it was possible to calculate how large a planet would have to exist, and what kind of an orbit it must have, to account for the anomalous motion of Mercury's perihelion. The only trouble was that they could never find that planet.

"Then Einstein modified Newton's theory of gravitation, made it more general, and showed that when the new, modified equations were used the motion of Mercury's perihelion was exactly accounted for. It also did a few other things, but never mind that."

Gonzalo said, "Why couldn't Moriarty have figured that out?"

Drake said, "Because then he would have called his treatise, *On the Dynamics of Mercury*. He couldn't possibly have discovered something that solved this prime astronomical paradox that had been puzzling astronomers for thirty years and have called it anything else."

Mason looked dissatisfied. "Then what you're saying is

that there isn't anything that Moriarty could have written that would have had the title *On the Dynamics of an Asteriod* and still have represented a first-class piece of mathematical work?''

Drake blew a smoke ring. ''I guess that's what I'm saying. What I'm also saying, I suppose, is that Sir Arthur Conan Doyle didn't know enough astronomy to stuff a pig's ear, and that he didn't know what he was saying when he invented the title. But I suppose that sort of thing is not permitted to be said.''

''No,'' said Mason, his round face sunk in misery. ''Not in the Sherlockian universe. There goes my paper, then.''

''Pardon me,'' said Henry, from his post at the sideboard. ''May I ask a question?''

Drake said, ''You know you can, Henry. Don't tell me you're an astronomer.''

''No, sir. At least, not beyond the average knowledge of an educated American. Still, am I correct in supposing that there are a large number of asteroids known?''

''Over seventeen hundred have had their orbits calculated, Henry,'' said Drake.

''And there were a number known in Professor Moriarty's time, too, weren't there?''

''Sure. Several dozen.''

''In that case, sir,'' said Henry, ''why does the title of the treatise read *The Dynamics of an Asteroid?* Why *an* asteroid?''

Drake thought a moment, then said, ''That's a good point. I don't know—unless it's another indication that Doyle didn't know enough—''

''Don't say that,'' said Mason.

''Well—leave it at 'I don't know,' then.''

Gonzalo said, ''Maybe Moriarty just worked it out for one asteroid, and that's all.''

Drake said, ''Then he would have named it *The Dynamics of Ceres* or whatever asteroid he worked on.''

Gonzalo said stubbornly, ''No, that's not what I mean. I don't mean he worked it out for one particular asteroid. I mean he picked an asteroid at random, or just an ideal asteroid, maybe not one that really exists. Then he worked out its dynamics.''

Drake said, "That's not a bad notion, Mario. The only trouble is that if Moriarty worked out the dynamics of an asteroid, the basic mathematical system, it would hold for all of them, and the title of the paper would be *The Dynamics of Asteroids*. And besides, whatever he worked out in that respect would be only Newtonian and not of prime value."

"Do you mean to say," said Gonzalo, reluctant to let go, "that not one of the asteroids had something special about its orbit?"

"None known in 1875 did," said Drake. "They all had orbits between those of Mars and Jupiter and they all followed gravitational theory with considerable exactness. We know some asteroids with unusual orbits *now*. The first unusual asteroid to be discovered was Eros, which has an orbit that takes it closer to the Sun than Mars ever goes and brings it, on occasion, to within fourteen million miles of Earth, closer to Earth than any other body its size or larger, except for the Moon.

"That, however, wasn't discovered till 1898. Then, in 1906, Achilles was discovered. It was the first of the Trojan asteroids and they are unusual because they move around the Sun in Jupiter's orbit though well before or behind that planet."

Gonzalo said, "Couldn't Moriarty have anticipated those discoveries, and worked out the unusual orbits?"

"Even if he had anticipated them, the orbits are unusual only in their position, not in their dynamics. The Trojan asteroids did offer some interesting theoretical aspects, but that had already been worked out by Lagrange a century before."

There was a short silence and then Henry said, "The title is, however, so definite, sir. If we accept the Sherlockian premise that it must make sense, can it possibly have referred to some time when there was only a single body orbiting between Mars and Jupiter?"

Drake grinned. "Don't try to act ignorant, Henry. You're talking about the explosion theory of the origin of the asteroids."

For a moment, it seemed as though Henry might smile. If the impulse existed, he conquered it, however, and said,

"I have come across, in my reading, the suggestion that there had once been a planet between Mars and Jupiter and that it had exploded."

Drake said, "That's not a popular theory anymore, but it certainly had its day. In 1801, when the first asteroid, Ceres, was discovered, it turned out to be only about four hundred fifty miles across, astonishingly small. What was far more astonishing, though, was that over the next three years three other asteroids were discovered, with very similar orbits. The notion of an exploded planet was brought up at once."

Henry said, "Couldn't Professor Moriarty have been referring to that planet before its explosion, when speaking of *an* asteroid?"

Drake said, "I suppose he could have, but why not call it a planet?"

"Would it have been a large planet?"

"No, Henry. If all the asteroids are lumped together, they would make up a planet scarcely a thousand miles in diameter."

"Might it not be closer to what we now consider an asteroid, then, rather than to what we consider a planet? Mightn't that have been even more true in 1875 when fewer asteroids were known and the original body would have seemed smaller still?"

Drake said, "Maybe. But why not call it *the* asteroid, then?"

"Perhaps Professor Moriarty felt that to call the paper *The Dynamics of the Asteroid* was too definite. Perhaps he felt the explosion theory was not certain enough to make it possible to speak of anything more than *an* asteroid. However unscrupulous Professor Moriarty might have been in the world outside science, we must suppose that he was a most careful and rigidly precise mathematician."

Mason was smiling again. "I like that, Henry. It's a great idea." He said to Gonzalo, "You were right."

"I told you," said Gonzalo.

Drake said, "Hold on, let's see where it takes us. Moriarty can't be just talking about the dynamics of the original asteroid as a world orbiting about the Sun, because it would be following gravitational theory just as all its descendants are.

"He would have to be talking about the explosion. He would have to be analyzing the forces in planetary structure that would make an explosion conceivable. He would have to discuss the consequences of the explosion, and all that would not lie within the bounds of gravitational theory. He would have to calculate the events in such a way that the explosive forces would give way to gravitational effects and leave the asteroidal fragments in the orbits they have today."

Drake considered, then nodded, and went on. "That would not be bad. It would be a mathematical problem worthy of Moriarty's brain, and we might consider it to have represented the first attempt of any mathematician to take up so complicated an astronomical problem. Yes, I like it."

Mason said, "I like it too. If I can remember everything you've all said, I have my article. Good Lord, this is wonderful."

Henry said, "As a matter of fact, gentlemen, I think this hypothesis is even better than Dr. Drake has made it sound. I believe that Mr. Rubin said earlier that we must assume that Professor Moriarty's treatise was suppressed, since it cannot be located in the scientific annals. Well, it seems to me that if our theory can also explain that suppression, it becomes much more forceful."

"Quite so," said Avalon, "but can it?"

"Consider," said Henry, and a trace of warmth entered his quiet voice, "that over and above the difficulty of the problem, and of the credit therefore to be gained in solving it, there is a peculiar appeal in the problem to Professor Moriarty in view of his known character.

"After all, we are dealing with the destruction of a world. To a master criminal such as Professor Moriarty, whose diseased genius strove to produce chaos on Earth, to disrupt and corrupt the world's economy and society, there must have been something utterly fascinating in the vision of the actual *physical* destruction of a world.

"Might not Moriarty have imagined that on that original asteroid another like himself had existed, one who had not only tapped the vicious currents of the human soul but had even tampered with the dangerous forces of a planet's interior? Moriarty might have imagined that this super-Moriarty of the original asteroid had deliberately destroyed his world, and all life on it, including his own, out of sheer joy in malignancy, leaving the asteroids that now exist as the various tombstones that commemorate the action.

"Could Moriarty even have envied the deed and tried to work out the necessary action that would have done the same on Earth? Might not those few European mathematicians who could catch even a glimpse of what Moriarty was saying in his treatise have understood that what it described was not only a mathematical description of the origin of the asteroids but the beginning of a recipe for the ultimate crime—that of the destruction of Earth itself, of all life, and of the creation of a much larger asteroid belt?

"It is no wonder, if that were so, that a horrified scientific community suppressed the work."

And when Henry was done, there was a moment of silence and then Drake applauded. The others quickly joined in.

Henry reddened. "I'm sorry," he murmured when the applause died. "I'm afraid I allowed myself to be carried away."

"Not at all," said Avalon. "It was a surprising burst of poetry that I was glad to have heard."

Halsted said, "Frankly, I think that's perfect. It's exactly what Moriarty would do and it explains everything. Wouldn't you say so, Ron?"

"I will say so," said Mason, "as soon as I get over being speechless. I ask nothing better than to prepare a Sherlockian paper based on Henry's analysis. How can I square it with my conscience, however, to appropriate his ideas?"

Henry said, "It is yours, Mr. Mason, my free gift, for initiating a very gratifying session. You see, I have been a devotee of Sherlock Holmes for many years, myself."

The good Doctor Asimov, author of nearly four hundred books on topics ranging from astronomy to Don Juan, not to mention limericks, detective stories, and many of the greatest classics of science fiction, seldom admits that there might be something which even he has difficulty writing.

There are exceptions. When he joined the Baker Street Irregulars (a very real organization of Sherlock Holmes afficiandos which have included among their ranks numerous illustrious literary folk) he thought it would be easy to write a Sherlockian article for that society's learned publication The Baker Street Journal. *But, alas, he suffered "the same miseries Mason did" until he finally did solve a Problem . . . and the result was the story you have just read.*

ALL YOU ZOMBIES—
by Robert A. Heinlein

In which a paradox is classically paradoctored.

2217 Time Zone V (EST) 7 Nov 1970 NYC—"Pop's Place": I was polishing a brandy snifter when the Unmarried Mother came in. I noted the time—10:17 P.M. zone five, or eastern time, November 7, 1970. Temporal agents always notice time and date; we must.

The Unmarried Mother was a man twenty-five years old, no taller than I am, childish features and a touchy temper. I didn't like his looks—I never had—but he was a lad I was here to recruit, he was my boy. I gave him my best barkeep's smile.

Maybe I'm too critical. He wasn't swish; his nickname came from what he always said when some nosy type asked him his line: "I'm an unmarried mother." If he felt less than murderous he would add: "—at four cents a word. I write confession stories."

If he felt nasty, he would wait for somebody to make something of it. He had a lethal style of infighting, like a female cop—one reason I wanted him. Not the only one.

He had a load on and his face showed that he despised people more than usual. Silently I poured a double shot of Old Underwear and left the bottle. He drank it, poured another.

I wiped the bar top. "How's the 'Unmarried Mother' racket?"

His fingers tightened on the glass and he seemed about to throw it at me; I felt for the sap under the bar. In temporal manipulation you try to figure everything, but there are so many factors that you never take needless risks.

139

I saw him relax that tiny amount they teach you to watch for in the Bureau's training school. "Sorry," I said. "Just asking, 'How's business?' Make it 'How's the weather?' "

He looked sour. "Business is okay. I write 'em, they print 'em, I eat."

I poured myself one, leaned toward him. "Matter of fact," I said, "you write a nice stick—I've sampled a few. You have an amazingly sure touch with the woman's angle."

It was a slip I had to risk; he never admitted what pen names he used. But he was boiled enough to pick up only the last: " 'Woman's angle!' " he repeated with a snort. "Yeah, I know the woman's angle. I should."

"So?" I said doubtfully. "Sisters?"

"No. You wouldn't believe me if I told you."

"Now, now," I answered mildly, "bartenders and psychiatrists learn that nothing is stranger than truth. Why, son, if you heard the stories I do—well, you'd make yourself rich. Incredible."

"You don't know what *incredible* means!"

"So? Nothing astonishes me. I've always heard worse."

He snorted again. "Want to bet the rest of the bottle?"

"I'll bet a full bottle." I placed one on the bar.

"Well—" I signaled my other bartender to handle the trade. We were at the far end, a single-stool space that I kept private by loading the bar top by it with jars of pickled eggs and other clutter. A few were at the other end watching the fights and somebody was playing the jukebox—private as a bed where we were.

"Okay," he began, "to start with, I'm a bastard."

"No distinction around here," I said.

"I mean it," he snapped. "My parents weren't married."

"Still no distinction," I insisted. "Neither were mine."

"When—" He stopped, gave me the first warm look I ever saw on him. "You mean that?"

"I do. A one-hundred-percent bastard. In fact," I added, "no one in my family ever marries. All bastards."

"Don't try to top me—*you're* married." He pointed at my ring.

"Oh, that." I showed it to him. "It just looks like a wedding ring; I wear it to keep women off." It is an antique I bought in 1985 from a fellow operative—he had fetched it from pre-Christian Crete. "The Worm Ouroboros . . . the World Snake that eats its own tail, forever without end. A symbol of the Great Paradox."

He barely glanced at it. "If you're really a bastard, you know how it feels. When I was a little girl—"

"Wups!" I said. "Did I hear you correctly?"

"Who's telling this story? When I was a little girl— Look, ever hear of Christine Jorgenson? Or Roberta Cowell?"

"Uh, sex-change cases? You're trying to tell me—"

"Don't interrupt or swelp me, I won't talk. I was a foundling, left at an orphanage in Cleveland in 1945 when I was a month old. When I was a little girl, I envied kids with parents. Then, when I learned about sex—and believe me, Pop, you learn fast in an orphanage—"

"I know."

"—I made a solemn vow that any kid of mine would have both a pop and a mom. It kept me 'pure,' quite a feat in that vicinity—I had to learn to fight to manage it. Then I got older and realized I stood darn little chance of getting married—for the same reason I hadn't been adopted." He scowled. "I was horse-faced and buck-toothed, flat chested and straight-haired."

"You don't look any worse than I do."

"Who cares how a barkeep looks? Or a writer? But people wanting to adopt pick little blue-eyed golden-haired morons. Later on, the boys want bulging breasts, a cute face, and an Oh-you-wonderful-male manner." He shrugged. "I couldn't compete. So I decided to join the W.E.N.C.H.E.S."

"Eh?"

"Women's Emergency National Corps, Hospitality and Entertainment Section, what they now call 'Space Angels'— Auxiliary Nursing Group, Extraterrestrial Legions."

I knew both terms, once I had them chronized. We use still a third name, it's that elite military service corps: Women's Hospitality Order Refortifying and Encouraging Spacemen. Vocabulary shift is the worst hurdle in time-jumps—did you know that "service station" once meant a dispensary for petroleum fractions? Once on an assignment in the Churchill Era, a woman said to me, "Meet me at the service station next door"—which is not what it sounds; a "service station" (then) wouldn't have a bed in it.

He went on: "It was when they first admitted you can't send men into space for months and years and not relieve the tension. You remember how the wowsers screamed?— that improved my chance since volunteers were scarce. A gal had to be respectable, preferably virgin (they liked to train them from scratch), above average mentally, and stable emotionally. But most volunteers were old hookers, or neurotics who would crack up ten days off Earth. So I didn't need looks; if they accepted me, they would fix my buck teeth, put a wave in my hair, teach me to walk and dance and how to listen to a man pleasingly, and everything else— plus training for the prime duties. They would even use plastic surgery if it would help—nothing too good for Our Boys.

"Best yet, they made sure you didn't get pregnant during your enlistment—and you were almost certain to marry at the end of your hitch. Same way today, A.N.G.E.L.S. marry spacers—they talk the language.

"When I was eighteen I was placed as a 'mother's helper.' This family simply wanted a cheap servant but I didn't mind as I couldn't enlist till I was twenty-one. I did housework and went to night school—pretending to continue my high school typing and shorthand but going to a charm class instead, to better my chances for enlistment.

"Then I met this city slicker with his hundred-dollar bills." He scowled. "The no-good actually did have a wad of hundred-dollar bills. He showed me one night, told me to help myself.

"But I didn't. I liked him. He was the first man I ever met who was nice to me without trying games with me. I quit night school to see him oftener. It was the happiest time of my life.

"Then one night in the park the games began."

He stopped. I said, "And then?"

"And then *nothing!* I never saw him again. He walked me home and told me he loved me—and kissed me good-night and never came back." He looked grim. "If I could find him, I'd kill him!"

"Well," I sympathized, "I know how you feel. But killing him—just for doing what comes naturally—hmm . . . Did you struggle?"

"Huh? What's that got to do with it?"

"Quite a bit. Maybe he deserves a couple of broken arms for running out on you, but—"

"He deserves worse than that! Wait till you hear. Somehow I kept anyone from suspecting and decided it was all for the best. I hadn't really loved him and probably would never love anybody—and I was more eager to join the W.E.N.C.H.E.S. than ever. I wasn't disqualified, they didn't insist on virgins. I cheered up.

"It wasn't until my skirts got tight that I realized."

"Pregnant?"

"He had me higher 'n a kite! Those skinflints I lived with ignored it as long as I could work—then kicked me out and the orphanage wouldn't take me back. I landed in a charity ward surrounded by other big bellies and trotted bedpans until my time came.

"One night I found myself on an operating table, with a nurse saying, 'Relax. Now breathe deeply.'

"I woke up in bed, numb from the chest down. My surgeon came in. 'How do you feel?' he says cheerfully.

" 'Like a mummy.'

" 'Naturally. You're wrapped like one and full of dope to keep you numb. You'll get well—but a Caesarian isn't a hangnail.'

" 'Caesarian,' I said. 'Doc—*did I lose the baby?*'

" 'Oh, no. Your baby's fine.'

" 'Oh. Boy or girl?'

" 'A healthy little girl. Five pounds, three ounces.'

"I relaxed. It's something, to have made a baby. I told myself I would go somewhere and tack 'Mrs.' on my name and let the kid think her papa was dead—no orphanage for *my* kid!

"But the surgeon was talking. 'Tell me, uh—' He avoided my name. '—did you ever think your glandular setup was odd?"

"I said, 'Huh? Of course not. What are you driving at?'

"He hesitated. 'I'll give you this in one dose, then a hypo to let you sleep off your jitters. You'll have 'em.'

" 'Why?' I demanded.

" 'Ever hear of that Scottish physician who was female

until she was thirty-five?—then had surgery and became legally and medically a man? Got married. All okay.'

" 'What's that got to do with me?'

" 'That's what I'm saying. You're a man.'

"I tried to sit up. '*What?*'

" 'Take it easy. When I opened you, I found a mess. I sent for the Chief of Surgery while I got the baby out, then we held a consultation with you on the table—and worked for hours to salvage what we could. You had two full sets of organs, both immature, but with the female set well enough developed for you to have a baby. They could never be any use to you again, so we took them out and rearranged things so that you can develop properly as a man.' He put a hand on me. 'Don't worry. You're young, your bones will readjust, we'll watch your glandular balance—and make a fine young man out of you.'

"I started to cry. 'What about my *baby?*'

" 'Well, you can't nurse her, you haven't milk enough for a kitten. If I were you, I wouldn't see her—put her up for adoption.'

" '*No!*'

"He shrugged. 'The choice is yours; you're her mother—well, her parent. But don't worry now; we'll get you well first.'

"Next day they let me see the kid and I saw her daily—trying to get used to her. I had never seen a brand-new baby and had no idea how awful they look—my daughter looked like an orange monkey. My feeling changed to cold determination to do right by her. But four weeks later that didn't mean anything."

"Eh?"

"She was snatched."

" 'Snatched?' "

The Unmarried Mother almost knocked over the bottle we had bet. "Kidnapped—stolen from the hospital nursery!" He breathed hard. "How's that for taking the last a man's got to live for?"

"A bad deal," I agreed. "Let's pour you another. No clues?"

"Nothing the police could trace. Somebody came to see

her, claimed to be her uncle. While the nurse had her back turned, he walked out with her.''

"Description?"

"Just a man, with a face-shaped face, like yours or mine." He frowned. "I think it was the baby's father. The nurse swore it was an older man but he probably used makeup. Who else would swipe my baby? Childless women pull such stunts—but whoever heard of a man doing it?''

"What happened to you then?"

"Eleven more months of that grim place and three operations. In four months I started to grow a beard; before I was out I was shaving regularly . . . and no longer doubted that I was male." He grinned wryly. "I was staring down nurses' necklines.''

"Well," I said, "seems to me you came through okay. Here you are, a normal man, making good money, no real troubles. And the life of a female is not an easy one."

He glared at me. "A lot you know about it!''

"So?"

"Ever hear the expression 'a ruined woman'?''

"Mmm, years ago. Doesn't mean much today."

"I was as ruined as a woman can be; that bum *really* ruined me—I was no longer a woman . . . and I didn't know *how* to be a man."

"Takes getting used to, I suppose."

"You have no idea. I don't mean learning how to dress, or not walking into the wrong rest room; I learned those in the hospital. But how could I *live?* What job could I get? Hell, I couldn't even drive a car. I didn't know a trade; I couldn't do manual labor—too much scar tissue, too tender.

"I hated him for having ruined me for the W.E.N.C.H.E.S., too, but I didn't know how much until I tried to join the Space Corps instead. One look at my belly and I was marked unfit for military service. The medical officer spent time on me just from curiosity; he had read about my case.

"So I changed my name and came to New York. I got by as a fry cook, then rented a typewriter and set myself up as a public stenographer—what a laugh! In four months I typed four letters and one manuscript. The manuscript was for *Real Life Tales* and a waste of paper, but the goof who wrote it, sold it. Which gave me an idea; I bought a stack of confession magazines and studied them.'' He looked cynical. ''Now you know how I get the authentic woman's angle on an unmarried-mother story . . . through the only version I haven't sold—the true one. Do I win the bottle?''

I pushed it toward him. I was upset myself, but there was work to do. I said, ''Son, you still want to lay hands on that so-and-so?''

His eyes lighted up—a feral gleam.

''Hold it!'' I said. ''You wouldn't kill him?''

He chuckled nastily. ''Try me.''

''Take it easy. I know more about it than you think I do. I can help you. I know where he is.''

He reached across the bar. *''Where is he?''*

I said softly, ''Let go my shirt, sonny—or you'll land in the alley and we'll tell the cops you fainted.'' I showed him the sap.

He let go. ''Sorry. But where is he?'' He looked at me. ''And how do you know so much?''

''All in good time. There are records—hospital records, orphanage records, medical records. The matron of your orphanage was Mrs. Fetherage—right? She was followed by Mrs. Gruenstein—right? Your name, as a girl, was 'Jane'—right? And you didn't tell me any of this—right?''

I had him baffled and a bit scared. ''What's this? You trying to make trouble for me?''

''No indeed. I've your welfare at heart. I can put this character in your lap. You do to him as you see fit—and I guarantee that you'll get away with it. But I don't think you'll kill him. You'd be nuts to—and you aren't nuts. Not quite.''

He brushed it aside. ''Cut the noise. *Where is he?*''

I poured him a short one; he was drunk but anger was offsetting it. ''Not so fast. I do something for you—you do something for me.''

''Uh . . . what?''

''You don't like your work. What would you say to high pay, steady work, unlimited expense account, your own boss on the job, and lots of variety and adventure?''

He stared. ''I'd say, 'Get those goddam reindeer off my roof!' Shove it, Pop—there's no such job.''

"Okay, put it this way: I hand him to you, you settle with him, then try my job. If it's not all I claim—well, I can't hold you."

He was wavering; the last drink did it. "When d'yuh d'liver 'im?" he said thickly.

"If it's a deal—*right now!*"

He shoved out his hand. "It's a deal!"

I nodded to my assistant to watch both ends, noted the time—2300—started to duck through the gate under the bar—when the jukebox blared out: *"I'm My Own Granpaw!"* The serviceman had orders to load it with old Americana and classics because I couldn't stomach the "music" of 1970, but I hadn't known that tape was in it. I called out, "Shut that off! Give the customer his money back." I added, "Storeroom, back in a moment," and headed there with my Unmarried Mother following.

It was down the passage across from the johns, a steel door to which no one but my day manager and myself had a key; inside was a door to an inner room to which only I had a key. We went there.

He looked blearily around at windowless walls. "Where is 'e?"

"Right away." I opened a case, the only thing in the room; it was a U.S.F.F. Co-ordinates Transformer Field Kit, series 1992, Mod. II—a beauty, no moving parts, weight twenty-three kilos fully charged, and shaped to pass as a suitcase. I had adjusted it precisely earlier that day; all I had to do was to shake out the metal net which limits the transformation field.

Which I did. "Wha's that?" he demanded.

"Time machine," I said and tossed the net over us.

"Hey!" he yelled and stepped back. There is a technique to this; the net has to be thrown so that the subject will instinctively step back *onto* the metal mesh, then you close the net with both of you inside completely—else you might leave shoe soles behind or a piece of foot, or scoop up a slice of floor. But that's all the skill it takes. Some agents con a subject into the net; I tell the truth and use that instant of utter astonishment to flip the switch. Which I did.

1030–VI–3 April 1963–Cleveland, Ohio–Apex Bldg.:
"Hey!" he repeated. "Take this damn thing off!"

"Sorry," I apologized and did so, stuffed the net into the case, closed it. "You said you wanted to find him."

"But—you said that was a time machine!"

I pointed out a window. "Does that look like November? Or New York?" While he was gawking at new buds and spring weather, I reopened the case, took out a packet of hundred-dollar bills, checked that the numbers and signatures were compatible with 1963. The Temporal Bureau doesn't care how much you spend (it costs nothing) but they don't like unnecessary anachronisms. Too many mistakes, and a general court-martial will exile you for a year in a nasty period, say 1974 with its strict rationing and forced labor. I never make such mistakes, the money was okay.

He turned around and said, "What happened?"

"He's here. Go outside and take him. Here's expense money." I shoved it at him and added, "Settle him, then I'll pick you up."

Hundred-dollar bills have a hypnotic effect on a person not used to them. He was thumbing them unbelievingly as I eased him into the hall, locked him out. The next jump was easy, a small shift in era.

7100–VI–10 March 1964–Cleveland–Apex Bldg.: There was a notice under the door saying that my lease expired next week; otherwise the room looked as it had a moment before. Outside, trees were bare and snow threatened; I hurried, stopping only for contemporary money and a coat, hat, and topcoat I had left there when I leased the room. I hired a car, went to the hospital. It took twenty minutes to bore the nursery attendant to the point where I could swipe the baby without being noticed. We went back to the Apex Building. This dial setting was more involved as the building did not yet exist in 1945. But I had precalculated it.

0100–VI–20 Sept 1945–Cleveland–Skyview Motel: Field kit, baby, and I arrived in a motel outside town. Earlier I had registered as "Gregory Johnson, Warren, Ohio," so we arrived in a room with curtains closed, windows locked, and doors bolted, and the floor cleared to allow for waver as the machine hunts. You can get a nasty bruise from a chair where it shouldn't be—not the chair of course, but backlash from the field.

No trouble, Jane was sleeping soundly; I carried her out, put her in a grocery box on the seat of a car I had provided earlier, drove to the orphanage, put her on the steps, drove two blocks to a "service station" (the petroleum products sort) and phoned the orphanage, drove back in time to see them taking the box inside, kept going and abandoned the car near the motel—walked to it and jumped forward to the Apex Building in 1963.

2200–VI–24 April 1963–Cleveland–Apex Bldg.: I had cut the time rather fine—temporal accuracy depends on span, except on return to zero. If I had it right, Jane was discovering, out in the park this balmy spring night, that she wasn't quite as "nice" a girl as she had thought. I grabbed a taxi to the home of those skinflints, had the hackie wait around a corner while I lurked in shadows.

Presently I spotted them down the street, arms around each other. He took her up on the porch and made a long job of kissing her good-night—longer than I thought. Then she went in and he came down the walk, turned away. I slid into step and hooked an arm in his. "That's all, son," I announced quietly. "I'm back to pick you up."

"You!" He gasped and caught his breath.

"Me. Now you know who *he* is—and after you think it over you'll know who you are . . . and if you think hard enough, you'll figure out who the baby is . . . and who *I* am."

He didn't answer, he was badly shaken. It's a shock to have it proved to you that you can't resist seducing yourself. I took him to the Apex Building and we jumped again.

2300–VII–12 Aug 1985–Sub Rockies Base: I woke the duty sergeant, showed my I.D., told the sergeant to bed my companion down with a happy pill and recruit him in the morning. The sergeant looked sour, but rank is rank, regardless of era; he did what I said—thinking, no doubt, that the next time we met he might be the colonel and I the sergeant. Which can happen in our corps: "What name?" he asked.

I wrote it out. He raised his eyebrows. "Like so, eh? *Hmm*—"

"You just do your job, Sergeant." I turned to my companion.

"Son, your troubles are over. You're about to start the best job a man ever held—and you'll do well. *I know.*"

"That you will!" agreed the sergeant. "Look at me—born in 1917—still around, still young, still enjoying life." I went back to the jump room, set everything on preselected zero.

2301-V-7 Nov 1970-NYC-"Pop's Place": I came out of the storeroom carrying a fifth of Drambuie to account for the minute I had been gone. My assistant was arguing with the customer who had been playing *"I'm My Own Granpaw!"* I said, "Oh, let him play it, then unplug it." I was very tired.

It's rough, but somebody must do it and it's very hard to recruit anyone in the later years, since the Mistake of 1972. Can you think of a better source than to pick people all fouled up where they are and give them well-paid, interesting (even though dangerous) work in a necessary cause? Everybody knows now why the Fizzle War of 1963 fizzled. The bomb with New York's number on it didn't go off, a hundred other things didn't go as planned—all arranged by the likes of me.

But not the Mistake of '72; that one is not our fault—and can't be undone; there's no paradox to resolve. A thing either is, or it isn't, now and forever amen. But there won't be another like it; an order dated "1992" takes precedence any year.

I closed five minutes early, leaving a letter in the cash register telling my day manager that I was accepting his offer to buy me out, so see my lawyer as I was leaving on a long vacation. The Bureau might or might not pick up his payments, but they want things left tidy. I went to the room back of the storeroom and forward to 1993.

2200-VII-12 Jan 1993-Sub Rockies Annex-HQ Temporal DOL: I checked in with the duty officer and went to my quarters, intending to sleep for a week. I had fetched the bottle we bet (after all, I won it) and took a drink before I wrote my report. It tasted foul and I wondered why I had ever liked Old Underwear. But it was better than nothing; I don't like to be cold sober, I think too much. But I don't really hit the bottle either; other people have snakes—I have people.

I dictated my report; forty recruitments all okayed by the Psych Bureau—counting my own, which I knew would be okayed. I was here, wasn't I? Then I taped a request for assignment to operations; I was sick of recruiting. I dropped both in the slot and headed for bed.

My eye fell on "The By-Laws of Time," over my bed:

Never Do Yesterday What Should Be Done Tomorrow.
If At Last You Do Succeed, Never Try Again.
A Stitch in Time Saves Nine Billion.
A Paradox May Be Paradoctored.
It Is Earlier When You Think.
Ancestors Are Just People.
Even Jove Nods.

They didn't inspire me the way they had when I was a recruit; thirty subjective-years of time-jumping wears you down. I undressed and when I got down to the hide I looked at my belly. A Caesarian leaves a big scar but I'm so hairy now that I don't notice it unless I look for it.

Then I glanced at the ring on my finger.

The Snake That Eats Its Own Tail, Forever and Ever . . . I *know* where *I* came from—but *where did all you zombies come from?*

I felt a headache coming on, but a headache powder is one thing I do not take. I did once—and you all went away.

So I crawled into bed and whistled out the light.

You aren't really there at all. There isn't anybody but me—Jane—here alone in the dark.

I miss you dreadfully!

The late Robert A. Heinlein (1907–1988) was one of the twentieth century's truly great science-fiction writers. His classics are too numerous to list. Breathes there a fan with soul so dead that he has not had his sense of wonder aroused and his intellectual horizons expanded by Double Star *or* The Moon Is a Harsh Mistress *or* The Past Through Tomorrow? *Heinlein was the great realist of modern science fiction who applied hard brainpower to making the future more plausible than it had ever been before.*

He also had a playful side, which is exhibited in "All You Zombies," surely the finest time-paradox story ever written.

THE IMMORTAL BARD

by Isaac Asimov

"Had I only known who he really was," we often say
when it's entirely too late. Over drinks, of course.

"Oh, yes," said Dr. Phineas Welch, "I can bring back
the spirits of the illustrious dead."

He was a little drunk, or maybe he wouldn't have said it.
Of course, it was perfectly all right to get a little drunk at
the annual Christmas party.

Scott Robertson, the school's young English instructor,
adjusted his glasses and looked to right and left to see if they
were overheard. "Really, Dr. Welch."

"I mean it. And not just the spirits. I bring back the
bodies too."

"I wouldn't have said it were possible," said Robertson
primly.

"Why not? A simple matter of temporal transference."

"You mean time travel? But that's quite—uh—unusual."

"Not if you know how."

"Well, how, Dr. Welch?"

"Think I'm going to tell you?" asked the physicist
gravely. He looked vaguely about for another drink and
didn't find any. He said, "I brought quite a few back.
Archimedes, Newton, Galileo. Poor fellows."

"Didn't they like it here? I should think they'd have been
fascinated by our modern science," said Robertson. He was
beginning to enjoy the conversation.

"Oh, they were. They were. Especially Archimedes. I
thought he'd go mad with joy at first after I explained a little
of it in some Greek I'd boned up on, but no—no—"

"What was wrong?"

"Just a different culture. They couldn't get used to our way of life. They got terribly lonely and frightened. I had to send them back."

"That's too bad."

"Yes. Great minds, but not flexible minds. Not universal. So I tried Shakespeare."

"*What?*" yelled Robertson. This was getting closer to home.

"Don't yell, my boy," said Welch. "It's bad manners."

"Did you say you brought back Shakespeare?"

"I did. I needed someone with a universal mind; someone who knew people well enough to be able to live with them centuries away from his own time. Shakespeare was the man. I've got his signature. As a memento, you know."

"On you?" asked Robertson, eyes bugging.

"Right here." Welch fumbled in one vest pocket after another. "Ah, here it is."

A little piece of pasteboard was passed to the instructor. On one side it said: *L. Klein & Sons, Wholesale Hardware.* On the other side, in straggly script, was written, *Willm Shaksper.*

A wild surmise filled Robertson. "What did he look like?"

"Not like his pictures. Bald and an ugly mustache. He spoke in a thick brogue. Of course, I did my best to please him with our times. I told him we thought highly of his plays and still put them on the boards. In fact, I said we thought they were the greatest pieces of literature in the English language, maybe in any language."

"Good. Good," said Robertson breathlessly.

"I said people had written volumes of commentaries on his plays. Naturally he wanted to see one and I got one for him from the library."

"And?"

"Oh, he was fascinated. Of course, he had trouble with the current idioms and references to events since 1600, but I helped out. Poor fellow. I don't think he ever expected such treatment. He kept saying, 'God ha' mercy! What cannot be racked from words in five centuries? One could wring, methinks, a flood from a damp clout!' "

"He wouldn't say that."

"Why not? He wrote his plays as quickly as he could. He said he had to on account of the deadlines. He wrote *Hamlet* in less than six months. The plot was an old one. He just polished it up."

"That's all they do to a telescope mirror. Just polish it up," said the English instructor indignantly.

The physicist disregarded him. He made out an untouched cocktail on the bar some feet away and sidled toward it. "I told the immortal bard that we even gave college courses in Shakespeare."

"*I* give one."

"I know. I enrolled him in your evening extension course. I never saw a man so eager to find out what posterity thought of him as poor Bill was. He worked hard at it."

"You enrolled William Shakespeare in my course?" mumbled Robertson. Even as an alcoholic fantasy, the thought staggered him. And *was* it an alcoholic fantasy? He was beginning to recall a bald man with a queer way of talking. . . .

"Not under his real name, of course," said Dr. Welch. "Never mind what he went under. It was a mistake, that's all. A big mistake. Poor fellow." He had the cocktail now and shook his head at it.

"Why was it a mistake? What happened?"

"I had to send him back to 1600," roared Welch indignantly. "How much humiliation do you think a man can stand?"

"What humiliation are you talking about?"

Dr. Welch tossed off the cocktail. "Why, you poor simpleton, you *flunked* him."

The good Dr. Asimov, author of nearly four hundred books on topics ranging from astronomy to Don Juan, not to mention limericks, detective stories, and many of the greatest classics of science fiction, may well be the greatest polymath since Pliny the Elder—an improvement on him even, since the Good Doctor tends to get his facts right.

He is of course uniquely qualified to have written the preceding story, being the author of Asimov's Guide to Shakespeare.

ANYONE HERE FROM UTAH?
by Michael Swanwick

Haven't you always wondered why so many people are wearing digital watches all of the sudden?

It was early evening when I drove into Manayunk. The fog was coming across the canal from the Schuylkill and creeping slowly up the hillside. A red neon sign over Keely's buzzed and crackled. I found a space not twenty yards away, under the elevated, and parked.

Keely's is a corner tappie of the old school, the kind that still has a side-door ladies' entrance. The old women of the neighborhood use it, too, huddling over their glasses of beer in the back room, never daring to go up front where the men are.

It's a quiet place. No television over the bar. A jukebox, only it wasn't in use, Monday being a slow night. There's a pool table in the back.

Midway through my first beer the little guy came in. He poked his head through the door, taking a quick peek, then whipped it back fast, like a turtle retreating into its shell. A pause, and then his round little face reappeared. He blinked rapidly, and nervously scanned the shelves over the bar. I craned my head to look, and saw only the usual assortment of bottles and such.

Finally the little guy actually *entered* the bar, took a stool to one side of me, and ordered a draught. We both drank in silence for a bit.

Then he nodded at the shelves over the bar. "No TV here," he said. And when I nodded, "Have you ever noticed how a TV set will suck you in? So that no matter how hard you try to ignore it, you always end up watching?"

He was an odd duck. There was a whiff of the streets about him, a hard, ingrained layer of poverty and grime. And yet he wore an expensive "Thinsulated" windbreaker, at least two hundred bucks in any store downtown, and though it was old and worn, it was worn to his body; he hadn't acquired it secondhand. "Why not tell me about it?" I suggested.

He eyed me nervously, then said, "Okay, listen. You ever notice how some pieces of technology seem like they're too *good* for us? Like you wonder how they can even *exist,* because they look as out-of-place as a Greyhound bus would in third-century Rome?"

"No," I said carefully. "Can't say that I have."

"Then you're not paying attention," he said angrily. "Take a look at computers—they've been around less than thirty years and already they're so small you can wear them *on your wrist,* for Chrissake. Then take a look at your car, and ask yourself why it only gets some four percent efficiency and falls apart before the payments are done. Are you trying to tell me the same people produced *both?*"

"Hey, now," I said soothingly.

The little guy clutched his glass so hard his knuckles whitened. "We got a country that can't produce a decent solar energy cell when the Arabs have got us up against the ropes, and yet we can transmit *pictures* through the *air*—and in color, too. And where did it come from? Television just appeared one day, complete and perfected! It didn't *evolve* the way that, say, films did."

"There was radio."

"Radio! I can make a radio out of a safety pin, an eraser and a chunk of quartz. But have you ever met anybody who actually *understands* television, who could build one from scratch?"

"Well . . ."

"And if you read up on it, it gets even weirder. Do you know what you see when you look at a TV screen?"

"Pictures, I presume."

"Wrong. You see this one little dot of light. It travels along all 525 lines of your screen sixty times a second, getting brighter and darker, and *your mind* puts this all together to form a picture. But there *is* no picture, only this little glowing dot that's like *hypnotizing* you, get it? And because the picture is assembled inside your head, it's gotten past your mental censors before you even know what it is. You believe it even when what it tells you contradicts what you actually experience."

"I take you don't watch much television, huh?"

He sighed, buried his nose in his drink. "I used to watch it just like everybody else—four, maybe five hours a night. I went on a camping trip in the Grand Tetons in Wyoming so I could be *by myself* and I took along a battery portable. Without even thinking about it.

"Second day out, I accidentally kicked the thing over a cliff. Boy, was I mad at myself! I almost turned around and went home. But I'd spent so much on the trip I went on without it. And you know what? After a week or so, I felt a lot better without the constant yammer-yammer-yammer of that damned box. My vision was better, I had more energy, and I thought a lot more clearly. But I was out in the wilderness all this time. When I came out again and picked up my car, I found out the truth."

"What *was* the truth?"

"Well, first of all, I wasn't in Wyoming, I was in Ohio."

I couldn't help it. I laughed.

The little guy glared. "Okay, okay—but it was damned scary to find that in the shops and lodges and tourist places people all talked as though we were in Wyoming, but out on the street, everyone was in Ohio. And if you *asked* them about this, they got this really blank expression, like zombies, and just walked away." He stared disconsolately into his beer. "After a while I noticed that people were a little *less* vague if they'd been away from the TV for a few hours, and I made the connection.

"I figured that *some*body was controlling our reality for *some* reason, and I set out to discover just what was going on. I drew out my savings from the bank and hit the road." He smiled self-deprecatingly. "Looking for America, you know? Only I *for sure* didn't find it. You do much traveling?"

"I'm a salesman. I get around."

"Well, have you noticed how about ten years ago the quality of life in New York City took a nosedive? I mean, it used to be the Queen of Cities, the Big Apple, right? How did it get so dirty and slummy and mean so fast? I went to New York City and looked, and you know what I found?"

"You tell me," I said.

"A crater. About a mile across and radioactive as hell. You stand on the lip and stare down through these wispy little clouds of steam and there's this blue glow down at the bottom. That's all that's left of Manhattan."

"Now wait a minute, I was *there* just last week."

He shook his head firmly. "Nope. That was Newark. They shifted the business and financial centers there, changed a few road signs, and brainwashed everyone to think they were in New York."

"Aw, come on. Millions of people go in and out of New York every day—you couldn't hush something like that up."

"You could if you controlled television. Listen, I've seen things that could practically fry your brains. Did you know that there are Communist Chinese troops in North Dakota? The entire state is under occupational rule! They've got concentration camps and slave labor and . . . And Utah— have you ever met anyone from Utah?"

"Well, not actually . . ."

He nodded emphatically. "Damn straight you haven't! My God, the things I've seen. I was in Los Angeles last month when the President of the United States presented the key to the city to Adolf Hitler—in *public*, mind you! Except for this little crowd who applauded, nobody seemed to notice."

"Reagan would never—" I began, but he cut me off.

"No, no, not that damned cowboy actor—the *real* President. Richard Nixon." He paused, stared thoughtfully into his drink. "Hitler was in a wheelchair, wearing a white suit. I think he was senile."

I'd heard enough. "So what are you doing about this?" I asked, cutting him off. "I presume you're doing *something*."

The little guy looked crestfallen. "Actually," he confessed, "I don't *know* what to do. I'm not the hero type. I just go around to bars—when I can find one without an infernal television set—and strike up conversations. I tell people that if they can just give up the TV for a few short weeks, they can set themselves free. Maybe if there were a *lot* of us, we could do something."

"I see. Made many converts?"

Now he looked downright heartbroken. "Not a one."

"Tell you what," I said, "If it makes you feel any better, *I'll* give it up—right here and now!"

The little guy looked me full in the eye, and there was a kind of dignity in defeat to him at that moment. "No you won't," he said. "You'll promise to, and you'll go back home or to your hotel room tonight, and you'll switch it on without even thinking about it." He finished his drink, and left a quarter on the bar for a tip. "But at least I've tried, and God knows that's all one man can do."

He slid off his barstool.

"Oh, Sammy?" I said casually. "I'd like to show you something."

He turned, puzzled. "How did you know my—" I pulled the device from my pocket. It was small, about the size of a pack of cigarettes, and it had a two-inch-square screen.

"Ever see one of these?" I asked. "It's hot off the assembly line. A year from now everybody will have one." I waved it back and forth gently. He tried to look away, but could not. His eyes were riveted to the little moving dot.

"Pretty nifty, huh?" I smiled. His trail had been cold when I picked it up in Utah. I had every reason to feel pleased with myself.

Sweat beaded up on his forehead. He clenched his teeth, but could not look away. "Who *are* you people?" he asked chokingly.

"Who are we, Sammy? We're the ones who matter. The power behind the multinationals. The guys who keep things going. The little voice that whispers in your ear," I said mockingly. "What do you care who we are?"

I didn't know how much he would hear. His eyes were glazing over quickly. But to my surprise he managed to say, "And now you kill me." He didn't sound as if he much cared anymore.

"Sammy, Sammy." I tousled his hair. "Imagine that you run a kennel and you find one of your dogs has burrowed halfway out. He's caught under the wire and is squirming to get free. Do you kill him?"

I waited for an answer, got none. "No, you do not," I answered for him. "Here." I placed the set in his hand. "It's a gift."

He stood there, numbly staring at it. All the contradictions, the fears and unacceptable memories were fading gently away.

On the way out, I paused to say, "Show it to your friends."

Michael Swanwick is the author of In the Drift *and* Vacuum Flowers *and is one of the most widely acclaimed new SF writers of the past decade. Two out of his first three published stories were Nebula Award finalists. His short fiction has appeared in* Isaac Asimov's SF Magazine, Amazing, New Dimensions, *and even in such out-of-genre publications as* Penthouse, High Times, *and* Triquarterly.

COLD VICTORY
by Poul Anderson

*A grim tale of war and heroism, in which many things are
revealed—and not revealed—in the telling . . .*

It was the old argument, Historical Necessity versus the
Man of Destiny. When I heard them talking, three together,
my heart twisted within me and I knew that once more I
must lay down the burden of which I can never be rid.

This was in the Battle Rock House, which is a quiet tavern
on the edge of Syrtis Town. I come there whenever I am on
Mars. It is friendly and unpretentious: shabby comfortable
loungers scattered about under the massive sandwood rafters,
honest liquor and competent chess and the talk of one's
peers.

As I entered, a final shaft of thin hard sunlight stabbed in
through the window, dazzling me, and then night fell like a
thunderclap over the ocherous land and the fluoros snapped
on. I got a mug of porter and strolled across to the table
about which the three people sat.

The stiff little bald man was obviously from the college;
he wore his academics even here, but Martians are like that.
"No, no," he was saying. "These movements are too great
for any one man to change them appreciably. Humanism,
for example, was not the political engine of Carnarvon—
rather, he was the puppet of Humanism, and danced as the
blind brainless puppeteer made him."

"I'm not so sure," answered the man in gray: undress
uniform of the Order of Planetary Engineers. "If he and his
cohorts had been less doctrinaire, the government of Earth
might still be Humanist."

"But being born of a time of trouble, Humanism was
inevitably fanatical," said the professor.

163

The big, kilted Venusian woman shifted impatiently. She was packing a gun and her helmet was on the floor beside her. Lucifer Clan, I saw from the tartar. "If there are folk around at a crisis time with enough force, they'll shape the way things turn out," she declared. "Otherwise things will drift."

I rolled up a lounger and set my mug on the table. Conversational kibitzing is accepted in the Battle Rock. "Pardon me, gentles," I said. "Maybe I can contribute."

"By all means, Captain," said the Martian, his eyes flickering over my Solar Guard uniform and insignia. "Permit me: I am Professor Freylinghausen—Engineer Soekarno—Freelady Nielsen-Singh."

"Captain Crane." I lifted my mug in a formal toast. "Mars, Luna, Venus, and Earth in my case . . . highly representative, are we not? Between us, we should be able to reach a conclusion."

I got out my pipe and began stuffing it. "There's a case from recent history in which I had a part myself. Offhand, at least, it seems a perfect example of sheer accident determining the whole future of the human race. It makes me think we must be more the pawns of chance than of law.

"I'll have to fill you in on some background." I lit my pipe and took a comforting drag. I needed comfort just then. It was not to settle an argument that I was telling this, but to re-open an old hurt which would never let itself be forgotten. "This happened during the final attack on the Humanists—"

"A perfect case of inevitability, sir," interrupted Freylinghausen. "Psychotechnic government had failed to solve the problems of Earth's adjustment to living on a high technological level. Conditions worsened until all too many people were ready to try desperation measures. The Humanist Revolution was the desperation measure which succeeded in being tried. A typical reaction movement, offering a return to a less intellectualized existence: the Savior with the Time Machine, as Toynbee once phrased it. So naturally its leader, Carnarvon, got to be dictator of the planet.

"But with equal force was it true that Earth could no longer *afford* to cut back her technology. Too many people, too few resources. The Humanists failed to keep their promises; their attempts led only to famine, social disruption, breakdown. Losing popular support, they had to become increasingly arbitrary.

"At last the oppression of Earth became so brutal that the democratic governments of Mars and Venus brought pressure to bear. But the Humanists had gone too far to back down. Their only possible reaction was to pull Earth-Luna out of the Solar Union.

"We could not see that happen, sir. Without a Union council to arbitrate between planets and a Solar Guard to enforce its decisions—there will be war until man is extinct. Earth could not be allowed to secede. Therefore Mars and Venus aided the anti-Humanist cabal which wanted to restore liberty and Union membership to the mother planet. Therefore, too, a space fleet was raised to support an uprising.

"Don't you see? Every step was an unavoidable consequence, by the logic of survival, of all which had gone before."

"All right so far, Professor," I nodded. "But the success of the anti-Humanists and the Mars-Venus intervention was by no means guaranteed. Mars and Venus were still frontiers, thinly populated. They didn't have the military potential of Earth.

"The cabal was well organized. Its well-timed mutinies swept Earth's newly created pro-Humanist ground and air forces before it. The countryside, the oceans, even the cities were soon cleared of Humanist troops.

"But Dictator Carnarvon and the men still loyal to him were holed up in a score of fortresses. Oh, it would be easy enough to dig them out or blast them out—except that the navy of Sovereign Earth, organized from seized units of the Solar Guard, had also remained loyal to Humanism. Its cinc, Admiral K'ung, had acted promptly when the revolt began, jailing all personnel he wasn't sure of—or shooting them.

"So there the pro-Union revolutionaries were, in possession of Earth but with a good 500 enemy warships orbiting above them. K'ung's strategy was simple. He broadcast that unless the rebels surrendered inside one week—or if meanwhile they made any attempt on Carnarvon's remaining strongholds—he'd start bombarding with nuclear weapons.

"Under such a threat, the general population was no longer backing the rebel cause. They clamored for surrender.

"Meanwhile, as you all know, the Unionist fleet under Dushanovitch-Alvarez had rendezvoused off Luna: as mixed a bunch of Martians, Venusians, and freedom-minded Earthmen as history ever saw. They were much inferior; it was impossible for them to charge in on Admiral K'ung and give battle with any hope of winning . . . but Dushanovitch-Alvarez had a plan. It depended on luring the Humanist fleet out to engage him.

"Only, K'ung wasn't having any. It was a costly nuisance, the Unionists sneaking in, firing and retreating, blowing up ship after ship of the Humanist forces. But K'ung would not accept the challenge until the rebels on the ground had capitulated; he was negotiating with them now, and it looked very much as if they would give in.

"So there it was, the entire outcome of the war—the whole history of man, for if you will pardon my saying so, gentles, Earth is still the key planet—everything hanging on this one officer, Grand Admiral K'ung Li-Po, a grim man who had given his oath and had a damnably good grasp of the military facts of life."

I took a long draught from my mug and began the story, using the third-person form which is customary on Mars.

The speedster blasted at four gees till she was a bare 500 kilometers from the closest enemy vessels; her radar screens were jittering with their nearness and in the thunder of abused hearts her crew sat waiting for the hawk-blow of a homing missile. Then she was at the calculated point, she spat her cargo out the main lock and leaped away still more furiously. In moments the thin glare of her jets was lost among crowding stars.

The cargo was three space-suited men, linked to a giant air tank and burdened with a variety of tools. The orbit into which they had been flung was aligned with that of the Humanist fleet, so that relative velocity was low.

In cosmic terms, that is. It still amounted to nearly a thousand kilometers per hour.

Lieutenant Robert Crane pulled himself along the light cable that bound him, up to the tank. His hands groped in

the pitchy gloom of shadowside—then all at once rotation
had brought him into the moonlight and he could see. He
found the rungs and went hand over hand along the curve
of the barrel, centrifugal force streaming his body outward.
Awkwardly, he got one foot into a stirruplike arrangement
and scrambled around until he was in the "saddle" with both
boots firmly locked; then he unclipped the line from his
waist.

The stars turned about him in a cold majestic wheel. Earth
was an enormous grayness in the sky, a half-ring of blinding
light from the hidden sun along one side.

Twisting a head made giddy by the spinning, he saw the
other two mounted behind him. García was in the middle—
you could always tell a Venusian, he painted his clan
markings on his suit—and the Martian Wolf at the end.
"Okay," he said, incongruously aware that the throat mike
pinched his Adam's apple, "let's stop this merry-go-round."

His hands moved across a simple control panel. A tangen-
tially mounted nozzle was opened, emitting an invisible
stream of air. The stars slowed their lunatic dance, steadied.

"Any radar reading?" García's voice was tinny in the
earphones.

"A moment, if you please, till I have it set up." Wolf
extended a telescoping mast, switched on the portable
'scope, and began sweeping the sky. "Nearest indication
. . . um . . . one o'clock, five degrees low, 422 kilometers
distant." García worked an astrogator's slide rule.

The baseline was not the tank, but its velocity, which
could be assumed straight-line for so short a distance.
Actually, the weird horse had its nose pointed a full 30
degrees off the direction of movement. "High" and "low,"
in weightlessness, were simply determined by the plane
bisecting the tank, with the men's heads arbitrarily desig-
nated as "aimed up."

The airbarrel had jets aligned in three planes, as well as
the rotation-controlling tangential nozzles. With Wolf and
García to correct him, Crane blended vectors until they were
on a course which would nearly intercept the ship. Gas was
released from the forward jet at a rate calculated to match
velocity.

There was nothing but the gauges to tell Crane that he was

braking. Carefully dehydrated air emerges quite invisibly, and its ionization is negligible; there was no converter to radiate, and all equipment was painted a dead nonreflecting black.

Soundless and invisible—too small and fast for a chance eye to see in the uncertain moonlight, for a chance radar beam to register as anything worth buzzing an alarm about. Not enough infrared for detection, not enough mass, no trail of ions—the machinists on the *Thor* had wrought well, the astrogators had figured as closely as men and computers are able. But in the end it was only a tank of compressed air, a bomb, a few tools, and three men frightened and lonely.

"How long will it take us to get there?" asked Crane. His throat was dry and he swallowed hard.

"About forty-five minutes to that ship we're zeroed in on," García told him. "After that, *¿quien sabe?* We'll have to locate the *Monitor*."

"Be most economical with the air, if you please," said Wolf. "We also have to get back."

"Tell me more," snorted Crane.

"If this works," remarked García, "we'll have added a new weapon to the System's arsenals. That's why I volunteered—if Antonio García of Hesperus gets his name in the history books, my whole clan will contribute to give me the biggest ranch on Venus."

They were an anachronism, thought Crane, a resurrection from old days when war was a wilder business. The psychotechs had not picked a team for compatibility, nor welded them into an unbreakable brotherhood—they had merely grabbed the first three willing to try an untested scheme. There wasn't time for anything else. In another forty hours, the rebel, pro-Union armies on Earth would either have surrendered or the bombardment would begin.

"Why are you lads here?" went on the Venusian. "We might as well get acquainted."

"I took an oath," said Wolf. There was nothing priggish about it; Martians thought that way.

"What of you, Crane?"

"I—it looked like fun," said the Earthman lamely. "And it might end this damned war."

He lied and he knew it, but how do you explain? Do you admit it was an escape from your shipmates' eyes?

Not that his joining the Unionists had shamed him; everyone aboard the *Marduk* had done so, except for a couple of CPOs who were now under guard in Aphrodite. The cruiser had been on patrol off Venus when word of Earth's secession had flashed; her captain had declared for the Union, and the crew cheered him for it.

For two years, while Dushanovitch-Alvarez, half idealist and half buccaneer, was assembling the Unionist fleet, intelligence reports trickled in from Earth. Just before the Unionists accelerated for rendezvous, a detailed list of all the new captains appointed by K'ung had been received. And the skipper of the *Huitzilopochtli* was named Benjamin Crane.

Ben . . . what did you do, when your brother was on the enemy side? Dushanovitch-Alvarez had let the System know that a bombardment of Earth would be regarded as genocide and all officers partaking in it would be punished under Union law. Lieutenant Robert Crane of the *Marduk* had protested: this was not a normal police operation, it was war, and executing men who merely obeyed the government they had pledged to uphold was opening the gates to a darker barbarism than the fighting itself. The Unionist force was shorthanded, and gave Lieutenant Crane no more than a public reproof for insubordination; but his messmates had tended to grow silent when he entered the wardroom.

If the superdreadnought *Monitor* could be destroyed, and K'ung with it, Earth might not be bombarded; then if the Unionists won, Ben would go free, or he would die cleanly in battle—reason enough to ride this thing into the Humanist fleet!

Silence was cold in their helmets.

"I've been thinking," said García. "Suppose we do carry this off, but they decide to blast Earth anyway before dealing with our boats. What then?"

"Then they blast Earth," said Wolf. "Though most likely they won't have to. Last I heard, the threat alone was making folk rise against our friends on the ground there." Moonlight shimmered along his arm as he pointed at the darkened planet-shield before them. "So the Humanists will be back in power, and even if we chop up their navy, we won't win unless we do some bombarding of our own."

"¡Madre de Dios!" García crossed himself, a barely visible gesture in the unreal flood of undiffused light. "I'll mutiny before I give my name to such a thing."

"And I," said Wolf shortly. "And most of us, I think."

It was not that the Union fleet was crewed by saints, thought Crane. Most of its personnel had signed on for booty—the System knew how much treasure was locked in the vaults of Earth's dictators. But the horror of nuclear war had been too deeply graven for anyone but a fanatic at the point of desperation to think of using it.

Even in K'ung's command, there must be talk of revolt. Since his ultimatum, deserters in lifeboats had brought Dushanovitch-Alvarez a mountain of precise information. But the Humanists had had ten years in which to build a hard cadre of hard young officers, to keep the men obedient.

Strange to know that Ben was with them—*why?*

I haven't seen you in more than two years now, Ben—nor my own wife and children, but tonight it is you who dwell in me, and I have not felt such pain for many years. Not since that time we were boys together, and you were sick one day, and I went alone down the steep bluffs above the Mississippi. There I found the old man denned up under the trees, a tramp, one of many millions for whom there was no place in this new world of shining machines—but he was not embittered, he drew his citizen's allowance and tramped the planet and he had stories to tell me which our world of bright hard metal had forgotten. He told me about Br'er Rabbit and the briar patch, never had I heard such a story, it was the first time I knew the rich dark humor of the earth itself. And you got well, Ben, and I took you down to his camp, but he was gone and you never heard the story of Br'er Rabbit. On that day, Ben, I was as close to weeping as I am this night of murder.

The vessel on which they had zeroed came into plain view, a long black shark swimming against the Milky Way. They passed within two kilometers of her. Wolf was busy now, flicking his radar around the sky, telling off ships. It was mostly seat-of-the-pants piloting, low relative velocities and small distances, edging into the mass of Earth's fleet.

The *Monitor* was in the inner ring; a deserter had given them the approximate orbit.

"You're pretty good at this, boy," said García.

"I rode a scooter in the asteroids for a couple of years," answered Crane. "Patrol and rescue duty."

Slowly over the minutes, the *Monitor* grew before him, a giant spheroid never meant to land on a planet. He could see gun turrets scrawled black across remote star-clouds. There was more reason for destroying her than basic strategy— luring the Humanists out to do battle. It would be the annihilation of a symbol: the *Monitor,* alone among all ships that rode the sky, was designed with no other purpose than killing.

Slow, now, easy, gauge the speeds by eye, remember how much inertia you've got . . . edge up, brake, throw out a magnetic anchor and grapple fast. Crane turned a small winch, the cable tautened and he bumped against the hull.

There was no talking. They had work to do, and their short-range radio might have been detected. García unshipped the bomb. Crane held it while the Venusian scrambled from the saddle and got a firm boot-grip on the dreadnought. The bomb didn't have a large mass. Crane handed it over, and García slapped it onto the hull, gripped by a magnetic plate. Stooping, he wound a spring and jerked a small lever. Then, with the spaceman's finicking care, he returned to the saddle.

In twenty minutes, the clockwork was to set off the bomb. It was a small one, plutonium fission, and most of its energy would be wasted on vacuum. Enough would remain to smash the *Monitor* into a hundred white-hot fragments.

Crane worked the air-jets, forcing himself to be calm and deliberate. The barrel swung about to point at Luna, and he opened the rear throttle wide. Acceleration tugged at him, he braced his feet in the stirrups and hung on with both hands. Behind them, the *Monitor* receded.

When they were a good fifteen kilometers away, he asked for a course. His voice felt remote, as if it came from outside his prickling skin; most of him wondered just how many men were aboard the dreadnought and how many wives and children they had to weep for them. Wolf squinted through a sextant and gave his readings to García. Corrections made, they rode toward the point of rendezvous: a point so tricky to compute, in this Solar System where the planets were never still, that they would doubtless never come within a hundred kilometers of the speedster that was to pick them up. But they had a hand-cranked radio which would broadcast a strong enough signal for the boat to get a fix on them.

How many minutes had they been going? Ten . . . Crane looked at the clock in the control panel. Yes, ten. Another five or so, at this acceleration, ought to see them beyond the outermost orbit of the Humanist ships—

He did not hear the explosion. There was a swift and terrible glare inside his helmet, enough light reflected off the inner surface for his eyes to swim in white-hot darkness. He clung blind to his seat, nerves and muscles tensed against the hammerblow that never came. And then the darkness parted raggedly, and he turned his head back toward Earth. A wan nimbus of incandescent gas hung there, and a few tattered stars glowed blue as they fled from it.

Wolf's voice whispered in his ears: "She's gone already. The bomb went off ahead of schedule. Something in the clockwork—"

"But she's gone!" García let out a rattling whoop. "No more flagship. We got her, lads, we got the stinking can!"

Not far away, there was a shadow visible only where it blocked off the stars. A ship . . . light cruiser— "Cram on the air!" said Wolf roughly. "Let's get the devil out of here."

"I can't." Crane snarled it, his brain still dizzy, wanting only to rest and forget all war. "We've only got so much pressure left, and none to spare for maneuvering if we get off course."

"All right—" They lapsed into silence. That which had been the *Monitor,* gas and shrapnel, dissipated. The enemy cruiser fell behind them, and Luna filled their eyes with barren radiance.

They were not aware of pursuit until the squad was almost on them. There were a dozen men in combat armor, driven by individual jet-units and carrying rifles. They overhauled the tank and edged in—less gracefully than fish, for there was no friction to kill forward velocity, but they moved in.

After the first harsh leap of his heart, Crane felt cold and numb. None of his party bore arms: they themselves had been the weapon, and now it was discharged. In a mechanical fashion, he tuned his headset to the standard band.

"Rebels ahoy!" It was a voice strained close to breaking, an American voice . . . for a moment such a wave of homesickness for the green dales of Wisconsin went over Crane that he could not move or realize he was about to be captured. "Stop that thing and come with us!"

In an animal reflex, Crane opened the rear throttles full. The barrel jumped ahead, almost ripping him from the saddle. There was a flaring of ions behind as the enemy followed. Their units were beam-powered from the ship's nuclear engines, and they had plenty of reaction mass in their tanks. It was only a moment before they were alongside again.

Arms closed around Crane, dragging him from his seat. As the universe tilted about his head, he saw Wolf likewise caught. García sprang to meet an Earthman, hit him and bounced away, but got his rifle. A score of bullets spat. Suddenly the Venusian's armor blew white clouds of freezing water vapor and he drifted dead.

Wolf wrestled in vacuum and tore one hand free. Crane heard him croak over the radio: "They'll find out—" Another frosty geyser erupted; Wolf had opened his own airtubes.

There was a man on either side of Crane, pinioning his arms—he could not have suicided even if he chose to. The rest flitted in, guns ready. He relaxed, too weary and dazed to fight, and let them face him around and kill forward speed, then accelerate toward the cruiser.

The airlock was opening for him before he had his voice back. "What ship is this?" he asked, not caring much, only filling in an emptiness.

"*Huitzilopochtli*. Get in there with you."

Crane floated weightless in the wardroom, his left ankle manacled to a stanchion. They had removed his armor, leaving only the thick gray coverall which was the underpadding, and given him a stimpill. A young officer guarded him, sidearm holstered—no reason to fear a fettered captive. The officer did not speak, but awe and horror lay on his lips.

The pill had revived Crane, his body felt supple and he sensed every detail of the room with an unnatural clarity. But his heart had a thick beat and his mouth felt cottony. . . .

Captain Benjamin Crane of the Space Navy, Federation of Earth and the Free Cities of Luna, drifted in through a ghostly quiet. It was a small shock to see him again . . . when had the last time been, three years ago? They had gone up to their father's house in Wisconsin. The old man was dead and the house had stood empty a long time. But it had been a fine pheasant shoot, on a certain cool and smoky-clear fall morning. Robert Crane remembered how the first dead leaves had crackled underfoot, and how the bird dog stiffened into a point which was all flowing line and deep curves, and the thin high wedge of wild geese, southward bound.

That was the first thing he thought of, and then he thought that Ben had put on a good deal of weight and looked much older, and then he recalled that he himself had changed toward gauntness and must seem to have more than the two-year edge on Ben he really did.

The captain stiffened as he came through the air. He grabbed a handhold barely in time, and stopped his flight ungracefully. After that there was another quietness. There was little to see on Ben's heavy face, unless you knew him as well as his own brother did.

He spoke finally, a whisper: "I never looked for this."

Crane of the *Marduk* tried to smile. "What are the mathematical odds against it?" he wondered. "That I, of all people, should be on this mission, and that your ship of all Earth's fleet should have captured me. How did you detect us?"

"That bomb . . . you touched it off too soon. The initial glare brought us all to the ports, and the gas-glow afterward, added to the moonlight, was enough to reveal a peculiar object. We got a radar on it and I sent men out."

"Accident," said Robert Crane. "It wasn't supposed to detonate till we were well away."

"I knew you were on . . . the other side," said Ben with slowness. "If it hadn't been for the *Marduk*'s special Venus patrol, you would probably have been right here when the . . . the trouble began, and you'd have had to remain loyal."

"Like you, Ben?"

The young officer of Earth floated "upright," at attention, but his eyes were not still. Ben nodded at him. "Mr. Nicholson, this prisoner happens to be my brother."

There was no change in the correct face.

Ben sighed. "I suppose you know what you did, Lieutenant Crane."

"Yes," said Robert. "We blew up your flagship."

"It was a brilliant operation," said Ben dully. "I've had a verbal report on your . . . vessel. I imagine you planted an atomic bomb on the *Monitor*'s hull. If we knew just where your fleet is and how it's arrayed, as you seem to know all about us, I'd like to try the same thing on you."

Robert floated, waiting. There was a thickening in his throat. He felt sweat forming under his arms and along his ribs, soaking into the coverall. He could smell his own stink.

"But I wonder why that one man of yours suicided," went on Ben. He frowned, abstractedly, and Robert knew he would not willingly let the riddle go till he had solved it. "Perhaps your mission was more than just striking a hard blow at us. Perhaps he didn't want us to know its real purpose."

Ben, you're no fool. You were always a suspicious son-of-a-gun, always probing, never quite believing what you were told. I know you, Ben.

What had Wolf's religion been? Crane didn't know. He hoped it wasn't one which promised hellfire to all suicides. Wolf had died to protect a secret which the drugs of Earth's psychotechs—nothing so crude as torture—would have dissolved out of him.

If they had not been captured . . . the natural reaction would have been for Earth's fleet to rush forth seeking revenge before the Unionists attacked them. They did not know, they must not know, that Dushanovitch Alvarez lacked the ships to win an open battle except on his own ground and under his own terms; that the Humanist fleet need only remain where it was, renew the threat of bombardment, carry it out if necessary, and the Union men could do nothing to interfere.

"Sir—"

Ben's head turned, and Robert saw with an odd little sadness that there were gray streaks at the temples. What was his age—thirty-one? *My kid brother is growing old already.*

"Yes, Mr. Nicholson?"

The officer cleared his throat. "Sir, shouldn't the prisoner be interrogated in the regular way?"

"Oh, yes, Intelligence will be happy to pump him," said Ben. "Though I suspect this show will be over before they've gotten much information of value. Vice Admiral Hokusai of the *Krishna* has succeeded to command. Get on the radio, Mr. Nicholson, and report what has happened. In the meantime, I'll question the prisoner myself . . . privately."

"Yes, sir." The officer saluted and went out. There was compassion in his eyes.

Ben closed the door behind him. Then he turned around and floated, crossing his legs, one hand on a stanchion and the other rubbing his forehead. His brother had known he would do exactly that. *But how well can he read me?*

"Well, Bob." Ben's tone was a gentle one.

Robert Crane shifted, feeling the link about his ankle. "How are Mary and the kids?" he asked.

"Oh . . . quite well, thank you. I'm afraid I can't tell you much about your own family. Last I heard, they were living in Manitowoc Unit, but in all the confusion since—" Ben looked away. "They were never bothered by our police, though. I have some little influence."

"Thanks," said Robert. Then bitterness lashed out: "Yours are safe in Luna City. Mine will get the fallout when you bombard, or they'll starve in the famine to follow."

The captain's mouth wrenched. "Don't say that!" After a moment: "Do you think I like the idea of shooting at Earth? If the rebels really give a curse in hell about the people their hearts bleed for so loudly, they'll surrender first. We're offering terms; they'll be allowed to go to Mars or Venus."

"I'm afraid you misjudge us, Ben," said Robert. "Do you know why I'm here? It wasn't just a matter of being on the *Marduk* when she elected to stay with the Union. I believe in what the rebels are trying to do."

"Believe in those pirates out there?" Ben's finger stabbed

at the wall, as if to pierce it and show the stars and the hostile ships swimming between.

"Oh, sure, they've been promised the treasure vaults. We had to raise men and ships somehow. What good was all that money doing, locked away by Carnarvon and his gang?" Robert shrugged. "Look, I was born and raised in America. We were always a free people. From the moment the Humanists seized power, I had to start watching what I said, who I associated with, what tapes I got from the library. My kids were growing up into perfect little parrots. It was too much. When the purges began, when the police fired on crowds rioting because they were starving—and they were starving because this quasi-religious creed cannot accept the realities and organize things rationally—I was only waiting for my chance. . . . Ben, be honest. Wouldn't you have signed on with us if you'd been on the *Marduk?*"

The face before him was gray. "Don't ask me that! No!"

"I can tell you exactly why not, Ben." Robert folded his arms and would not let his brother's eyes go. "I know you well enough. We're different in one respect. To you, no principle can be as important as your wife and children—and they're hostages for your good behavior. Oh, yes, K'ung's psychotechs evaluated you very carefully. Probably half their captains are held by just such chains."

Ben laughed, a loud bleak noise above the steady murmur of the ventilators. "Have it your way. And don't forget that your family is alive, too, because I stayed with the government. I'm not going to change, either. A government, even the most arbitrary one, can perhaps be altered in time. But the dead never come back to life."

He leaned forward, suddenly shuddering. "Bob, I don't want you sent Earthside for interrogation. They'll not only drug you, they'll set about changing your whole viewpoint. Surgery, shock, a rebuilt personality—you won't be the same man when they've finished.

"I can wangle something else. I have enough pull, especially now in all the confusion after your raid, to keep you here. When the war is settled, I'll arrange for your escape. There's going to be so much hullabaloo on Earth that nobody will notice. But you'll have to help me, in turn.

"What was the real purpose of your raid? What plans does your high command have?"

For a time which seemed to become very long, Robert Crane waited. He was being asked to betray his side voluntarily; the alternative was to do it anyway, after the psychmen got through with him. Ben had no authority to make the decision—it would mean court-martial later, and punishment visited on his family as well, unless he could justify it by claiming quicker results than the long-drawn process of narcosynthesis.

Robert Crane wet his lips. "How do you know I'll tell the truth?" he asked.

Ben looked up again, crinkling his eyes. "We had a formula once," he said. "Remember? 'Cross my heart and hope to die, spit in my eye if I tell a lie.' I don't think either of us ever lied when we took that oath."

"Ben, the whole war hangs on this, maybe. Do you seriously think I'd keep my word for a kid's chant if it could decide the war?"

"Oh, no." There was a flickering smile in the captain's eyes. "There's going to be a meeting of all the skippers, if I know Hokusai. He'll want the opinions of us all as to what we should do next. Having heard them, he'll make his own decision. I'll only be one voice among a lot of others.

"But if I can speak with whatever information you've given me—do you understand? The council will meet long before you could be sent Earthside and quizzed. I need your knowledge *now*. I'll listen to whatever you have to say. I may or may not believe you . . . but it's the only way I can save you, and myself, and everything else I care about."

He waited then, patiently as the circling ships. They must have come around the planet by now, thought Robert Crane. The sun would be drowning many stars, and Earth would be daylit if you looked out.

A captains' council . . . it sounded awkward and slow. But they all, nearly all, had kindred on Earth. None of them wished to explode radioactive death across the world they loved. K'ung's will had been like steel, but now they would—subconsciously, and all the more powerfully for that—be looking for any way out of the frightful necessity.

A respected officer, giving good logical reasons for postponing the bombardment, would be listened to eagerly.

Robert Crane shivered. It was a heartless load to put on any one man. The dice of all future history . . . he could load the dice, because he knew Ben as any man knows a dear brother, but maybe his hand would slip as he loaded them.

"Well?" It was a grating in the captain's throat.

Robert drew a long breath. "All right," he said.

"Yes?" A high, cracked note; Ben must be near breaking too.

"I'm not in command, you realize." Robert's words were blurred with haste. "I can't tell for sure what— But I do know we've got fewer ships. A lot fewer."

"I suspected that—"

"We have some plan—I haven't been told just what— it depends on making you leave this orbit and come out and fight us where we are. If you stay here, there's not a damn thing we can do. This raid of mine . . . we'd hoped that with your admiral dead, you'd join battle out toward Luna."

Robert Crane hung in the air, twisting in its currents, the breath gasping in and out of him. Ben looked dim, across the room, as if his eyes were failing.

"Is that the truth, Bob?" The question seemed to come from light-years away.

"Yes. Yes. I can't let you go and get killed and— Cross my heart and hope to die, spit in my eye if I tell a lie!"

I set down my mug, empty, and signalled for another. The bartender glided across the floor with it and I drank thirstily, remembering how my throat had felt mummified long ago on the *Huitzilopochtli*.

"Very well, sir." Freylinghausen's testy voice broke a stillness. "What happened?"

"You ought to know that, Professor," I replied. "It's in the history tapes. The Humanist fleet decided to go out at once and dispose of its inferior opponent. Their idea—correct enough, I suppose—was that a space victory would be so demoralizing that the rebels on the ground would capitulate immediately. It would have destroyed the last hope of reinforcements, you see."

"And the Union fleet won," said Nielsen-Singh. "They chopped the Humanist navy into fishbait. I know—my father was there. We bought a dozen new reclamation units with his share of the loot, afterward."

"Naval history is out of my line, Captain Crane," said the Engineer, Soekarno. "Just how did Dushanovitch-Alvarez win?"

"Oh . . . it was a combination of things. Chiefly, he disposed his ships and gave them such velocities that the enemy, following the usual principles of tactics, moved at high accelerations to close in. And at a point where they would have built up a good big speed, he had a lot of stuff planted, rocks and ball bearings and scrap iron . . . an artificial meteor swarm, moving in an opposed orbit. After that had done its work, the two forces were of very nearly equal strength, and it became a battle of standard weapons. Which Dushanovitch-Alvarez knew how to use! A more brilliant naval mind hasn't existed since Lord Nelson."

"Yes, yes," said Freylinghausen impatiently. "But what has all this to do with the subject under discussion?"

"Don't you see, Professor? It was chance all along the line—chance which was skillfully exploited when it arose, to be sure, but nevertheless a set of unpredictable accidents. The *Monitor* blew up ten minutes ahead of schedule; as a result, the commando that did it was captured. Normally, this would have meant that the whole plan would have been given away. I can't emphasize too strongly that the Humanists would have won if they'd only stayed where they were."

I tossed off a long gulp of porter, knocked the dottle from my pipe, and began refilling it. My hands weren't quite steady. "But chance entered here, too, making Robert Crane's brother the man to capture him. And Robert knew how to manipulate Ben. At the captains' council, it was the *Huitzilopochtli*'s skipper who spoke most strongly in favor of going out to do battle. His arguments, especially when everyone knew they were based on information obtained from a prisoner, convinced the others."

"But you just said—" Nielsen-Singh looked confused.

"Yes, I did." I smiled at her, but my thoughts were all in the past. "But it wasn't till years later that Ben heard the story of Br'er Rabbit and the briar patch; he came across it

in his brother's boyhood diary. Robert Crane told the truth,
swore to it by a boyhood oath—but his brother could not
believe he'd yield so easily. Robert was almost begging him
to stay with K'ung's plan. Ben was sure it was an outright
lie . . . that Dushanovitch-Alvarez must actually be planning
to attack the navy in its orbit and could not possibly survive
a battle in open space. So that, of course, was what he
argued for.''

"It took nerve, though," said Nielsen-Singh. "Knowing
what the *Huitzilopochtli* would have to face—knowing you'd
be aboard—"

"She was a wreck by the time the battle was over," I
said. "Not many who were in her survived.''

After a moment, Soekarno nodded thoughtfully. "I see
your point, Captain. The accident of the bomb's going off
too soon almost wrecked the Union plan. The accident of
that brotherhood saved it. A thread of coincidences—yes, I
think you've proved your case.''

"I am afraid not, gentles.'' Freylinghausen darted birdlike
eyes around the table. "You misunderstood me. I was not
speaking of minor ripples in the mainstream of history—
certainly those are ruled by chance. But the broad current
moves quite inexorably, I assure you. *Vide:* Earth and Luna
are back in the Union under a more or less democratic
government, but no solution has yet been found to the
problems which brought forth the Humanists. They will
come again; under one name or another, they will return.
The war was only a ripple, after all.''

"Maybe.'' I spoke with inurbane curtness, not liking the
thought. "We'll have to see.''

"If nothing else," said Nielsen-Singh, "you people
bought for Earth a few more decades of freedom. They can't
take that away from you.''

I looked at her with sudden respect. It was true. Men died
and civilizations died, but before they died they *lived*. It was
not altogether futile.

But I could not remain here. I had told the story, as I must
always tell it, and now I needed aloneness.

"Excuse me.'' I finished my drink and stood up. "I have
an appointment . . . just dropped in . . . very happy to have
met you, gentles.''

Soekarno rose with the others and bowed formally. "I trust we shall have the pleasure of your company again, Captain Robert Crane."

"Robert—? Oh." I stopped. I had told what I must in third person, but it had seemed so obvious to me— "I'm sorry. Robert Crane was killed in the battle. I am Captain Benjamin Crane, at your service, gentles."

I bowed to them all and went out the door. The night was lonesome in the streets and across the desert.

Poul Anderson is one of the most prolific writers in all of science fiction and fantasy, the recipient of many awards, and author of titles too numerous to list. A few favorites that spring immediately to mind are The Broken Sword, Tau Zero, *and the Nicholas van Rijn and Dominic Flandry series. His most recent work includes a historical fantasy trilogy,* The King of Ys, *written in collaboration with his wife, Karen Anderson.*

C.O.D.
by Jonathan Milos

Sometimes you can misplace little things when you shuffle too many papers . . . like the fauna of a whole planet, for instance.

Greetings, people of RC 7761, otherwise known as Earth. No, that's silly. I didn't spend all that time and trade balance stuffing my monitor-brain with your idioms to address you like that. Not even the few of you I talk to directly.

You see—and you may never read this particular line, I don't know what kind of censorship goes on down there— you may have been told there was only the one contact with the Consortium of the Thousand Stars, but you weren't told the truth. We keep a line of communication open, which your people with access to it call the Spacevine. Interesting idiom. If you'd like to talk on it too, sorry, you don't qualify. We don't need talkers, we need listeners. Especially from Re—uh, Earth. You'll see why.

I was in a tavern on Ef'tle, chewing berries to forget; the silly things are toxic if you take too many, but then, so is *chil*, my favorite tipple. And if I didn't clean out my holding-brain every few turns I wouldn't have any place to put stories, and I make a pretty good living off those stories. MedServ gives me pills for berry hangover, but it's money that keeps me in *chil*.

So there I was, chewing berries and swallowing the seeds—thus cleaning out mind and body at once—when a Zhanzherezhin—oops, a Zhanzherezh*ine*—came up to see me and eyed my plate. "Honor," she said.

"Honor to you," I said. I noticed then she was wearing a RescueService plate and a Captain's pendant, and her claws were empty. "You must be fresh landed. Drink, your choosing?"

"I am *not* frezzh-fallen," she buzzed, "and I am *not* intoxicating."

Now that was news worth recording, right there. Zhanzherezhini pilots are common enough—they've got it all over us poor creatures without faceted eyes or gyroscopes built into our skulls—but a Zizzy Captain grounded and sober not only wasn't common, it to my knowledge just *wasn't*.

I shoved the bowl of berries away and fired up my recording-nerves. "Transact at your word," I said.

"How much for a tale of the world RC 7761?"

I bit down hard, hurting my mouth on a stray berry-pit. RC 7761 is an outThousand planet whose inhabitants, prespace sapients, call it Dirt, or Earth, or Soil. I know that a RescueService ship had made some kind of a deal there that had raised the twin spirits of Rumor and Secrecy; some facts, any facts, in the matter were worth my plate. So I just counted my trade balance, deducted an eighth for emergency, and offered the Zizzy the rest.

She *bzzz*ed at me and said "It'll do." I should have thought it would; it was twice a deepspace Captain's Guaranteed Trade Wage for a full turn. But I just said, "I transfer," and pressed our plates together. Click, hum. It's so easy to spend balance these days. I ordered a mug of *chil* out of my remaining finances, switched brains and listened.

Some seven million turns ago (said the Captain) ScienceService detected a magnetic flare about to blow in the C Segment of R Galaxy; not much of a flash, but enough to raise the Great Beast with neurally advanced creatures. So RescServ was dispatched to scan and evacuate if necessary.

RescueService was overloaded then as now, and nobody expected to have to evacuate anything anyway, so all that actually got sent were a light scientific cruiser and an automated sublight massfreezer of the *Obon* class—which haven't, incidentally, been made for five million turns. I know all this; I've looked it all up, with JustiServ at my wingtip—but that part comes later.

When that long-ago Rescue team got to RC 7761, they found intelligent life after all—not technociv, but tool use, limited control of fire, villages. A nice solid start down the road to the Thousand, about to get pinched off hard.

Beastslayer only knows how they communicated with the natives. Meta-Linking was still in the fry-your-brains stage. Maybe they had some natural telepaths. Anyway, somehow they convinced the locals, who called their planet Reeth, that the big bright yellow thing was going to get big and eat them all up, unless they got aboard the little silver brother-to-moon in parking orbit. I did say this place had a moon, didn't I? Big one, the size of an Outpost of the Thousand.

So the natives and some of their livestock got in and got cold. RescServ had to hustle to get them in before the magstorm, but they managed, just like we usually manage.

They had to find them a planet to resettle on. They couldn't just wait out the flash and take them home; the ecosystem would have been all broken-winged, they'd never have adjusted to it. So another place had to be found.

Every race is the same in one way: they're all impossible to please. This one likes it hot, this one cold, this one needs UV to keep its genetic tension down, this one needs hot sulfur pools—

And while they looked for an appropriate place to dump fifty thousand frozen Reethi, there was a, well, clerical error.

I maintain that makes it CompServ's liability—yes, I know what the InterService contract says down the side, but still—sorry. I'll go on.

(She shaded her eyes from the sight of a party of carousing Zhanzherezhini.) What happened was, they got misfiled. Lost. Forgotten. For seven million turns, that old *Obon*-class kept going nowhere, everyone on board it cold and happy. At that, they were lucky they were on an underlight ship; time dilation took over, and the machinery didn't wear out and nobody thawed too soon.

CompServ claims that they never really lose anything; they just build up long access times. Maybe they're right. They finally found that old massfreezer. And guess who got tagged to repatriate them? Me and my ship, of course. A hundred thousand crews on the board, and—

Well, it *was* our idea to take the Reethi back to 7761. The planet-finding situation hasn't gotten any better in seven megaturns, and things back home should certainly have stabilized in that amount of time. Evolution? Of course there'd have been evolution, but the Thousand's lasted, what, a hundred million turns? We know how evolution operates. Sure as the Queen's drones love her, we do.

What we found was a whole planet radiating noise into the middle ranges, pumping combustion products into the atmosphere at an incredible rate—we couldn't have breathed it for a nanoturn without passing out—and what looked like starship maintenance stations, all over the surface. *Looked* like. We tried to lock and land at one—and the Beast-netted thing was a habitat complex. Imagine: a city spread out to the size of a medium cruiser! And that wasn't even the biggest. They directed us to that one, which didn't have any facilities either, except a big paved area named for a tribal deity.

This place, Advancedyork, had an intertribal negotiations center, apparently the only one operating. Tribalism and fusion demolitions, they turned out to have, but no fusion generators. Yet. May the Net ensnare them.

We shuttled down, making sure to take plenty of portable environment with us. We told them what we were there for; that we had a shipload of their ancestors, coming out of freeze, and that they were being returned pending the usual fee.

(The Captain paused to smooth her fur. For the benefit of my listeners, the fee she refers to is negotiated by RescServ with the group they service. They can ask for whatever they can get, and it goes on the indestructible receipt. If—and only if—the receipt for services is blank, EconoServ will pay the team back their expenses, and no more. RescueService has gotten very good at negotiating fees. And after all, how much is not burning up worth to you?)

At least (the Zizzy continued) our Linker tried to send that. When I said earlier that I didn't know how they communicated with natives before the Meta-Link—I certainly on't understand it now. Our Linker's in MaintServ now. If she so much as sees a mindset she bounces off the ceiling.

For that reason, I can't tell you much of what happened among the inhabitants. Apparently one tribe said they didn't have room for the Reethi because their economy was planned in advance. Then another tribe said they'd take the whole group because they were the land with streets of soft metal, and the first tribe accused them of an untranslatable expression and offered to pay the whole fee plus a tenth extra in lightly armored ground combat vehicles. And then some little tribes said they'd take the Reethi if it would start a fight between the first two tribes—this is just what a hysterical Linker told me, you understand. There even seemed to be some kind of relevant local legend, but it involved a deluge of neutron-moderating fluid rather than electromagnetic radiation.

We brought up the fee again, and everybody got quiet. It seems the tribes never discuss trade in council; only the restraint of other tribes' trade. And then it turned out that they knew just about nothing about deuterium and didn't have enough of it collected in one place to be worth the loading aboard. And they'd never even *heard* of *wykoras kansi*. We asked what was locally valuable, and they named some easily-synthesized metals.

I had the Linker, who was jittery but not quite gone, scan some of them for what they actually thought was worth something. The first answer was universal, but I doubt that the novelty would last. The second is hard to export, there being only one Universe to be the absolute master of. We went past some things you wouldn't *believe*—and finally got to something called "oil." Stuff was Beastly near magical, so read the Linker—and it wasn't her fault, I suppose, poor worker.

Now, the thing about this "oil" was, no two tribal spokesmen visualized it the same way. With the valuable soft metal, they all had the same picture—shiny yellow ingots of it piled up—but "oil" was different. Some of them saw towers of some kind, some saw metal cylinders, some saw a sand field, some huge metal surface vessels—*now* do you perceive why the image didn't get across to us? Queen's curse on CommServ! —Apologies.

So we said we'd take a shipload of "oil." And they started protesting at once. There was one little cluster o tribes who seemed absolutely insane over the stuff. Finally we caught something about energy sources, and shortages—that was when we found out they had uncontrolled fusion but not generators.

So I said, may my mouth chew the Net forever, "Wil you sign the receipt if we add a d-pack to the exchange?' After all, the ship only needed two of its three; and I can' tell you how much I wanted to get off that place.

They called us "Bs," did I mention—it's the second symbol in their script system. Beeez—like the noise an airlock alarm makes. Maybe they called us after our speech pattern. Beeeeez—do I talk like that?

(Sobriety seemed to be taking a dreadful toll on the Captain. I told her that her voice was beautiful, nothing at all like an airlock alarm.) Well. There was a creature we observed during descent that resembled you, Informator, but it was called "moose."

Finally, with a hold full of "oil"—which seemed to be metal cylinders after all—off we went, hoping never to return.

And then . . . and then . . . sometimes, Informator, I think that we are all in the Great Beast's Net already, and we merely have not reached the cords. About a thousand light-turns out, we had a failure—and was it maneuver thrust? Was it waste recirculation? No. It was a d-pack, of course, putting us on half power. Which dropped us a full overlight quantum, so that a tenth-turn trip would now require a whole one.

As we crept along, our wings clipped, one of the Scientors aboard suggested we run tests on the priceless alien "oil," to discover its characteristics.

We found out. We had gotten a paid-in-full slip—given up our EconoServ expense subsidy—for a holdful of completely unrefined liquid hydrocarbons. A shipload of raw booze!

"So what did you do then?" I asked—the first time I'd had to prompt the Captain.

"What do you think we did? I apologize—your cognitive

brain is off, of course.'' She looked bitterly at my *chil* mug.
'We distilled it and drank it, of course. And drank it and
drank it—I must admit it was not bad stuff; but can you
imagine a full turn in space, drunk, with a crew in the same
condition? I Queen's-life wonder about those Earthi, living
with a solar period of only a tenth-turn, breathing an
atmosphere that'd sozzle any thinking creature.

''Now you know why I am not intoxicated, and may never
be again; at least, not until JustiServ finds a loophole in that
payment slip.''

I switched my nerves back and inclined my horns. I had
trade's worth, all right.

Well, now you know why so few of you on RC 7761,
known to many as Earth, get to hear things through the
Spacevine. Do you think the Captain would have told that
story to an, ah, Earthi? *I*'ve given you the story straight,
remember, just as it appears in release to All the Thousand.
Any omissions are the fault of your own people, just as it
wasn't our fault you chose to translate our turns into your
''years,'' misjudged the age of your returning ancestors, and
assumed that you were getting a shipload of early cavemen
or whatever. The RescueService Captain didn't say a *word*
about the Reethi being human, or primate, or even mammal.

But be of good cheer, Earthi. (Damn idiom pill again.)
Tonight, walk out on a street lit by the clean fusion power
we gave you as part of the deal, and then say something nice
to a Reethi—a name they prefer to what you called them
when you thought them extinct so many millions of turns,
or tens of millions of years ago—and of course they are a
lot smarter than the dinosaurs that *did* get wiped out by that
magnetic flare.

Remember, you *won* the horse trade.

*Jonathan Milos arrived in the United States a few months
after the Hungarian Revolution, ''of which I have several*

strong recollections, primarily that it did not succeed.'' He has commanded Soviet forces in war games against U.S. Army officers, plodded over battlefields in much of the English-speaking world, and been to Munich without an umbrella. He is the author of a number of obscure books and papers, is a recognized authority on vaguely defined areas of knowledge, and as a dinner speaker his popularity rivals that of Jean Armand du Plessis, whom he in no other way resembles. Asked to comment on his fiction, he points out that even Mussolini wrote a novel, ''and if Dorothy Parker would give me the same sort of review she gave him, life would hold no further terrors.''

PENNIES FROM HELL

by *Darrell Schweitzer*

A tale of madness, obsession, and loose change . . .

I met Jim Bowen for the first time in over ten years in a
Fifties Revival bar in Philadelphia. It was the sort of place
with posters of James Dean, Marilyn Monroe, and Elvis on
the walls, the waiters in regulation Duck's Ass hairdos, an
interior decorating style which can only be described as Art
Tacko, and of course, inevitably, a dance floor. The sign
over the entrance said: BOP TILL YOU DROP.

It wasn't Jimbo's style, but there he was. I called him
over to my table. He looked up, didn't seem to recognize
me at first, and then slid off his barstool, glass in hand, not
stumble-down drunk but walking, ah, *carefully*. That, too,
wasn't his style.

"You've changed," I said.

"Well, I'm *forty-three*, Chuckie-boy. I can still call you
that, I hope, for all you're a big-time novelist now. For me
the downhill slide into senility has already begun. Not much
longer and I'll be decrepit enough to get a job as an extra
in *Night of the Return of the Revenge of the Living Dead,
Part II.*"

I could tell that he was, as we literary types phrase it, into
his cups.

"This isn't like you."

"At least it's a grown-up obsession." He nodded toward
his glass.

I glanced at the picture of Roy Rogers and Trigger on the
wall behind him.

"So why are you suddenly worried about being grown-up
all the sudden?"

"You remember what I used to say, Chuckie-boy? In American society we remain adolescents until they issue us bifocals. Well, I wear contacts, but the time has come, as inevitably it must. I think that's why I come here." He lifted his glass and pointed one finger at Jimmy Dean, then at Elvis. "This place is a mausoleum of lost youth. It reminds us that time is passing."

"Awfully morbid of you, Jimbo, old buddy."

"Well, God damn it, I have every *right* to be morbid. Sometimes I get to thinking about Joe Eisenberg—"

"The cartoonist who . . . died?"

"Yeah. He was after your time. You'd gone off to commit literature by then."

"I met him in your office once," I said. "Besides, after I stopped writing for underground comics, I still read them, at least the ones you published. I loved Eisenberg's stuff. As far out as S. Clay Wilson, only he could draw. I particularly remember the upside-down face series, this guy with his nose pointing up, and corks with little crucifixes stuck in his nostrils, and the caption: *Damned uncomfortable, but it sure keeps the snot vampires away.* Great stuff, elegant, tasteful—"

"But he never grew up, and it was a childish obsession that killed him."

"I never knew exactly how he died."

Jim went back to the bar for another drink. I had a hunch I was going to need an excuse to linger for some time yet, so I called a waitress over and ordered a Brown Cow and a Wangadangburger.

My friend came back, sat down again, and drank in silence for several minutes. Then, finally, he said, "I suppose I've set myself up for this. I might as well tell you the whole story. You don't have to believe a word of it, but you can listen. Maybe you can use some of it in a book."

"Jimbo, I may have called you a lot of things, but never a liar."

"Just listen."

"Okay," I said.

"Well, the first thing you have to remember," Jim began, "is that Joe Eisenberg was like one of the characters in his own cartoons. Mock-pedantry was definitely his schtick. You *couldn't tell* when he was serious and when he wasn't. He'd explain something like the Spooch Theory in the driest professorial tone, like an arcane point of real linguistics.''

"The *what* theory?''

"The idea was that *spooch* is an inherently funny word on the phonetic level. The double-*o* sound is inherently funny. The *sp* sort of slides you in there, and the hard *ch* traps you inside the word, so the *oo* can resonate until it reaches the humor threshold. A soft sound at the end, and you'd escape. That's why *spoon* isn't funny, but *spooch* is.''

I snickered. Jim took another sip of his drink and said, "You *see?* That proves it. Or that's what Joe used to say. And he had lots more where that came from.''

"Weird.''

"Yeah, but creative people are allowed to be weird. The same secret committee that issues the bifocals assigns weirdness quotas, and underground comic-book artists get more than most people. And Joe was fun that way. We used to call him Spoocho Marx. The other Marx Brothers had locked him in the refrigerator and forgotten about him, sometime back in the '30s, so here he was. He looked the part too, like a dark-haired version of Harpo.

"But somewhere he went too far, and the silliness turned into craziness of a less pleasant sort. I think it began about a year after he'd started working for me, one evening in December. I was still prosperous then, and lived in the suburbs, and Joe and I used to go home on the same train.

"We had been working late over some storyboards. It was the beginning of Joe's *Miracles of Saint Toad* series that later got such a tremendous response in *Zipperhead Funnies*. He had the art wrapped in a plastic trashcan liner under one arm, and we ran for the train, the wind and rain blasting in our faces. I reached the entrance first, and I could hear the train rumbling in downstairs. We would have made it, but Joe suddenly called out, 'Jim! Help!'

"He'd spilled the artwork, all of it, half inside the doorway, half out. Rain splattered over the floor. Late commuters rushed in, not too careful where they stepped.

"I ran back and helped him recover it, but by then several panels had been ruined. They'd have to be redone. We missed the train, and had to wait another hour inside the station. Much of that time was spent drying the storyboards with paper towels from the men's room.

" 'How the Hell did you drop them?' I asked.

" 'Oh,' he said, digging into his coat pocket. 'Here's why.' He held up a penny. 'You know what they say, *See a penny, pick it up; all the day you'll have good luck—*'

" 'That was real dumb,' I said. 'Grade-A Idiota Maximus. You're running to catch a train, in the rain, and you're carrying art that took you days or even weeks to produce, and you risk it all for *one crummy cent.* Not what I would call sound financial planning, my dear fellow. Not at all.'

"He went on for a minute drying a spot where the ink had run badly, then he gave me his best Harpo smile and said, 'It isn't the money, Jimbo. It's more *luck.* If I don't have luck, I might lapse into superstition, which is *really* bad luck. It's where I get my inspiration from. I've found that out. It works like this: I have to find at least one penny every day. That's basic recognition from the gods.'

" 'The gods?'

" 'Yeah, Zeus and all that crowd. Nobody sacrifices oxen or goes to oracles anymore, so this is how they stay in touch with the few remaining faithful.'

" '*Uh-huh . . .*'

" 'Like I said, you find one penny a day and that's a sign that at least nothing disastrous will happen. Find more, or dimes or quarters, and you're ten times blessed, or twenty-five times, and things will turn out real nice. Find a bright, shiny penny, and something *new* will come into your life, while an old, tarnished thing means that you'll find something or do something which is old and familiar, but still good. It's a form of divination, I suppose. There are lots of ramifications. I could go on for hours.'

"He proceeded to do so. He explained away the accident with the art by the fact that he hadn't yet picked up a penny that day, and so was sailing under a curse, so to speak. But the evening would be better. He would probably get a lot of work done, or inherit money from a long-lost uncle, or hear from his old girlfriend, or something. The penny foretold it. He had a whole system worked out, as elaborate as anything in an astrology manual, and he was absolutely serious as he explained it all, in the station while we waited, then on the train all the way to his stop.

"Any other time it might have been hilarious, but I was thinking about deadlines and distributors, and the sort of scene my then-wife Carol was going to cause when I got home late and her special organic dinner was cold.

" 'Christ, Joe,' I said at last. 'I don't have time for this bullshit.'

"He turned to me, a hurt look on his face. 'It isn't bullshit,' he said quietly.

"Before I could say anything, the train arrived at his stop, and he got up and left.

"Things got rapidly weirder after that, but I didn't care, because Joe was hot. He was turning in great stuff. Before long I gave him his own book, *Saint Toad's Cracked Chimes*, and by the time the third issue was out and the returns were in on the first, I knew we had a hit. If he had discovered the secret of success by picking up pennies on the street, well, all I could say was more power to him.

"It's hard for me to think of any scene in what was left of his life that didn't have a penny in it. I mean, he found them *everywhere*. In a dark alley, during a *blackout*, for God's sake, he stopped, bent over, and said, 'Ah, here we go!'

"That summer we went to a comic-art convention in Boston. The two of us shared the taxi from the train station to the hotel, and, sure enough, there was a penny on the floor in front of him. He held it up to the window, doing his best Harpo act, and, true to character, whipped out an oversized magnifying glass and began to scrutinize the coin minutely.

" 'What do you expect to find on it, the secret of the ages?' I asked.

" 'Something like that, Jimbo.'

"Joe was a big success with the fans. He could be a real charmer when he wanted to be. But he got a lot of odd looks, always bending over to pick up pennies. There were a lot of jokes about how badly I paid my artists, that they had to scrounge change to stay alive. And once, in the middle of a panel discussion, all the microphones went dead.

Joe calmly unscrewed the top of his, shook it, and a penny dropped onto the tabletop. He gave the audience his trademarked grin, and there was nervous laughter, as if most people didn't get the joke.

" 'There's a fortune written on it,' he told them. 'It says: *You will find true love and get laid.*'

"That got a laugh, and, you know, the prediction came true, at least in part. There was a groupie in the audience, who used Joe's schtick to bait him . . . literally. She laid out a trail of pennies, up a flight of stairs, along a corridor, and under the door to her room. The door was unlocked. And that, to make a steamy story short, is how Joe Eisenberg lost his virginity, at the age of twenty-seven. Because the gods had revealed that he would, he told me afterward.

" 'I'm sure glad I picked up *that* penny,' he said.

"I think he used his silliness to hide social awkwardness. And somewhere along the line, all this very much ceased to be amusing.

"He found I don't know *how* many pennies during the remainder of the convention, and on the train ride back. The way he pounced on them told me that the totally overdone gag was turning into a mania. It was a wonder he didn't walk right into people. He was always scanning the floor, looking for pennies.

" 'Awright! Enough of this!' I told him in my best Graham-Chapman-as-a-British-Army-Officer voice. 'This has got to stop. It's getting silly.'

" 'I only wish it were, Jimbo,' he said softly, then turned to stare out the train window.

"It was early November when he came into my office one evening late with a stack of new artwork. Things were going badly for me by then, for all Joe's stuff sold better than anything else I had. The early '70s were bad times for undergrounds. Sex and obscenity had lost a good deal of their novelty, and the Moron Majority was after us. Head shops were closing, and with them went much of the distribution. Books that had sold seventy-five thousand copies five years previously now were lucky to do twenty thousand. And so I was *living* in that dingy office above the record store on

South Street. My suburban apartment, and my wife Carol, had gone in the course of belt-tightening.

"I was working late with some bills, and Joe knew I'd be there. He had a key and he just came in. I hardly glanced up.

"Just as he stepped through the door my Selectric jammed and began making a hideous rattle.

"Somehow he was expecting it. Joe dropped his artwork on a chair and ran to my desk, leaning over my shoulder, reaching into my typewriter with the longest pair of tweezers I have ever laid eyes on, and extracted—you don't have to guess—a shiny, new, goddamn *penny* from the innards of my typewriter. As soon as he did, the machine reverted to a contented hum.

"Out came the magnifying glass again. I knew better than to expect an explanation.

" 'This is great!' he said in something that was almost a tone of reverential awe. 'The pattern is complete. I have all the answers now.'

"Without another word, he left, not bothering to even discuss the artwork. But, as I said, I was pretty used to his, ah, eccentricities by now. So I just got up and looked at the art myself.

"And in a minute, I'd forgotten my troubles, how weird Joe was getting, and everything. The stuff was brilliant. It was the first of that final sequence of the *Saint Toad* strips, in which the warty sage sets out on his pilgrimage to find the Meaning of Life in the Land of Reversible Cups. I was laughing aloud. It was a breakthrough, which put Joe on a level with the immortal R. Crumb, or even a notch above.

" 'Wow,' I said to myself. 'Mister Natural, move over.'

"It was part of a sustained burst of creativity on Joe's part. I didn't see him much after that. He sent his stuff in Federal Express. There was enough there to keep *Saint Toad* going for several years. Weird, metaphysical stuff, all full of dooms and prophecies—and some of his predictions were just uncanny, as things turned out. You know, about the World Series and Comet Kohoutek and the President's brain.

"There were pennies in every panel. It became a trademark, a game, to see where he had hidden them. Even in the *Fantastic Voyage* parody sequence, where the hero sails a tiny submarine up his own asshole, if you look very closely, there's an Indian-head cent lodged in the pancreas.

"It was completely impossible for me to think of Joe Eisenberg without thinking of pennies, and vice versa. '*My God*,' I told myself, '*he must have buckets of them by now.*'

"By the time the following January came around, the sale of Joe's work was all that was keeping my operation afloat. So you can understand my alarm when I tried to call him one day and got a recorded message saying his phone had been disconnected.

"It was a mistake, I told myself. Or maybe he had just forgotten to pay the bill. I sent him a letter, certified, so he'd have to come to the door and sign for it.

"The letter was returned undeliverable.

"There was another Joe Eisenberg schtick that came to mind: mock-childish eagerness over the question, *Can we panic now? Huh? Huh? Can we?*

"*Yes,* I thought, *we can panic now*.

"I decided to pay him a visit. It was raining that evening as I walked to the train station. I couldn't help but think of the night when the penny-mania had all begun. Joe no doubt would have called it a sign from the gods, a meaningful symmetry or something.

"There was a discarded newspaper on the seat beside me as the train pulled out of Thirtieth Street and headed for the suburbs. I glanced out at the familiar scenes for a while, then picked up the paper. It was a back section, and there, under a snide headline, was a little piece about a 'local character,' the Penny Man, who spent whole days wandering the streets after loose change, the bulging pockets of his old overcoat jangling. For all there was no photo and no names were mentioned, I knew it was Joe.

"'*Oh shit*,' I muttered to myself, crumbling the newspaper. '*Oh shit . . .*'

"Joe lived on one of the few sleazy side streets in the posh Main Line town of Bryn Mawr, in an upstairs apartment over a drugstore. I went up the back stairs—wooden stairs outside the building—and tapped gently on his door. No answer. I peered through the glass. The apartment was dark. It was just my luck. Maybe he was out picking up pennies again, hoping to find the secret of the universe that way—and in my state of mind, I didn't doubt he could actually do it—or else the pennies had revealed that he should move without telling me. I was ready to believe anything.

"Then I heard slow, shuffling footsteps, a metallic clang, and the sound of coins pouring onto the floor, followed by incoherent obscenities. But I knew that tired, almost-sobbing voice.

"He opened the door, then lunged for my feet. I jumped back, startled. He picked up a penny off the mat, looked at it, then put it in his pocket and turned to go back inside.

" 'Not yet,' he said to himself. 'A little more time.'

"He made to shut the door, as if he hadn't noticed me at all.

" 'Joe, aren't you going to ask me in?'

" 'Uh, hello, Jim' he said, a little disoriented.

"I got a good look at him then, and I hardly recognized him. Now you'll recall that there were still a lot of hippies then, and squalor hadn't totally fallen into disfavor yet—but Joe had gone beyond acceptable limits. It was a cold, damp winter night, and there he was barefoot, wearing old jeans with both knees out, and a bathrobe held shut with safety pins. He hadn't shaved in at least a week, and he smelled like he hadn't bathed in twice that. And he was haggard, his face pale and sunken, his eyes bloodshot, his gaze wild and distracted. Like a crazy man's. Like the look you see on bag people, when they sit for hours in a corner somewhere, staring into nothing.

" 'How are you, Joe?'

" 'Jimbo, I'm . . . I knew you would come by eventually. I suppose you deserve an explanation. Come in.'

"I followed him silently along an unlighted corridor, stepping over boxes and piles of papers. His studio was a mess, paint chipping from the walls, trash in cardboard boxes heaped in corners, orange peels on the floor. Something moved behind the boxes. Maybe it was a cat, maybe not

"I wondered how he could work here. The only window looked out on a brick wall. The overhead light apparently didn't work, so the only illumination came from a small lamp he'd clamped onto his drawing table.

"I waded forward, careful not to step on any artwork, and looked at the drawing on the table. It was a rough pencil sketch of the opening spread for what turned out to be the final issue of *Saint Toad,* the scene where they sacrifice Little Nell to Odin. I was selfishly relieved to see that, for all Joe Eisenberg might be going mad, his creative powers were not failing. His stuff would continue to sell comic books.

"Still Joe didn't say anything. I turned away from the table, and began to scan the bookshelves, reading titles as best I could in the gloom. You know, you can tell a lot about someone by what is on their bookshelves. Joe was full of surprises. Oh, there were lots of comics, and the hardcover reprints of the E. C. classics, but also lots of classics in the literary sense. He had most of the Elizabethans, and even Latin and Greek writers. And there were scholarly books on religion, folklore, magic, that sort of thing. I could only make out a few titles: Franz Cumont books on Roman paganism, *The Hero with a Thousand Faces,* the Joshi translation of *Al Azif,* and a few more. Not what you'd expect for the average cartoonist. Of course Joe wasn't the average cartoonist, and his strips were fantastically erudite sometimes.

" 'Jim,' he said at last, 'you are probably wondering . . .'

" 'You could say that.'

" 'I'll bet you have.' Then he bent over and I noticed something I hadn't seen before. All along one wall was a row of buckets, and they were indeed filled with pennies. He picked up a handful of them, and let them dribble through his fingers. '*See a penny, pick it up; all the day you'll have good luck.* Do you know what the next verse is, Jimbo?'

" 'No, but I think you've going to tell me.'

" '*See a penny, leave it lay; death will claim you that same day.* I learned that from the Penny Elves. That's one of the many things they told me.'

" 'The what kind of elves?'

" ' Penny Elves, Jim. Like tooth fairies who have been

promoted, only they're not good enough to work for Santa Claus. I used to think it was the old gods, and that was a grand and serene and beautiful way to look at it—the Olympian powers exiled, forgotten, reduced to communicating to the few mortals who still acknowledge them by penny-divination. There's a certain pathos in the idea. But it isn't true. It's all the work of these loser elves. They resent the job. They want the prestige of being in the employ of the Big Claus, but they know they haven't made the grade. So they put us humans through the paces, just to make us look ridiculous. They bait the trap with real knowledge, real predictions, and lead us on.'

"He said all this with such conviction, such passive yet intense resignation, that the effect was *scary*. I can't put it any other way.

" 'Is this . . . like the Spooch Theory, Joe?'

Suddenly he was angry. I had never seen him angry before. He threw the remaining pennies down hard, and started shooing me toward the door.

" 'Forget it, Jimbo. You keep asking me if I can be serious. Well, *you* can't. That's pretty obvious. You won't understand. Don't worry about your goddamn artwork. You'll get it on time. What you need to worry about is, *What are you going to do when this starts happening to you?* Huh, Jimbo? What?'

"He slammed the door in my face. I stood there for a minute at the top of the stairs, stunned, and then I headed for the Bryn Mawr train station. There was nothing I could do. I had never felt so helpless in all my life. Joe had no family that I knew of, and I couldn't very well spend seventy-five dollars an hour—even if I had it—explaining to a shrink that I had *this friend* who was suffering from extraordinary delusions. What was left? Call up the police and tell them Joe was behaving irrationally? There are lots of irrational people in our society, and nobody cares a bit about them. You see them in every big city, sleeping on vents.

"So I caught the last train back into Philly and did nothing.

"I was disturbed to notice that there was an unusual

amount of loose change on the floor of the train car I was riding in. Nobody stooped to pick any of it up.

"Joe Eisenberg was as good as his word. He remained punctual until the end. His work came in on time, as brilliant and wonderful as ever. Somewhere in the deep recesses of his tangled mind, *genius* still remained. I don't use the word lightly. *Genius.*

"My own behavior in the following couple of months was selfish, even shameful. That whole scene had been a cry for help from a very disturbed individual, but I tried to put him out of my mind. He was an adult, I told myself, his own responsibility. I was his publisher, not his daddy.

"Mostly I retreated into my work. When I'd started out publishing undergrounds, it was a lark, a mixture of joking and idealism, a way of showing what we called The Establishment in those days that the true spirit of freaky America had not been stifled. I never imagined that it would become a desperate, grinding *business* frequently interrupted by messages from the sponsor, that is to say the landlord, who swore he would turn me and mine out on the sidewalk if the rent was late one more time. Then there were the artists. I managed to pay some of them, some of the time. I felt bad about that.

"But Joe never complained. He was faithful till the end.

"The end came on the last evening of April, Walpurgisnacht. I suppose that figured. I had been out most of the day, trying to find a secondhand typewriter to replace my Selectric, which had rattled and gurgled its last. When I got back to the office-cum-apartment, there was a package between the inner and outer doors, with no markings at all, save a single word scribbled on the back in magic marker: GOODBYE.

"I recognized Joe's handwriting, of course. I hurried inside and slit open the package. Several pennies fell out, onto the carpet. The package contained artwork, another—the final—installment of *Saint Toad's Cracked Chimes,* beginning with the sacrifice scene I'd seen on his drawing table during my visit. Well, fine, I thought. He's delivering them himself now.

"Then the phone rang. It was the printer, who wasn't

going to print the next *Zipperhead* unless I paid him for the jobs he'd done on the previous *four*. As soon as I got myself out of that one, another artist called and threatened to *go on strike* if I didn't pay him what I owed him.

"One thing followed another, and I didn't manage to even think of Joe again until quite late that night. It must have been around eleven when I noticed that one of the coins on the rug was much larger than the others. I picked it up. It wasn't an American penny, but a very old, large-sized British one, with Queen Victoria on the front.

"On the back were the words: WATCH THIS SPACE FOR FURTHER DEVELOPMENTS.

"I dropped it with a yelp, as if it were red hot. I was sure I was seeing things, going a bit mad myself. The coin lay on the rug at my feet, the message fading in and out: WATCH . . . WATCH . . . WATCH . . .

"Then the phone rang one more time. I assumed it was another creditor. It's never too late at night when people are after you for money.

" 'Hello!' I snarled.

"It was Joe. He sounded exhausted, his voice cracking as he spoke. I think he had been crying.

" 'Jim,' he said. 'You've been good to me, as good as anyone. I think you ought to know. It's too late to do anything for me, but I ought to tell you the truth.'

"There was a long pause, as if he couldn't bring himself to speak.

" 'What is it, Joe?' I asked him gently. 'You can tell me.'

" 'It isn't elves. There are no such things as Penny Elves.'

"For an instant I felt a rush of relief, as I hoped that somehow Joe had snapped out of it, had become sane again. But he didn't sound any saner. If anything, he sounded worse.

" 'It's *devils*,' he said. 'Devils right out of Hell. A special subdivision of them. They work for Mammon, the demon of avarice, and they lead people to damnation through, well . . . *money*. I made a pact with them, Jim. I did it before I knew who they really were. It all started as a game, picking up pennies, tying them in to coincidences, pretending they were omens and prophecies. But then, somehow, I discovered that they *really worked*. Forbidden knowledge, Jim. That's what it was. They told me . . . all sorts of things . . . wonderful, terrible. I made a deal. I wanted to be good, Jim. I wanted to be the best, so I made a deal, and I learned how to read the signs more closely than ever before. That's where my inspiration came from, *Saint Toad*, all the rest. Made in Hell. You know what they say about me—devilishly funny.'

" 'No, Joe,' I said. 'This is crapola. It's *you*. You're a genius. It comes out of *your* head. You didn't get it off the back of any stupid penny.'

" 'The back, Jimbo? How did you know the message is always on the back? I never told you that.'

"I looked down at the coin on the rug. There, on the back of it, was something new: JOE IS DYING.

" 'Joe!' I said. 'Don't do anything! Stay where you are! I'm coming out there right now!'

" 'I appreciate the thought, my friend, but you can't help me. They're coming for me tonight. They're coming to collect on an old debt. They told me this, on the last penny I found.'

"He babbled for a while after that. I could barely make out one word in five. Then he was weeping, and reciting poetry:

'*Cut is the branch that might have grown full straight,
and burned is Apollo's laurel-bough,
That sometime grew within this learned man.
Faustus is gone; regard his hellish fall,
Whose fiendful fortune may exhort the wise—*'

" 'I'm coming out there,'' I said, and hung up on him.

"I ran for the train station, only to find when I got there that I had missed the last train. I was desperate. I would have to take a cab, but then I realized that I didn't have enough money on me.

"The floor of the train station was littered with coins, which no one else seemed to notice. A cop paced calmly, kicking hundreds of nickels and dimes this way and that.

"I didn't look at any of them. They burned in my hands as I gathered them, but after a few minutes I had my pockets full, just like the Penny Man the newspaper writer had found so amusing.

"It was a long ride to Bryn Mawr. I didn't even bother to ask the cabbie why there was so much loose change on the floor in the back of his cab. Something scratched beneath the seat, and I thought I caught a whiff of sulfur. This same cabbie was more surprised than angry when I paid my fifteen-dollar fare with a double handful of coins.

"'You count it!' I yelled, as I ran up the stairs to Joe's apartment.

"There was a thunderous racket coming from the alley beneath the studio window. Coins were pouring out, rattling off the tops of trashcans like rainwater. When I got to Joe's door, the sound from inside was like what you'd hear if every slot machine in Atlantic City hit the jackpot at once.

"Of course I was too late. He was already dead by the time I forced open the door and crawled the length of that hall, through three or four *feet* of loose change, which seemed to wriggle and heave beneath me, while millions of coins poured out of the darkness overhead, battering, nearly suffocating me.

"I think Joe had been trying to draw at the very end. His table was still standing, and there were a few random lines across a sheet of paper clamped there. His stool was buried. I dug frantically.

"I found him at last, facedown on the floor, half underneath the drawing table. I pulled him to the surface and clung to him, as if somehow that would do some good, but he was already dead. I just sat there for a while as the coins rained down and the whole structure of the building creaked from the weight of them. My mind blanked out. His corpse was a kind of life preserver. I hung on because I couldn't let go. I was still holding him when the police arrived."

Jim Bowen stopped talking, and took another sip of his drink. My Wangadangburger had gotten cold on the plate. The waitress was staring at us.

"That's the story," he said. "I don't expect you to believe it, but that's the story."

"Wait a goddamn minute," I said, almost convinced I was the victim of the most inscrutable, poker-faced put-on in history. "You can't end it *there*. I mean, the police find you half-buried in something like forty million dollars worth of small change, and Joe Eisenberg is in your arms, crushed to death—you must have had quite a time explaining."

"He wasn't crushed. He'd choked on a single coin. Otherwise the apartment was its usual mess. All those pennies were gone."

"Except the one he'd choked on."

"That wasn't a penny, Chuck. It was a *solidus*."

"A *what?*"

"An ancient Roman coin, gold, about the size of a nickel. The figure on it was Julian the Apostate, who was the last emperor to honor the old gods. He was heavily into divination, I understand."

"But what has that got to do with—?"

"I think the devils, or whatever they were, thought it would make a particularly fine finishing touch, that's all. It was embedded in his esophagus. A doctor showed it to me after the autopsy."

I didn't know what to say next. Jim Bowen seemed so sincere about all this. That, as he'd put it, was the scary part.

I rose to leave.

"I suppose it is about that time," Jim said.

The waitress came with our checks on a little tray. I reached for my wallet, but Jim said, "No, you listened to my story. I'll treat you."

He put some bills down, and the waitress took them away. Then he picked up his napkin. There were coins under it, nickels, dimes, but mostly pennies.

He recoiled in disgust, as if the tabletop were covered with live spiders.

What are you going to do when this starts happening to you? Joe Eisenberg had supposedly asked. Jim was clearly wondering. So was I, just a little bit.

I thought he was going to faint. But instead, very gingerly, he brushed the tabletop clear.

Then the waitress came back, offering him a little tray.

"For God's sake! *Keep the change!*"

Darrell Schweitzer is a prolific writer of short stories, and has been published in Twilight Zone, Amazing, Night Cry, Whispers, *and other magazines and anthologies. He has published two novels,* The White Isle *and* The Shattered Goddess, *and two story collections,* Tom O'Bedlam's Night Out *and* We Are All Legends, *along with numerous reviews, essays, poems, nonfiction anthologies, and interviews. He is currently co-editor of* Weird Tales.

Darrell remarks that "Pennies from Hell" is all true, *"except for the parts that aren't," and the Fifties Revival bar described therein actually did exist in Philadelphia a couple of years ago, for all he never sampled either the Brown Cow or the Wangadangburger. Further, he actually did save up all the found money he had come upon in a single year, counting it on New Year's Eve as part of an occult ritual, and discovered that the awesome Meaning of Life and Mystery of the Universe is $50.63.*

NOT POLLUTED ENOUGH
by George H. Scithers

Sometimes one being's meat is another's toxic waste . . . or vice versa . . . or lunch.

"Now take pollution—" began Professor Timble, raising his voice over the rumble of the club car's wheels on the trackwork at Mollusc Junction.

"*You* take pollution," said Mrs. Jonas, a bit sourly. The last hand had been a perfect disaster. Old Dr. Wimple usually played superb bridge with a couple of Manhattans, but Ricky, the club-car attendant, must have mixed them stronger than usual.

"No, no, I mean figuratively," said Professor Timble. "Not that way either," he added hastily, with a glance at old Dr. Wimple. The doctor, who was looking a bit glassy-eyed, ignored him. "I mean all this excitement about DDT and so on, all this political issue-making—"

"Issue-making?" said Mrs. Jonas. "*Political?* With the California brown pelican practically extinct already, and human milk—you know"—she made a gesture, at once explicit and ladylike—"with more parts per million or whatever than the WPA people allow—"

"You mean FDA," said Professor Timble. "Food and Drug Administration. That's what I was talking about. They set the limits far too low, really. People aren't affected by DDT at those levels; it's all a headline hunt. The stuff's no more poisonous than aspirin. And when you consider how many lives have been saved from malaria, and that typhus epidemic in Naples during the war—"

"Jus'—I mean, just means there'll be more people t' starve, next time there's a crop failure," said old Dr. Wimple.

"But with DDT, the insect damage—"

"An' wha' happens next time there's a drought?" asked the doctor. "DDT *and* medicine, they're the banes of—of humanity, lately." He beckoned to the attendant. "Ricky? Here."

"Now look," said Professor Timble. "Have you ever *seen* a case of anybody dying because of DDT? Or heard of one, even? This parts-per-million stuff—"

"What about these crop dusters you hear about, coming down with convulsions and things," interrupted Mrs. Jonas. She gathered the cards, folded her hands on top of them. "And those grape-pickers—or am I thinking of the lettuce people? Anyway—"

Old Dr. Wimple blinked at the cup of coffee Ricky had brought for a moment, then sighed, "I suppose you're right." He drank, took a deep breath, and drank again. He turned to Professor Timble's partner and said, "You're always taking the unpopular side in an argument, Jim. Why don't you say something?"

Jim looked up from the score pad and grinned. "In the first place, biology isn't my field."

"That never stopped you before, when you wanted to argue."

"True, true." Jim scribbled a last sum and pocketed the pad. "In the second place, though, both sides of the argument seem pretty well represented already. Both wrong, unfortunately, but well represented."

"Wrong?" snapped Mrs. Jonas. "What's your theory, then?"

"It isn't theory that's wanted here, but data and experience. Of course, you can still draw the wrong conclusions from right data, like Columbus being so convinced that the world was only eight thousand miles in circumference when—"

"Now, now, young man," said Mrs. Jonas, "don't wriggle out of it. You said we're both wrong. Prove it."

"Well, I've but a couple of data, but they do make for a pretty strange story—"

"Go 'head. My bridge isn' too good today," said Dr. Wimple. He took another slurp of coffee, then burped gently.

Jim grinned again. "It happened a little over a year ago, when my company had a government contract to make some mods on a big radio navigation transmitter down in the South Pacific. Now, you got to remember that the South Pacific goes all the way down to the Antarctic, and this island was so small a heavy wake would have sunk it. I never did find out whether the U.S. actually owns the island, or just rents it from the French or Norse or somebody. It's too small for most maps, even. Also, being too small for a proper landing strip and out of 'copter range of anything big, the place is *really* isolated.''

"And you had oil slicks washing up on the beach?'' asked Mrs. Jonas, as she tucked the cards back into her cardcase.

Jim shook his head. "Like Thor—you know who I mean— or is it Cousteau?—writing about mid-ocean oil? We didn't see anything like that; too far south, I suppose. We did *talk* about pollution, though, when we weren't trying to get the transmitter to work—me, the other tech rep, and the dozen Coast Guard guys that made up the whole population of the island. One of 'em was a biologist, and he and Ralph—'' Jim paused, remembering the clean, chill whip of the wind, salted by thousands of miles of blue water; remembering the sound of breakers on the half-submerged rocks that shielded the little isle, the sound of wind whistling over the concrete building and whining through the lattice of the transmitting antenna. He frowned, remembering the easy grin of Ralph, the biggest of the Coastguardsmen, as he argued with Ted one morning as they stood in front of the island's one building.

"It was about DDT that they were arguing, that very morning," Jim said slowly. "Ted had been studying biology before he signed up for a hitch in the Guard, and he was trying to convince Ralph . . .''

"I hear what you're sayin' O.K., Ted," Ralph interrupted at last, "but I been handlin' the stuff all my life, practically swimmin' in it. The County Agent always says, pour the DDT on heavy; and Pop and me, we sure did. And with sprayin' and dustin' and all, I must of got me soaked about as well as the crops, and it never hurt me any. What I really wish'd be for me to get enough in me to kill mosquitoes and things when they take a nip. That would—''

"Never work," said Ted, shaking his head. "Didn't you

listen t' what I been telling you, Ralph? Besides, even if that much DDT didn't screw up *your* metabolism, the stuff'll get stored in your fat, not your bloodstream. So by the time—"

"Well, it was a good idea, even if it wouldn't work. Not much place to store the stuff in me, as little fat as I'm carryin', just muscle." He patted the solid bulge of biceps swelling his uniform sleeve, then grinned complacently.

"How 'bout between the ears?" asked another man who stood in the doorway of the concrete building, a few feet away.

"Now look," said Ralph, "who went and found that bad cap in the driver stage of the transmitter yesterday? And who got the generator started the day before, when you'd been workin' on it for—"

"O.K., O.K., you win," said the man in the doorway, throwing up his hands. "Hey, you and the tech reps gonna take the transmitter down again this morning? If you are, I want to work on the generator cut-over circuit some more."

The men scattered then, to the day's work. Just before lunch, a yell of "Everybody out here to catch this action—hey, you guys, outside—*quick!*" brought everyone running. Jim followed Ralph out the door, then bounced off his broad back when the big man stopped short.

"What *is* it?" asked someone.

"A—a moon rocket or somethin'?"

"Can't be; we'd of heard, and—"

"Maybe Russian? Gawd, that thing's *big!*"

Jim worked his way through the little crowd and looked up. The thing—whatever it was—looked like a small oil refinery wrapped rather tightly around a large, illuminating-gas storage-tank, and the whole affair—nearly a quarter the size of the whole island—was descending for a landing. A set of antenna-tower guy wires was in the way. Beams of light lanced out from the top of the gigantic thing and found the guys. In a moment, they glowed red, then they parted.

"Hey! You stop that!" yelled Ralph. He dashed forward, shook his fist up at the descending thing, then retreated cautiously as it majestically settled onto the island.

Behind him, Jim heard the antenna tower, with one set of guy wires gone, topple into the sea, but none of the men turned to watch its fall. Every eye was on the thing that towered over them.

"Now what?" said Ralph. "Ted, you're in charge; aren't you supposed—my Gawd! Look at that—at those—"

Hatches had popped open around the lower circumference of the thing, and animals—creatures—*things* were scuttling out. They were, Jim saw, about man-sized, with upright bodies, but there were four legs supporting the chunky hip structure, and those legs, though thick and straight, bent outward at the joints, so that the creatures moved with a strangely bowlegged, almost crab-wise scuttle. The arms were hardly manlike either; the creatures held them half-raised, half-folded, but for a few that were carrying various objects. And as for the heads—Jim looked, swallowed hard, and shuddered.

"Well, at least they ain't the Russians," said a voice from the back of the little huddle of humans.

"But what *is* it?"

"Flying saucer, silly."

"Some damn saucer. Hey, Ralph, say somethin' to 'em!"

"Uh, what'll I say?" asked Ralph, turning to look at the men clustered behind him, then jerking his head back to keep an eye on the advancing horde. One, carrying a two-foot cube, scuttled within a couple of yards, put the cube down on the sand, and stood motionless while another creature—about a foot taller than the rest—moved slowly up to the cube.

The tallest creature chattered his mandibles for a second, then the cube bellowed, "RITUAL INITIAL GREETINGS!"

Everyone jumped; Jim saw Ralph wince, then heard the big man growl, "Not so damn loud; we're not deaf—least, not yet."

The cube chattered; the tallest creature chattered back. The cube spoke again, "Ritual and appropriate apologies, we give you. Your deafness, we do not intend. So, English, we are speaking?"

"Uh—ah—you mean, are we speaking English?" asked Ralph. "Yeah, sure. But we're United States—uh—I mean, we're Americans and—"

While Ralph explained, Jim took a careful look at the

creature. The sturdy torso and thick limbs seemed to be encased in some kind of armor or shell—like a crab? No, the legs were too thick for a crab, and there weren't enough of them. Still, it reminded him of something familiar . . . He turned to Ted, touched his shoulder. "What—?"

"Extraterrestrial," said Ted, almost in a whisper. "But that isn't saying anything, really. Six limbs, and those jaws! I'd say it's a kind of giant insect, redesigned for the size, semi-graviportal legs and a good circulatory system, only—"

"Like one of those—whatcha-call-ems—praying mantises?" asked someone behind Jim.

Jim took a deep breath. The creature had none of the spidery grace of a mantis, but it was built along the same general plan. Maybe.

"No way," said Ted, firmly. "If it's extraterrestrial— extrasolar, too—it couldn't be related to any of our insects. It just happens—"

"Speaking one at a time, we ask you!" the cube said loudly. The tallest creature pointed a claw-tipped arm at Jim and resumed chattering his mandibles; the cube spoke a second later. "Speaking several at a time, you confuse the speak circuit."

"Uh, that's a—a translation machine?" asked Jim.

"Ritual and appropriate apologies, the wrong word we used. This, a translation machine is. So, similar to us, you have an insect?"

Jim was still puzzling out the sentence when Ted nodded, said, "Yes," and held up a hand with thumb and forefinger spread to show size. "Little thing, like so. But you can't be *related* to our—"

"On this island, you have not any?" interrupted the cube. Ted shook his head; the chattering creature and its translating machine went on: "Incompletely, we explored this planet; although many times, we have visited it. Ritual apologies, but the word *related* confuses us. Related, meaning common ancestors, we are not to your insects. But related, meaning of the same meat, we are precisely like so."

Ted asked, "You mean you're really—uh—just the same

as insects, only bigger and smarter and—and you evolved on another planet and all?''

"We are so," the creature said through his translating cube. "By the nature of things, only the five chief kinds of large land life are possible. As every mid-school Dreth knows, these five occur—but for a life-science lecture, we are not with an appropriate instant. But, on full intereatability, we assure you.''

"Uh—intereatability?" asked Ralph.

"A word of your language, it is not?'' The creature opened his claws wide in what seemed to be the equivalent of a shrug. ''Ritual apologies; new your language is to our translation machine. In different words I say my meaning. So: safely and easily, we Dreth and you internal skeleton animals can eat each other.''

"*Eat* each other!" said Ralph. "Now look here—"

"Cool it, Ralph," said Ted. "He doesn't mean the—uh—Dreth go around eating people, just—" He turned to the tallest of the insectile Dreth and asked, ''What have you been eating, anyway? Around here, about the only thing would be whales and porpoises and—''

"Whales? The large ocean air-breathing animals about eighteen glirts in size?'' asked the tallest visitor. "To us, *you* should give ritual apologies. Being now rare animals in risk of disappearing, of course we do not eat them. Ever conscious of the balance of life, we Dreth do not do such things. Always after proper study of abundances and overpopulation, we establish our feeding routes. So, if tilted is the balance of life, we do to restore it. So also, if overpopulations we find, then therefore—''

"*What* feeding stations?'' asked Ralph abruptly.

"In our interstellar journeys, we establish stopping places for feeding our crews. For carrying adequate prey aboard, our ships are too small.''

"Too small?'' snorted Ralph, glancing up at the spaceship that towered over them all. "Just what are you leadin' up to, anyway?'' he demanded.

"Since at last you have asked, it is no longer impolite to say this,'' said the Dreth. "Ritual apologies nevertheless, but your kind are too numerous for the balance of life on your planet. So also, in selecting your own feeding, your kind does yet more harm to the balance of life. In our recent survey, the air poisons from your population clusters we—''

"O.K., O.K., what are you bugs plannin' to do about it?'' asked Ralph. The broad-shouldered man stood a pace in front of the rest of the men, facing the tallest Dreth with the translation cube at his feet. "Kill us off with A-bombs or poisons or somethin'?''

The tallest Dreth drew himself up to his full height and clattered his claws for a moment, while the cube said, "Expression of extreme anger!'' The Dreth's mandibles chattered, and the cube went on with, "Ritual apologies, I should demand of you. Your question is a great discourtesy. That we Dreth are without the science of the balance of life, you are suggesting? This is quite—but I forget, you are still primitive.'' He snapped his claws again; Jim saw the chelae were somewhat like both the pincers of a crab and the grasping arms of a mantis.

"So,'' continued the tallest Dreth, "many dozens of erbtors ago, when your kind were not so numerous, a regular stopping place this planet was. Since they were in proper numbers then, whales we took. So, since even then your kind were not rare, for variety we would catch an ocean vessel or even on one of the islands to the north we would land—''

"The *Marie Celeste*—that ship with the crew gone,'' gasped someone behind Jim.

"Been enough ships vanished without a trace,'' said Ted. "Maybe *that's* why the Polynesians were that way about cannibalism.''

"Perhaps,'' said the tallest Dreth, through the translation machine at his feet. "You are of their tribe? Most excellent and admirable, we found them.''

"No,'' said Ralph.

"Ritual apologies,'' replied the Dreth. "But traffic lapsed for many dozen erbtors, during the Nurithan disturbances.'' He shuffled all four of his feet for a moment. "So now, the disturbances being disposed of, I and this scoutship and my crew are re-establishing the interstellar routes. So also, the feeding stations, we—''

"Hey! You're not going to—to eat one of *us!*'' interrupted Ralph.

"Minor apologies; not one, all."

"*All* of us? But you can't—" Jim glanced around; the little group of men was surrounded by the man-high Dreth now. "Look, there's lots of bigger islands—maybe up north—"

"Jim," objected Ralph, "we can't send these—these things somewheres else. They'll—damn, they'll do us in. But—"

"Perhaps," said the tallest Dreth, "a demonstration we can show you?"

He pointed to the island's one tree, then drew back his claw. "The plant I should not damage. Instead, the corner of the building." He pointed there, clicked his pincers twice. Light, white and intense, beamed down from the top of the spaceship, and a cubic foot of concrete exploded into dust. "So," the Dreth said through the cube, "of the uselessness of resistance, we have—"

"Yeah, yeah, we're convinced," growled Ralph. "That and gettin' outnumbered by a hundred or so to fourteen." He bit his lip, then turned to Ted. " 'Member what we were talkin' about this mornin'?"

"Yes, but—"

"Might work?"

"If it doesn't—" Ted glanced at the waiting Dreth. "You going to—uh—take us all at once, or—"

"One at a time, we would prefer. So, in this way, any indigestion will be restricted to the first feeders. Does your custom—"

"One at a time," said Ralph, firmly. "And me first."

"But I'm the senior," objected Ted. "I'm in charge; I should—"

"Ted, shut *up*," growled Ralph. "If this doesn't work, you can get ate next all you like, but I'm goin' first if I gotta paste you one."

"Ritual apologies for interrupting a discussion," said the tallest Dreth via the translator, "but our custom is to save the biggest and best to last. With appropriate apologies for touching on your customs, why—"

Ralph yanked off his shirt, tossed it aside. He glared at the Dreth, then ripped off his trousers and kicked them away.

I don't give a howlin' hoot fer your damn customs,'' he growled. "I'm goin' first 'cause I want to. O.K.?''

The Dreth spread his pincers wide; behind him, the rest of his horde pressed close, pincers twitching. One, standing just behind the tallest, chattered his mandibles; the translation machine picked up his remark as, "Extreme fortune; he is in moult!''

Another chatter of mandibles came through: "He is shedding his integument. The records did not mention—''

"O.K.,'' said Ralph, completely stripped now. "What next? Do I go in your kitchen and get cooked there, or do you bring the stuff out here or what?''

"No, no, we'll eat you right here,'' replied the tallest of the insectile Dreth. "Is there something—?'' he asked, at Ralph's startled yelp.

"No, there's an old joke—well, it isn't very funny this way. But, aren't you going to—''

"Quite unbearable, your insults are becoming,'' interrupted the Dreth. "You should submit a major ritual apology for even hinting that we would eat you without a pain-stop spray first.'' He gestured; a smaller Dreth scuttled forward, thrust a small implement under Ralph's nose. Jim heard a hiss, saw Ralph sneeze. "So, in a moment you should have no pain feeling. Now about that apology—''

"I'm gettin' ate alive; isn't that enough apology for ya?'' growled Ralph. In a calmer tone, he went on, "What is that stuff, anyway?''

"General purpose pain-stop for internal skeleton animals,'' explained the small Dreth. "Quick acting and, of course, not persisting; none of any civilized race's chemicals persist, you know. There should be enough interval now. Would you pinch yourself anywhere?''

Ralph did. He looked surprised, pinched harder. "Damn! It works,'' he said. Jim saw the small Dreth move in again, pincers extended. "Hey!'' Ralph said, looking up at the tallest of the giant insects. "Aren't you goin' to—you know—lead off?''

"Ritual apologies I give you for even hinting such a thing,'' said the tallest Dreth, "but in case you should be unsuitable eating, it is our custom—but I should be intro-

ducing you to my spouse's second eldest brother, who ha
the honor to have the post of first taster of the expedition.

"Yeah, yeah," growled Ralph, frowning down at th
small Dreth. "Glad t' meet ya, I suppose. Only—"

Professor Timble interrupted with a firm, "I don't believ
it."

"Now really," said Mrs. Jonas. "Don't be rude. I know
what you think about saucers and things, but—"

"No, no, that's not it at all. I just can't see a man *volun
teering* to go first, much less being polite to the little horro
that was about to start—" The professor took a long drin
of his whiskey and soda.

"He wasn't, as you put it, being all that polite," said Jim
defensively. "Anyway, he was just—you know—still, it wa
pretty brave," he added, shaking his head as he remembere
Ralph glaring at the Dreth.

"*That* brave?" Professor Timble took another sip of hi
drink.

"Oh, come now," said Old Dr. Wimple. "Did the la
play bridge? No? Well, it shtill—sorry—still applies. Th
way the morning paper's bridge writer keeps saying, if yo
can make your bid only if the cards lie a particular way, the
you have to play the hand as if they do lie that way." H
sighed. "I'm not making it very clear, am I?"

"No, no; I mean yes," said Mrs. Jonas. "You mean if—
ah—Ralph's DDT didn't work, they'd get to him no matte
whether he was first or last in line; but if the DDT did wor
after all, they'd have to—to eat him to find out, so th
sooner the better, at least for the rest of you." She smiled
"Of course, Jim, your being here does spoil the story'
suspense."

"Sorry to disappoint you like that," said Jim. "It wa
pretty damn suspenseful for us on the island, that morning
especially for Ralph."

"Only, if you guys are all that worried about us being
intereatable—" Ralph turned and loped toward the island'
one building, calling back over his naked shoulder, "Bac
in a sec. And Ted, if they get t' chompin' at th' bit, stall."

After a short, uneasy wait, another of the Dreth scuttle

ver to the tallest of the giant insects; the pair chattered
mandibles for a few seconds. Then, the tallest Dreth turned
to the waiting men; the cube translated his words: "A minor
zoology, but a question is asked. The word *stall,* used by
our first-to-be-eaten but now-for-the-moment-departed-one:
did he command you to delay for an interval of time, or is
that you have an accommodation for horses?"

To Jim, Ted whispered, "What'n hell do I do now?"

"Like Ralph said, *stall,*" hissed Jim. Inspiration struck.
Get real insulted; demand an apology for everything in
sight. The way these bugs are on politeness and—"

"How *dare* you?" yelled Ted, taking a long pace
forward. "The very *idea!*" He snatched off his cap, hurled
to the ground, and jumped on it with both feet. The tallest
Dreth backed up a scuttling step; most of his horde retreated
two. "Never in the history of—of—of *history* has so
insulting an—an insult been m-made!" Ted continued.
Calling us horses, are you?" He jumped on his cap again,
ground his heels into it, then yanked his shirt off, over his
head, and began to rip it to shreds. "Horses indeed," he
growled, hurling bits of cloth this way and that. He stopped,
pointed at the little island's one building. "Does *that* look
like the work of horses?" He grabbed a handful of his
undershirt, jerked hard, and tore it half off his torso. "Do I
look like a horse?" he yelled, snatching off the rest of his
undershirt in grabs and handfuls. "Does he—or him—or
him—do they look like horses?" he demanded, pointing at
one man, then another.

Ted stood a moment, panting, then stalked forward until
he stood just inches from the tallest Dreth. "WELL?" he
bellowed.

"Most major and intense apologies," replied the chief
Dreth, retreating another sidelong pace. "The translation
the—the language—our ignorance—that you are to delay an
interval of time, it is now clear. So—"

Jim took a deep breath, strode forward. "Oh, that's it,"
he snarled. He swallowed hard, forced a scowl on his face.
"First you insult us by calling us horses, and now you say
we're stalling—calling us cowards—claiming we're afraid!"
His voice broke on the last word. He swallowed again,
glanced around desperately. "Here he is," he said, putting

a hand on Ted's bare shoulder, "m-moulting his—I mean
stripping off his clothing, practically climbing into your-
your c-claws, and you say he's *stalling?*"

"Hey!" came a yell from the building. Jim stopped
searching for his next words, whirled, and stared. Ralph, still
naked, was trotting toward the group of men and Dreth, with
a package under one arm and what looked like a large ham
in his hands. "I *told* you guys to wait till I got back," Ralph
said, as he joined the group.

"I *was* waiting, but these things—you know." Ted jerked
his thumb at the waiting crowd of giant insects. "Wait a
minute; that's the ham for lunch."

"Yeah?" Ralph grinned, lifted it to his mouth, and bit out
a big chunk. "Good, too," he mumbled as he began
chewing, then held out the ham to a nearby Dreth. "Before
you begin trying us out, take a few bites of this first, see if
we're really as intereatable as you say."

The Dreth scuttled backwards a step, waving its antenna
suspiciously. "Do you mean you do eat each other after all?
In that case, an apology—"

"Nope," said Ralph. "Just ham. Off of hogs. I'll take
another bite, while you're making up your minds." He
started to raise the ham to his mouth again, but the closest
Dreth scuttled to him and snatched the meat from Ralph's
hands. "Hey, there," said Ralph. "There's no call for ya to
get grabby; I was just gonna take one more bite."

"Ritual apologies," said the Dreth with the ham, "but
you were seeming about to devour it all for yourself." The
creature lifted the ham in its claws, rotated it for a moment,
then started to nibble. There was a moment of frozen silence
while the rest, men and Dreth, watched a quarter of the ham
disappear. Finally the little Dreth lowered the ham, licked
its mandibles clean, and announced, "Delicious!"

"Well, I suppose so," sighed Ralph. He pulled the
package from under his arm and unwrapped it.

"What are you doing with that?" demanded the station's
cook, from the huddled group of Coastguardsmen. "That
corned beef was for supper."

"Way I figger it," said Ralph, "either we won't be
around for supper, or else we'll be having more of a
celebration than corned beef's good for." He took a bite of

e beef, then said, "Not bad, though." He chewed for a
oment. "Lemme take another bite, before you—hey,
ere!" One of the Dreth had grabbed the corned beef away
om Ralph; now, out of Ralph's reach, the creature was
rying its mandibles in the pink meat.

"Medium apologies," said the tallest Dreth, "but they
ve been for so long' without variety in their diet that they
e being hasty." He gestured at the surrounding crowd of
reth, where the remains of the ham were going from claw
claw, with each biting off a mandible-full before passing
on. "They are forgetting that, since we will eat you,
thing of what you devour beforehand will be lost to us."

"Uh, you eat *everything*?" asked Ted. "Innards and all?"

"Rudeness is a custom among you internal-skeleton
ings, it appears to me," said the tallest Dreth, while the
anslation cube put a tone of disapproval into the words.
No civilized being would leave the landscape littered, nor
ave eatable parts uneaten. Even the bones, especially if you
e stiffened with calcium and phosphate, will be devoured
the last." A sharp grinding noise interrupted it; when the
isc subsided, the Dreth went on, "That was the bone of
e ham, I believe. Now, your first-to-be-eaten?"

Ralph gulped hard, paled, but stepped bravely up to the
ief Dreth. "Aren't ya gonna wait until there's been time
r—"

"It would be a discourtesy to keep you waiting longer,"
id the Dreth. "Clearly our previous expeditions found your
anet's meat proper, and the small sample you provided has
en assimilated without distaste. We Dreth metabolize
ickly. That you ate from your samples shows no poison
s been added; a minor apology, but thoughts such as this
ust be thought on a not recently visited planet. Now, the
rst taster again." He gestured; the small Dreth—Jim
ssumed it was the one who had been introduced before—
uttled to Ralph, claws at the ready.

"Hey, don't grab me *there*," protested Ralph.

"Is not the pain-stop effective?" asked the small Dreth.
It is just the right—"

"Look, who's gettin' ate, me or you?" growled the big
an. "As long as it's me, you'll do it my way!" He
owled at the Dreth, then patted his rump. "Start here."

"As you insist," said the small Dreth, reluctantly letti
go its first hold and moving around to Ralph's side. T
small Dreth spread its mandibles, reached for Ralph's hi
Jim felt his own stomach turn over; he looked hastily awa

Jim saw some of the men watching in sick fascinatio
others had squeezed their eyes shut. One man, the cook, h
turned almost green. The Dreth, however, were all watchi
with what Jim could only interpret as avid interest. At leas
all but one that was beginning to twitch its antenn
aimlessly. Jim stared a moment, then turned back to Ral
and the Dreth who had taken a nip out of the big man
rump. "Whatever your name is—you, the one in charge,
said Jim. He jerked his thumb back over his shoulde
"Something's wrong with one of your—uh—people." H
turned away quickly, away from the Dreth that was about
take another nip out of Ralph, just in time to see t
twitching Dreth stumble and fall over its own legs. Anoth
Dreth limped to the tallest of the horde.

"Ritual apologies," the cube translated, "but since I a
the ham, I am tending to forget to breathe."

"Forgetting to *breathe?*" said the Dreth leader. "At onc
to the ship, *go!*" The tallest waved its chelae; his mandibl
chattered. "Give assistance to those unable! The alertin
of—" and the cube lost the rest as the big insect scuttle
around, directing the evacuation of the half-dozen Dreth wh
were now helplessly twitching on the ground or staggerin
in circles.

"Just in time," whispered Ted, as the men watched th
confusion swirl around them. "Ralph, are you—?"

"I'm O.K.," said the big man, looking down at the poi
where a trickle of blood was welling from a small woun
on his hip. "It don't hurt none, and I won't miss what h
bit off; I'm too big there anyways." He glanced around
"Wonder what happened to th' little—oh, oh; here come
the boss critter now."

The tallest of the Dreth, flanked by two more of the gian
insects, halted their approach a half-dozen paces away
"Whether apologies are required, I do not yet know,
announced the Dreth. "It is visible to all that the sample
you brought us are giving some problem. Whether you

sociate is digestible, we will have to discover with caution.
e first taster—"

"Isn't that the one," said Ralph, pointing behind Jim,
unning in circles? That must be; his claws are all bloody."

"Yes, it appears so. One hesitates to say, out of polite-
ss, but it is almost as if there is a poison—"

"There is, there is," said Ralph, with a broad grin.
Touch of DDT. You bugs, with big brains and all, must
awful sensitive t' th' stuff, but it don't bother us internal
eleton animals a bit. Whole planet's soaked in th' stuff by
w."

"Deepest condolences," said the Dreth. "You have been
ertaken by a natural disaster?"

"Nope," said Jim. "We make the stuff. By the ton."

"*Make* it? Disgusting—utterly uncivilized. We shall quit
is—this polluted place at once." The giant insect turned
ay while the cube translated, "At once; *board ship!*"

"Wait!" yelped Ralph. "How about—?" He pointed at
c Dreth with the bloody claws, who was now rushing
adly around the space ship, claws waving in the air.

"No time," said the tallest Dreth. A medium-sized one
cked up the translation cube; together the pair scuttled for
e ship. "We would be all day catching him, and doubtless
e very sands are saturated with your horrid poison; ritual
ologies but you must dispose of him yourselves. Perhaps
place of—" The two insectile horrors sidled through a
tch, and the ungainly craft lurched into the air and fled
ward the sky.

"My God!" said Ted, as the men watched the Dreth ship
sappear. "I had no idea we were that soaked with DDT."

"Well, I was afraid th' ham might not be," said Ralph,
so I sprayed it and th' slab of beef with a bug-bomb I
und in th' galley. Some farmers don't lay on the DDT like
e and dad."

"And then you took a few bites to show the bugs it was
.K.?" asked Ted. "Gave you a chance to spray yourself
o."

"Spray me?" demanded Ralph, indignantly. "That would
e cheating, wouldn't it? I *told* you guys I got enough DDT
me already."

"Well, granting your adventure really happened, shall v say, as you told it," said Professor Timble, "I can see ho it proves the point about a pesticide saving your lives. A for that matter, a lot more lives too; it would be rath awkward for those, how did you name them, Dreth usir Earth for a quick lunch counter. But the other side of t picture—"

"How come nothing ever showed in the papers or TV? asked Mrs. Jonas. "With all these leaks, I don't see ho the government could keep it all secret."

"Government never heard about it," said Jim. "We a agreed we'd rather not go through a big scene, so we worke out a story about lightning hitting the guy wire and droppin the antenna, and Ralph getting a little chunk taken out whe the wire shipped around and hit him in the butt. What els could we have done? And who would have believed us?"

"I suppose you're right." Mrs. Jonas paused for thoughtful moment. "Still—with overpopulation and the A bombs and all, maybe being a lunch stop wouldn't be s bad, the way we're messing up things on our own." Sh patted her hair absently. "And you had that translatin machine and that anesthetic; I'm not completely sure it such a good thing that it turned out the way it did."

"Oh, come on now, Mrs. Jonas," said the professor, " you really want to see overpopulation, go take a look at th inside of a livestock feeding pen. If we're going to solve ou overpopulation problems, we're going to have to do ourselves. However, that anesthetic—"

"I do not think so," interrupted Old Dr. Wimple. "] there is anything we do not need, it is another 'perfect anesthetic. When I think of all the misery and trouble we'v had from one perfect painkiller after another, I think we' be off better having none and spending the effort on curin causes instead of symptoms." He looked up, called "Ricky—another cup, please?"

"You are right about that," said Jim. "Even in the three four days the painkiller was working on Ralph, he found h was bruising himself and getting cuts and burns and things because he couldn't feel them hurt; that kid was *glad* whe he could feel pain again."

The doctor blinked gravely around the table. "And o

course, the last of the insect monsters—ah, thank you, Ricky—that's where the example on the other side of the pollution argument comes in, doesn't it?" He picked up the refilled cup and sipped.

"Yes, it does," said Jim. He grinned at the obvious puzzlement on Mrs. Jonas's face. "The last of the Dreth, the first taster, eventually ran into the side of the building and knocked himself cold, and somebody suggested that since the Dreth had eaten our lunch—dinner too—and even took a couple of nips out of Ralph—" Jim grinned again and licked his lips.

"You didn't!" said Mrs. Jonas.

"We did," said Jim. "Tasted like king crab, only more so, if you know what I mean."

"But the other side of the pollution argument?" said the professor. "I don't—"

"Don't you see it?" asked Old Dr. Wimple. He took another sip of coffee. "Just think how lucky it was for Jim and his friends that the—how did you call them—the Dreth were too civilized and ecologized to let themselves get polluted with some kind of pesticide that kills off vertebrate animals."

George Scithers has won four Hugo awards as editor, two for his sword-and-sorcery magazine Amra, *and two more for his work on* Isaac Asimov's Science Fiction Magazine, *of which he was the founding editor. He has since been editor of* Amazing *and is currently co-editor (with Darrell Schweitzer and John Betancourt) of* Weird Tales. *He has written little fiction, but has an enviable record of selling to some of the most distinguished editors in the history of the field: John W. Campbell, Jr.; Frederik Pohl; and this one, to Ben Bova.*

WELL BOTTLED AT SLAB'S
by John Gregory Betancourt

There are worse things waiting . . . inside some bottles.

A young man dressed all in blue pushed his way into Slab's Tavern. He had the thin good looks and light brown hair of a native Zelloquan, I saw, and his robes were of good material, well cut.

Glancing around, he swallowed nervously, then started for my table. As he neared I looked him over. He couldn't have been more than sixteen, I thought, and no one that young had much business *here*.

My tavern catered to none but the most bloodthirsty of clientele. Slab's had a certain reputation—well nurtured over the years—of being the toughest, roughest bar in all of Zelloque. I ought to know: I'd spread many of the rumors myself. When I took a quick glance around the main serving room, I saw pirates haggling in one corner, slavers throwing dice in another, and all manner of cutthroats bellied up to the bar for wine.

They didn't seem to discourage the boy, though. Ignoring all else, he slid into the seat opposite mine.

"Ulander Rasym, I presume?" he said.

"Perhaps." I studied him: pale lips, a paler complexion, the watery eyes of someone who read too much. Indeed, far from my normal run of customers. Something extraordinary had to have brought him here. I demanded, "Who are you?"

"My name is Vriss Arantine. I'm one of Pondrane's students. Perhaps you've heard of him?"

"He's a wizard. So? What do you want?"

"Your tavern has ghosts."

"Of course. Everyone knows that." It was true: among

226

the various magical happenings in Slab's over the years, ghosts often appeared. They were patrons who had died, mostly. And there was a table where chilled wine tasted like warm blood, and a spot (which moved around from night to night) where, if you stepped too close, monsters sometimes appeared.

"Good," Vriss said. "I had to make sure. I need to study them."

"What?"

"Yes." He nodded. "I'm writing a book—*Manifestations of the Dead*. It will prove conclusively that ghosts are no more than mental projections of latent magical talents."

He said it with such sincerity that I was left speechless for a moment—a very rare occurrence, I assure you. Unfortunately, I wasn't the only one who'd heard these preposterous statements. Slowly, behind the boy's back, a luminous white mist had begun to gather.

Ignoring the ghost, I said, "So what do you want me to do?"

"I want permission to sit at a small table in the back of your tavern for a month—to watch for spectral phenomena, of course."

The mist grew thicker, began to swirl up into a human form. "What do I care," I said, watching it, "so long as you pay for your wine?"

"Ah," he said eagerly, "you have put your finger on precisely the problem. I have developed a rigid scientific method for studying such phenomena—"

"Ghosts, you mean."

"—and I can't drink anything but water while I'm here, since it might cloud my judgment."

The luminous fog coalesced into a short, broad man in a flowing cape. I recognized him at once: Slab Vethiq himself, my tavern's founder and former owner, whom I'd served for twenty odd years. After his untimely death I'd taken over his establishment and run it myself. Even dead, though, Slab wouldn't surrender his property; he had a tendency to show up at the most inopportune times to try to run things . . . like now, when I was about to have this would-be scholar thrown out.

I just sighed. Such were the problems of owning a haunted tavern.

Slab nodded to me and winked knowingly. "Let him stay," he said in a way only I could hear. "He amuses me."

"But—"

Slab shook his head in warning. Then he was gone.

I sighed again. There would be trouble, I knew, if I didn't cooperate . . . walls dripping blood, loud, mysterious groans, clanking chains: petty annoyances which had a habit of scaring people away. Why did Slab always have to make things difficult?

Knowing it was a mistake, knowing I'd regret my decision, I turned to the lad and said, "Very well. But stay out of the way, and I don't want you bothering the paying customers!"

"Thank you!" Vriss said, beaming. "I'll start tonight!" Rising, he went to a small, empty table, sat down, and drew a small parchment from some hidden pocket in his cloak. Next to the parchment he set a small jar of ink and a quill pen. Then he began eyeing the various areas of the tavern and taking copious notes. He was as obvious as a boar at a feeding trough.

I motioned to Lur, my doorman and bodyguard, and he lumbered over. Lur was a large man—about seven feet tall— with broad shoulders and muscles enough to intimidate all but the most suicidal of drunks.

"What?" he asked, with his usual eloquence.

I nodded toward Vriss. "See to it he's not disturbed. Let the word get around that he's a . . . a nephew of mine. That should take care of it."

"Yes, master." He lumbered off.

As I studied my patrons with a dispassionate eye, I noticed half the men at the bar giving young Vriss Arantine the once-over. I knew what they were thinking: he'd be an easy mark, some nobleman's son out slumming, or just a lad who'd walked into the wrong bar on the wrong side of town.

But then Lur wandered among them, bending to whisper into an ear here, inserting a terse word or two into a conversation there. I don't know what he said, but it seemed to do the trick. The cutthroats tended to pale very suddenly, then turn back to their drinks, making almost painful efforts not

to even glance in Vriss's direction. Even so, I couldn't lose
the feeling that the boy would be trouble.

It started out simply enough: I felt a chill breeze, then a
beautiful glowing woman with long, glistening silver hair
emerged from the thick stone wall to my right. I jumped a
bit as her gown brushed my foot, sending little knives of
cold shooting the length of my leg, but it was nothing
unusual: I'd seen her kind of ghost every now and then.

Ignoring everyone else, she walked straight to Vriss,
curtsied a bit, then held out her hand as though asking him
to dance. He scarcely glanced up from his note taking.

Finally the ghost-woman walked on, moving through his
table, through the stack of parchments he'd already filled
with his tiny, cribbed writing. As she vanished into the wall,
I saw a look of puzzlement blended with frustration on her
face.

Interesting, indeed! Something was going on, and I didn't
like it, not at all. I vowed then and there to see it stopped.
But how? Why would ghosts bother Vriss Arantine? And
why would Slab Vethiq, who was never a man (or ghost)
known for his generosity, take an interest in the lad?

I had to find out more about young Arantine. Rising, I
fetched my cloak from the storeroom. A visit to Vriss's
master, the wizard Pondrane, seemed in order.

The wizard lived in the better part of town, in a tall,
rambling old house surrounded by a high stone wall. I
walked up to the gate, Lur at my side, and rang a little silver
bell. Instantly, it seemed, a gray-bearded servant appeared
from the shadows. He unlocked the gate, pulled it open, and
bowed humbly to me.

"This way, Ulander Rasym," he said.

I didn't move. "How do you know me?" I demanded.

"The master is expecting you." Turning, he started up an
overgrown path toward the house.

I glanced around once and, seeing nothing to alarm me,
followed. Lur fell in step behind, mace at his side.

The servant led us through a series of dimly lit rooms that
stank of mold and decay. Books and scrolls and bizarre
objects of all sorts had been piled on every available surface.

I recognized human bones among the jumble and wondered if they were the wizard's former servants.

Finally we came to a steep, narrow staircase. Boards creaking ominously underfoot, we climbed, the stench of decay growing stronger around us. At the top of the stairs was a hall, and at the end of the hall a dark, overcrowded little workroom. The servant ushered us in, then turned and shuffled off. Tables lined the walls. On them sat still more books and scrolls, plus bottles and tubes and all manner of jars filled with what looked like magical ingredients. Scattered here and there were trophies from fifty years of wizardry: mummified animals, polished bones, teeth, and strangely shaped pebbles. Lur moved awkwardly here, like an animal in a room full of glass, fearful of breaking something. I didn't blame him; wizards were a difficult lot at best, and there was no telling what Pondrane would do if either of us damaged his possessions, accidentally or not.

I heard a low cough behind me. A board shifted and groaned under my feet when I turned, but I saw no one in the shadows. "Who's there?" I called. "Is that you, wizard?"

Light suddenly flickered around us, jags of gold and silver dancing through the air like fireflies. Then the sparks coalesced into a glowing sphere that drifted up to the ceiling and stationed itself there. By its light I could see an old man sitting on a chair in the corner: Crollion Pondrane.

He was a small man, and old beyond measure. His face had been wrinkled and creased by years spent outdoors, but now his skin was pallid as a slug's belly, his cheeks hollowed, his eyes dark and deep as stagnant pools of water. His hands shook as he raised himself to his feet and took a step forward. The smell of decay seemed to radiate from him, thick and damp.

"Your servant said you were expecting me," I said. It was half a challenge, half a question.

"You are Ulander Rasym, owner of Slab Vethiq's tavern, yes?"

I frowned. "Yes. I've come to ask about one of your students . . ."

He seemed to be ignoring me. "Good, good," he

murmured to himself. Slowly he circled me, examining my face, my clothes in great detail.

"About Vriss—" I began.

"I have a proposition," he said. "It's worth five thousand gold royals to you."

That caught my interest. "I'm listening," I said.

"I knew Beren Vethiq—Slab Vethiq to you. When we were young we played together, travelled together, drank and whored together. We were the best of friends until one sad summer day in Pavania, when we both fell in love with the same girl. That night Beren drugged me, sold me into slavery, and sent me off to Harandel with a trader caravan. I ended up in that despicable city for ten years. I blamed him for all my troubles, swore vengeance. It was hatred that kept me going.

"I pursued him across half the world and finally cornered him in Frissa. We fought, I with magic, he with a sword. He won again by a fluke, and again he sold me into slavery. It took me fifteen years to get away that time. When I escaped, again I pursued him, but he had already died when I reached Zelloque. Only a few months ago did I learn of his ghost."

"So?" I said cautiously.

"I shall trap his spirit, put him in a tiny bottle where no one can ever find him." He cackled with glee. "That will be my revenge: an eternity of solitude, an eternity of punishment for what he did to me so long ago!"

It seemed to me Slab had once mentioned a wizard he'd known in Pavania, something about the wizard trying to kill him . . . My forehead wrinkled as I tried to remember. And finally it came to me.

"Slab mentioned you," I said slowly. "It was *you* who tried to kill him over the girl!"

"That's not the way it happened."

"I remember now—he said a princess of the Fourth House fell in love with him, and a wizard became jealous. The wizard burned the inn in which they were staying to the ground, and the princess rushed into the building to try and save him, and the roof collapsed on top of her—"

"No!"

"*Yes!* That's what he said!"

He shrugged a bit. "It was a long time ago. Who can remember the exact details? I will have my old friend's ghost, and I will pay you not to interfere."

I swallowed, my mouth dry. "And Vriss?"

"My apprentice. He is the instrument that will capture Beren Vethiq."

Lur began to growl ever so faintly, like an angered dog, and I knew I had to but give the word and he'd strangle the wizard—or, more likely, die trying. His loyalty to a dead man was touching. But what did *I* owe Slab? It might be worth it to sit back and let Vriss capture him. The thought of those five thousand royals jingling in my pouch made my fingers itch.

But then I remembered all Slab had done for me. Sure, he'd made my life miserable at times. But he'd also done his best to keep Slab's Tavern open and running, even when an Oracle tried to tear the place apart in search of a splinter from one of his god's bones, even when One-eyed Seth tried to muscle in on business, and even when the Great Lord of Zelloque's counsellors decided I was a menace and ordered my assassination.

I owed him my life many times over. The thought of Slab spending the rest of eternity alone, with Crollion Pondrane torturing him, made me distinctly uncomfortable.

Abruptly, I started for the door, before my morals took second place to my greed. Over my shoulder I called, "We have nothing to discuss. And if your apprentice dares set foot in my tavern again, I'll sell him into slavery myself, just like Slab would have done!"

"Fool!" Pondrane shouted after me, and then he began to laugh again, voice high and warbling. It made me realize how much I hated him.

When we came in sight of my tavern, I saw a large crowd had gathered in front, all of them looking in through doors and windows, all of them shouting and passing bets back and forth. At once I realized a brawl must have broken out, and without Lur to break it up, things had gotten out of hand.

"Come on!" I shouted, and I raced down the street, Lur thundering after me.

I forced my way through the mass of people around the

oor, entered the musty pleasantness of my tavern—and ound myself surrounded by a whirling, screaming, shrieking torm of ghosts. Spectral figures stalked between the tables. evered heads floated over the bar, bellowing snatches of ong. Skeletons sipped wine in the booths. In every corner omething writhed or slithered or chortled. The din was deafening.

At the center of it all, still scribbling notes furiously, sat Pondrane's apprentice. Vriss seemed oblivious to all the apparitions around him. Now, however, I knew the truth: he was waiting for Slab Vethiq to show himself.

With a roar of sheer rage—at Slab for sending these ghosts, at Pondrane for sending his apprentice, at all the money they both had cost me by frightening off my customers—I ran into the room and seized Vriss by the collar. Hauling him to his feet, I shook him as hard as I could. His teeth rattled; he trembled all over.

"Get out!" I snarled. "If I ever see you or your master again, I'll beat you both to bloody pulp!"

I cuffed his ear, and with a yelp, he went sprawling across the floor. Lur dragged him to his feet and propelled him forcibly toward the door. The crowd there scattered.

It was then that I became aware of the deathly silence around us. All the various ghosts had vanished, gone back to whatever nightmare they'd crawled from. I began to breathe a bit easier, confident that my troubles had ended.

However, as soon as I turned, I noticed Lur had stopped. He still held Vriss by collar and belt, dangling the lad half a foot above the floor, but his attention seemed focused on something else. Then I saw Slab slowly materializing in front of them, blocking their way. Slab's arms were crossed and he looked more than a bit peeved. I saw it all, then, knew he'd wanted to frighten a boy who didn't believe in ghosts. He wouldn't let Vriss leave yet; his fun wasn't over.

"No!" I shouted to him, a sinking feeling inside, knowing it was too late. "It's a trap—"

But Vriss had whipped a small bottle from some hidden pocket. He popped the cork, pointed its mouth at Slab, and shouted a magic word with such sadistic glee I knew inside his innocence had all been an act, that he would grow up to be exactly like his master.

I heard a sucking sound, felt a rush of wind all around me, and then Slab was gone. The wizard had won after all, it seemed. I felt positively sick.

Lur had turned Vriss Arantine upside down and begun shaking him by one leg. Bits of parchment, several small coins, and various pouches flew in all directions. At last the bottle dropped free.

Flinging Vriss to one side, Lur grabbed it up and uncorked it. He began shaking it, trying to release Slab. Nothing happened. And Lur began to growl again—a sure sign of his anger.

Vriss had, meanwhile, climbed from the wreckage of two chairs and a table. He seemed dazed, unsure as to where he was and what he was doing. Then he saw Lur and seemed to remember, for he lunged after the bottle.

Lur held it well out of reach, raising the hole to one eye. Peering inside, he said, "Slab?"

Again Vriss shouted that magic word, and again I heard the sucking noise. In the blink of an eye my bodyguard had vanished.

The bottle clattered loudly on the floor. Vriss grabbed it up and bolted, but I tackled him before he'd taken three steps.

As I sat on his chest, pinning his arms, I stuffed my bulging money purse in his mouth to keep him quiet. Only then did I pry the bottle from his clenched fist.

After corking it securely, I held it up to the light, turning it this way and that, looking for some way to release its contents. The thing wasn't made of glass, I thought; it wasn't transparent and the texture felt wrong. It seemed more like ivory or bone of some kind.

Finally, giving up, I decided to have Vriss reverse the magic. I could live without Lur, I was certain—hired muscle could be found anywhere—but I certainly needed Slab. He'd always watched out for me, always made sure the tavern turned a profit. And, beyond that, he'd become almost as much a fixture in the place as the huge block of marble that served as the bar, or the old tapestries on the walls, or the huge brick fireplace where toasts were made and glasses thrown on cold winter nights. Slab's Tavern without its

atron ghost would be just another bar. I could never let that
appen.

Pulling the makeshift gag from Vriss's mouth, I let him
asp and take large gulps of air until he could talk again.

"All right," I said angrily, "how do I get them out?"

"I don't know."

"I don't believe you." I let one hand tighten around his
aroat for a second. His eyes bulged.

When I released him, he coughed and wheezed for several
ainutes. "It's true!" he managed to gasp. "My master did
ll the magic. I just had to say the word—"

Jal and Ferrin, two of my least timid servants, had dared
o venture back inside by then. They tended the bar and
ometimes helped out at the door, when things got too busy
or Lur to handle alone.

Now I glared at them: "It's about time!"

"Yes, Ulander," Jal said, wiping his hands on his apron.
Ie didn't meet my gaze. "It's just that—"

"Never mind. Give me a hand here. Hold him while I get
ap."

They seized Vriss with ill-concealed pleasure. The boy
truggled a bit when I stood, but Jal bent one of his arms
ack until he cried for mercy.

"Mercy?" I said, mocking him. "What mercy did you
how my friends?" I waved the bottle under his nose. "How
he Hell am I supposed to get them out of here?"

He just stared at me, gritting his teeth as Jal continued to
wist his arm. I finally decided he really *didn't* know.

Perhaps, I decided, smashing the bottle would do the trick.
I fetched a hammer from the back room, set the bottle on
the stone floor, and struck it as hard as I could. The hammer
bounced off with a ringing sound. Again and again I
pounded on it, but to no effect. It wouldn't break.

Sighing, I rose to my feet. If nothing else I'd always
prided myself on my inventiveness. If I couldn't get them
out, I'd get someone else to do it for me. The wizard
Pondrane would certainly know how. All I had to do was
persuade him.

I looked at his apprentice and smiled. "Tell me," I said,
"the magic word that makes the bottle work."

He thrashed his arms and tried to break free, but Jal and

Ferrin held him securely. After I'd hit him a few times, he
stopped struggling and began to whimper a bit.

"Stop that sniveling," I said. "You brought it on
yourself. I made a perfectly sensible request. Now answer
me!"

"You're going to put me in there!"

"Of course," I said. "That will make sure Pondrane
empties the bottle."

Vriss bit his lip and shook his head, but I saw the fear in
his eyes. I knew then that he'd tell.

"Save yourself a lot of pain," I said. "What's the word?"

Slowly, grudgingly, he told me. When he'd done so, I
drew out the bottle, uncorked it, and pointed the opening at
him. He closed his eyes and turned his head away. Then I
said the magic word and in a split second he vanished.

Unfortunately, Jal and Ferrin vanished with him. It
seemed the thing sucked up whoever or whatever was in
front of it.

Shaking my head, I tucked the bottle into a pocket, closed
up shop, and headed for the wizard Pondrane's house.

The same servant who'd met Lur and me earlier that night
brought me back to Pondrane's damp, dank workshop. The
wizard was bent over several small jars, carefully measuring
ingredients into each. He looked up when I came in, then
set aside his instruments.

His voice held a hint of a sneer when he said, "So,
you've changed your mind, have you? Come crawling back
for the money?"

I smiled. "No. Rather, I've got a present for you."

"Oh? What?"

I produced the bottle. "Your apprentice."

Frowning, Pondrane demanded, "What's he doing in
there?"

"He was a bit careless. After putting my bodyguard
inside, he managed to do the same to himself. Needless to
say, I want Lur back, and I imagine you'd like Vriss."

He carried the bottle over to one of his tables, set it down,
and rummaged through a stack of papers. Finding the one
he wanted, he pulled it out and read it aloud. The bottle

gan to shimmer with a weird, pulsing light. He held it up
d squinted.

"You told the truth," he admitted a bit sadly. "From the
ra, there *are* living humans in there."

"You would doubt my word?" I smiled.

"I had hoped you were lying. There *is* a slight problem
th getting them out."

"What?"

"The bottle is not supposed to hold people. It was
signed for a ghost, something ethereal. I don't know what
ill happen if I try to release its contents. The strain might
ove too great and shatter them."

"The people or the bottle?"

"Both. Either. The cage took me months to make and I
n't go wasting it, now can I?"

I made a mental note not to mention Jal or Ferrin. If two
ople inside the bottle worried him, four might well frighten
m off. Rather, I changed tactics and said, "Don't you have
ore time than that invested in your apprentice?"

Slowly, almost reluctantly, he nodded. "I suppose so.
cry well, then, I'll let them out. Please stand back."

I retreated into the hall. As I watched through the
oorway, he removed the cork, set the bottle in the middle
the floor, then took two steps back and stretched out his
ms. His eyes closed; he seemed to be concentrating deeply.
Finally he began to speak, the words strange, slurred,
eavy. The air around us took on an odd, liquid quality, as
ough I gazed at him through a great depth of water. I
oticed a blue mist rising around the bottle, tendrils circling,
vining upward, then coursing down into the bottle's open
outh. The room grew chill; I felt a cold sweat trickle down
e small of my back.

Pondrane shouted a word, then came a blinding flash of
ght and an explosion that knocked me off my feet. Dust
olled around me, smothering, and I choked and gasped for
reath. When the air cleared, I gathered my wits enough to
agger into the wizard's workroom.

Everything lay in shambles, the glass bottles broken, the
irniture smashed, debris all over. Pondrane himself
orawled across one of his tables, a mummified cat pillowing
is head.

Lur and Jal and Ferrin lay in a jumble on the floor. heard one of them groan and begin to stir so I knew the were still alive. I didn't see Vriss at first, but then I spotte his foot sticking out from under Lur. Fortunately he'd broke my bodyguard's fall, as well as Jal's and Ferrin's.

Slab stood off to one side, looking faintly amused by th whole mess. I frowned. "At least you could show a littl gratitude for my rescuing you!"

He laughed at me, then slowly faded away. His lack c grace in being saved hurt a bit, but he *was* a ghost an allowances had to be made. When all I'd done for him ha sunk in, I knew he'd be grateful.

Meanwhile, there were important things to think abou like my men. Pulling them off of Vriss, I slapped their face and called their names until they opened their eyes an looked blearily at me. After that I breathed easier. The skulls were hard; they didn't seem hurt by their ordeal. I fact, it took surprisingly little to get them on their feet an moving.

On my way out I spotted the magic bottle lying on th floor, its cork beside it. Smiling, I picked it up.

Then I crossed to the wizard Pondrane, pointed it at him and spoke the magic word. With a sucking sound and a gus of wind, he vanished. Grinning happily, I tamped the cor back into place. Then I put it on the workbench, in plai sight—just next to fifty-odd other bottles that looked exactl the same. It would probably take Vriss months to notice . . . if he ever did.

Smiling, I followed after my men. It felt good to hav saved Slab. Dead or alive, a fellow had to look out for hi friends.

I just hoped Slab felt that way, too.

John Gregory Betancourt is a rapidly rising star in th field of fantasy and science fiction, the author of five book published within the past two years. The most recent is hi ience-fiction novel, Johnny Zed, *but he reports that he has* *no means abandoned pirates, Slab's tavern, giant ants,* *the world of Zelloque.*

Watch for, among other upcoming Betancourt opuses, Dr. nes and the Dragons of Camelot *and* The Pirates of lloque.

THE THREE SAILORS' GAMBIT
by Lord Dunsany

Some games not even the Devil can win . . .

Sitting some years ago in the ancient tavern at Over, on afternoon in spring, I was waiting as was my custom fo something strange to happen.

In this I was not always disappointed, for the very curiou leaded panes of that tavern, facing the sea, let a light int the low-ceilinged room so mysterious, particularly a evening, that it somehow seemed to affect the events within Be that as it may, I have seen strange things in that taver and heard stranger things told.

And as I sat there three sailors entered the tavern ju: back, as they said, from sea and come with sunburned skin from a very long voyage to the South; and one of them ha a board and chessmen under his arm, and they wer complaining that they could find no one who knew how t play chess. This was the year that the Tournament was i England. And a little dark man at a table in a corner of th room, drinking sugar and water, asked them why the wished to play chess; and they said that they would play an man for a pound. They opened their box of chessmen then a cheap and nasty set, and the man refused to play with suc uncouth pieces, and the sailors suggested that perhaps h could find better ones; and in the end he went round to hi lodgings near by and brought his own, and then they sa down to play for a pound a side. It was a consultation gam on the part of the sailors, they said all three must play.

Well, the little dark man turned out to be Stavlokratz.

Of course he was fabulously poor, and the sovereig meant more to him than it did to the sailors, but he didn'

240

seem keen to play, it was the sailors that insisted; he had made the badness of the sailors' chessmen an excuse for not playing at all, but the sailors had overruled that, and then he told them straight out who he was, and the sailors had never heard of Stavlokratz.

Well, no more was said after that. Stavlokratz said no more, either because he did not wish to boast or because he was huffed that they did not know who he was. And I saw no reason to enlighten the sailors about him; if he took their pound they had brought it on themselves, and my boundless admiration for his genius made me feel that he deserved whatever might come his way. He had not asked to play, they had named the stakes, he had warned them, and gave them first move; there was nothing unfair about Stavlokratz.

I had never seen Stavlokratz before, but I had played over nearly every one of his games in the World Championship for the last three or four years; he was always, of course, the model chosen by students. Only young chess-players can appreciate my delight at seeing him play firsthand.

Well, the sailors used to lower their heads almost as low as the table and mutter together before every move, but they muttered so low that you could not hear what they planned. They lost three pawns almost straight off, then a knight, and shortly after a bishop; they were playing in fact the famous Three Sailors' Gambit.

Stavlokratz was playing with the easy confidence that they say was usual with him, when suddenly at about the thirteenth move I saw him look surprised; he leaned forward and looked at the board and then at the sailors, but he learned nothing from their vacant faces; he looked back at the board again.

He moved more deliberately after that; the sailors lost two more pawns, Stavlokratz had lost nothing as yet. He looked at me, I thought, almost irritably, as though something would happen that he wished I was not there to see. I believed at first he had qualms about taking the sailors' pound, until it dawned on me that he might lose the game; I saw that possibility in his face, not on the board, for the game had become almost incomprehensible to me. I cannot describe my astonishment. And a few moves later Stavlokratz resigned.

The sailors showed no more elation than if they had won some game with greasy cards, playing amongst themselves.

Stavlokratz asked them where they got their opening. "We kind of thought of it," said one. "It just come into our heads like," said another. He asked them questions about the ports they had touched at. He evidently thought, as I did myself, that they had learned their extraordinary gambit, perhaps in some old dependency of Spain, from some young master of chess whose fame had not reached Europe. He was very eager to find who this man could be, for neither of us imagined that those sailors had invented it, nor would anyone who had seen them. But he got no information from the sailors.

Stavlokratz could very ill afford the loss of a pound. He offered to play them again for the same stakes. The sailors began to set up the white pieces. Stavlokratz pointed out that it was his turn for first move. The sailors agreed but continued to set up the white pieces and sat with the white before them waiting for him to move. It was a trivial incident, but it revealed to Stavlokratz and myself that none of these sailors was aware that white always moves first.

Stavlokratz played on them his own opening, reasoning of course that as they had never heard of Stavlokratz they would not know of his opening; and with probably a very good hope of getting back his pound he played the fifth variation with its tricky seventh move, at least so he intended, but it turned to a variation unknown to the students of Stavlokratz.

Throughout this game I watched the sailors closely, and I became sure, as only an attentive watcher can be, that the one on their left, Jim Bunion, did not even know the moves.

When I had made up my mind about this I watched only the other two, Adam Bailey and Bill Sloggs, trying to make out which was the mastermind; and for a long while I could not. And then I heard Adam Bailey mutter six words, the only words I heard throughout the game, of all their consultations, "No, him with the horse's head." And I decided that Adam Bailey did not know what a knight was, though of course he might have been explaining things to Bill Sloggs, but it did not sound like that; so that left Bill Sloggs. I watched Bill Sloggs after that with a certain wonder; he was no more intellectual than the others to look at, though rather more forceful perhaps. Poor old Stavlokratz was beaten again.

Well, in the end I paid for Stavlokratz, and tried to get a game with Bill Sloggs alone; but this he would not agree to, it must be all three or none. And then I went back with Stavlokratz to his lodgings. He very kindly gave me a game: of course it did not last long, but I am more proud of having been beaten by Stavlokratz than of any game that I have ever won. And then we talked for an hour about the sailors, and neither of us could make head or tail of them. I told him what I had noticed about Jim Bunion and Adam Bailey, and he agreed with me that Bill Sloggs was the man, though as to how he had come by that gambit or that variation of Stavlokratz's own opening he had no theory.

I had the sailors' address, which was that tavern as much as anywhere, and they were to be there all that evening. As evening drew in I went back to the tavern, and found there still the three sailors. And I offered Bill Sloggs two pounds for a game with him alone and he refused, but in the end he played me for a drink. And then I found that he had not heard of the *en passant* rule, and believed that the fact of checking the king prevented him from castling, and did not know that a player can have two or more queens on the board at the same time if he queens his pawns, or that a pawn could ever become a knight; and he made as many of the stock mistakes as he had time for in a short game, which I won. I thought that I should have got at the secret then, but his mates who had sat scowling all the while in the corner came up and interfered. It was a breach of their compact apparently for one to play chess by himself; at any rate they seemed angry. So I left the tavern then and came back again next day, and the next day and the day after, and often saw the three sailors, but none were in a communicative mood. I had got Stavlokratz to keep away, and they could get no one to play chess with at a pound a side, and I would not play with them unless they told me the secret.

And then one evening I found Jim Bunion drunk, yet not so drunk as he wished, for the two pounds were spent; and I gave him very nearly a tumbler of whiskey, or what passed for whiskey in that tavern in Over, and he told me the secret at once. I had given the others some whiskey to keep them quiet, and later on in the evening they must have gone out, but Jim Bunion stayed with me by a little table, leaning across it and talking low, right into my face, his breath smelling all the while of what passed for whiskey.

The wind was blowing outside as it does on bad nights in November, coming up with moans from the south, toward which the tavern faced with all its leaded panes, so that none but I was able to hear his voice as Jim Bunion gave up his secret.

They had sailed for years, he told me, with Bill Snyth; and on their last voyage home Bill Snyth had died. And he was buried at sea. Just the other side of the line they buried him, and his pals divided his kit, and these three got his crystal that only they knew he had, which Bill got one night in Cuba. They played chess with the crystal.

And he was going on to tell me about that night in Cuba when Bill had bought the crystal from the stranger, how some folks might think that they had seen thunderstorms, but let them go and listen to that one that thundered in Cuba when Bill was buying his crystal and they'd find that they didn't know what thunder was. But then I interrupted him, unfortunately perhaps, for it broke the thread of his tale and set him rambling awhile, and cursing other people and talking of other lands, China, Port Said, and Spain: but I brought him back to Cuba again in the end. I asked him how they could play chess with a crystal; and he said that you looked at the board and looked at the crystal and there was the game in the crystal the same as it was on the board, with all the odd little pieces looking just the same though smaller, horses' heads and what-nots; and as soon as the other man moved, the move came out in the crystal, and then your move appeared after it, and all you had to do was to make it on the board. If you didn't make the move that you saw in the crystal things got very bad in it, everything horribly mixed and moving about rapidly, and scowling and making the same move over and over again, and the crystal getting cloudier and cloudier; it was best to take one's eyes away from it then, or one dreamt about it afterwards, and the foul little pieces came and cursed you in your sleep and moved about all night with their crooked moves.

I thought then that, drunk though he was, he was not

telling the truth, and I promised to show him to people who played chess all their lives so that he and his mates could get a pound whenever they liked, and I promised not to reveal his secret even to Stavlokratz, if only he would tell me all the truth; and this promise I have kept till long after the three sailors have lost their secret. I told him straight out that I did not believe in the crystal. Well, Jim Bunion leaned forward then, even further across the table, and swore he had seen the man from whom Bill had bought the crystal and that he was one to whom anything was possible. To begin with, his hair was villainously dark, and his features were unmistakable even down there in the South, and he could play chess with his eyes shut, and even then he could beat anyone in Cuba. But there was more than this, there was the bargain he made with Bill that told one who he was. He sold that crystal for Bill Snyth's soul.

Jim Bunion, leaning over the table with his breath in my face, nodded his head several times and was silent.

I began to question him then. Did they play chess as far away as Cuba? He said they all did. Was it conceivable that any man would make such a bargain as Snyth made? Wasn't the trick well known? Wasn't it in hundreds of books? And if he couldn't read books, mustn't he have heard from sailors that that is the Devil's commonest dodge to get souls from silly people?

Jim Bunion had leant back in his own chair quietly smiling at my questions, but when I mentioned silly people he leaned forward again, and thrust his face close to mine and asked me several times if I called Bill Snyth silly. It seemed that these three sailors thought a great deal of Bill Snyth, and it made Jim Bunion angry to hear anything said against him. I hastened to say that the bargain seemed silly, though not, of course, the man who made it; for the sailor was almost threatening, and no wonder, for the whiskey in that dim tavern would madden a nun.

When I said that the bargain seemed silly he smiled again, and then he thundered his fist down on the table and said that no one had ever got the better of Bill Snyth, and that that was the worst bargain for himself that the Devil ever made, and that from all he had read or heard of the Devil he had never been so badly had before as the night when he

met Bill Snyth at the inn in the thunderstorm in Cuba, for
Bill Snyth already had the damnedest soul at sea; Bill was
a good fellow, but his soul was damned right enough, so he
got the crystal for nothing.

Yes, he was there and saw it all himself, Bill Snyth in the
Spanish inn and the candles flaring, and the Devil walking
in out of the rain, and then the bargain between those two
old hands, and the Devil going out into the lightning, and
the thunderstorm raging on, and Bill Snyth sitting chuckling
to himself between the bursts of the thunder.

But I had more questions to ask and interrupted this
reminiscence. Why did they all three always play together?
And a look of something like fear came over Jim Bunion's
face; and at first he would not speak. And then he said to
me that it was like this; they had not paid for that crystal,
but got it as their share of Bill Snyth's kit. If they had paid
for it or given something in exchange to Bill Snyth that
would have been all right, but they couldn't do that now
because Bill was dead, and they were not sure if the old
bargain might not hold good. And Hell must be a large and
lonely place, and to go there alone must be bad; and so the
three agreed that they would all stick together, and use the
crystal all three or not at all, unless one died, and then the
two would use it and the one that was gone would wait for
them. And the last of the three to go would bring the crystal
with him, or maybe the crystal would bring him. They didn't
think, he said, they were the kind of men for Heaven, and
he hoped they knew their place better than that, but they
didn't fancy the notion of Hell alone, if Hell it had to be.
It was all right for Bill Snyth, he was afraid of nothing. He
had known perhaps five men that were not afraid of death,
but Bill Snyth was not afraid of Hell. He died with a smile
on his face like a child in its sleep; it was drink killed poor
Bill Snyth.

This was why I had beaten Bill Sloggs; Sloggs had the
crystal on him while we played, but would not use it; these
sailors seemed to fear loneliness as some people fear being
hurt; he was the only one of the three who could play chess
at all, he had learnt it in order to be able to answer questions
and keep up their pretense, but he had learnt it badly, as I
found. I never saw the crystal, they never showed it to

anyone; but Jim Bunion told me that night that it was about the size that the thick end of a hen's egg would be if it were round. And then he fell asleep.

There were many more questions that I would have asked him but I could not wake him up. I even pulled the table away so that he fell to the floor, but he slept on, and all the tavern was dark but for one candle burning; and it was then that I noticed for the first time that the other two sailors had gone; no one remained at all but Jim Bunion and I and the sinister barman of that curious inn, and he too was asleep.

When I saw that it was impossible to wake the sailor I went out into the night. Next day Jim Bunion would talk of it no more; and when I went back to Stavlokratz I found him already putting on paper his theory about the sailors, which became accepted by chess-players, that one of them had been taught their curious gambit and the other two between them had learnt all the defensive openings as well as general play. Though who taught them no one could say, in spite of enquiries made afterwards all along the Southern Pacific.

I never learnt any more details from any of the three sailors, they were always too drunk to speak or else not drunk enough to be communicative. I seem just to have taken Jim Bunion at the flood. But I kept my promise; it was I that introduced them to the Tournament, and a pretty mess they made of established reputations. And so they kept on for months, never losing a game and always playing for their pound a side. I used to follow them wherever they went merely to watch their play. They were more marvellous than Stavlokratz even in his youth.

But then they took to liberties such as giving their queen when playing first-class players. And in the end one day when all three were drunk they played the best player in England with only a row of pawns. They won the game all right. But the ball broke to pieces. I never smelt such a stench in all my life.

The three sailors took it stoically enough, they signed on to different ships and went back again to the sea, and the world of chess lost sight, forever I trust, of the most remarkable players it ever knew, who would have altogether spoiled the game.

Lord Dunsany (Edward John Moreton Drax Plunkett, 18th Baron Dunsany, 1878–1957) practically invented the fantastic bar story. Certainly he wrote more than anyone else, with his five volumes (and a few uncollected stories) of the adventures of that modern Munchausen, Mr. Joseph Jorkens, who under the influence of bottled spirits would relate tales of his extraordinary and adventurous youth. The catch was, of course, that no matter how fantastic his claims, none of the listeners could ever prove that Jorkens was lying—or telling the truth.

A Jorkens story appeared in the first volume of this series. "The Three Sailors' Gambit" is one of Dunsany's non-Jorkens tales, which also happens to be a bar story.

Dunsany, in addition to being one of the greatest and most prolific fantasy writers ever (sixty-three books and nearly a thousand short stories) was also a soldier, Peer of the Realm, world traveller, sportsman, and, at one point, chess champion of Ireland.